NAKED PASSION

Eron took a deep, shuddering breath and came to his senses, realizing how ridiculous he must look, standing there in the river fully clothed, dripping wet. Feeling like an idiot, he peeled off his sodden clothes and tossed them on the bank.

The icy water had solved his problem for the moment, but he wasn't sure how long it would last. He glanced around. Juelle was nowhere in sight. She must have returned to the camp in a huff. Unable to blame her, he decided to take advantage of the situation and cleanse the day's grime from his hide.

When he finished, he climbed out of the water and prepared to put his wet clothes back on, but a towel hit him in the face.

"Here," said Juelle, "use this."

Startled, Eron stood there dumbly as he wiped the water out of his eyes. Juelle half smiled while her gaze wandered over his body as freely as his had roamed hers earlier. When her gaze fell below his waist, her eyebrows lifted. Quickly, Eron wrapped the towel around his waist. "Enjoy the view?" he said.

She tossed him a wicked grin and swiveled to return to the camp, hips swaying provocatively. "Very much," she called back over her shoulder.

Eron groaned. It was going to be a long night.

PAM McCUTCHEON

QUICKSILVER

LOVE SPELL ◈ NEW YORK CITY

LOVE SPELL®

September 1996

Published by

Dorchester Publishing Co., Inc.
276 Fifth Avenue
New York, NY 10001

The name "Love Spell" and its logo are trademarks of Dorchester Publishing Co., Inc.

Printed in the United States of America.

Dedicated to my friends for their unconditional support whenever, wherever I need it: to the GEnie Romexers for keeping me informed on this crazy business, to the AMEBOIDs for making me "leave my sanity at the door," and, as always, to the Wyrd Sisters for always being there.

Special appreciation to Rick Walton, Becky Hamilton, and Deb Stover for going above and beyond the call of friendship to read and critique huge chunks of this story in an incredibly short period of time. Thanks!

QUICKSILVER

Prologue

The small querent chamber, deep in the dark caverns of Oasis, glowed with the eerie violet light of a thousand exotic caroline flowers. Eron entered slowly, sinking reverently onto the cushion opposite the prophetess, and waited.

Though fiercely proud of the rank that brought him into the presence of the oracle, he dreaded the experience even more. Dreaded the carolines—beautiful flowers with five spiky white petals shading to a deep purple in the center, crowned by a circlet of golden filaments. Beautiful . . . yet terrifying. For, in the absence of light, they emitted a mind-drugging fragrance that was impossible to resist.

He reminded himself that he had nothing to fear. The pythia—the prophetess—was his twin sister Alyssa, through whom he had been granted the status of Councilman. She, and the empathic moncat who helped her foretell the future, would keep him safe during the ritual that was about to commence.

Alyssa indicated her readiness to begin, and Eron reluctantly, slowly, gave in to the lure of the carolines, knowing they were essential to the prophecy. He inhaled the heady scent and stared deep into the whirling, hypnotic eyes of Alyssa's moncat, letting his mind slide into the oblivion they offered.

His senses spun in a dizzying blur and he receded far into a trance, letting go more fully than ever before, trusting Alyssa to keep him unharmed. As he closed his eyes, tranquillity descended upon him. In gradual, measured increments, he sank into the depths of his own unconscious.

When he finally achieved the proper receptive state, he heard the oracle intone the time-honored declaration through his sister. "State your question."

His query burst forth and spilled into the waiting silence. "How will the Terrans affect Delphi?"

A part of himself detached from his consciousness to hover over the scene. Mild surprise filled him—this had never happened before. He usually felt and heard nothing after the question was stated.

He watched in calm detachment from above as the moncat's eyes whirled faster and Alyssa threw her head back in the throes of the prophetic trance. Then, without warning, he was swept up into a whirlwind.

Startled, Eron grimly hung on to the small thread that was his lifeline to Alyssa.

The storm wrenched him to and fro, tossing his large body about as if it were nothing but a straw on the mighty ocean of the gods.

After what seemed like hours of battle, the storm ceased abruptly, throwing Eron to his knees in front of a magnificent altar. He pushed the dark hair out of his eyes and raised his gaze to the being of light that pulsed in radiant splendor behind the altar—the oracle itself.

A beam shot out of the oracle to illuminate the altar, where a glowing image coalesced slowly. There, he saw an adolescent girl—no, a very small woman—with a short cap of silvery blonde hair, wearing a strange one-piece outfit. Clearly, this was a Terran, for no Delphian woman would wear such unfeminine garb. She stood pixie-like, her hands on her hips, laughing down at him.

She held his gaze and turned her head slowly to her right where a vision formed. Eron's gaze followed as the scene portrayed pythias and their moncats joyously celebrating Delphi's prosperity beneath the shining light of the oracle.

The woman demanded his attention with an imperious lift of her hand and swung her head to the left. There, a far different scene took form—weeping pythias lay across shattered altars, their moncats looking on piteously, the glow of the oracle dimmed forever. Horror filled him at the sight. *This can never be!*

He snapped his gaze back to the woman and silently demanded an explanation. The scenes disappeared and she held her arms out, beseeching his help, her startling blue eyes clouded with indecision.

His answer was clear. This slight woman, this Terran, had the power to bring prosperity to Delphi or to destroy it forever—it was up to him to ensure she made the right decision.

Chapter One

Juelle Shanard pushed aside the half-open curtains that screened the doorway to the Council Captain's private chambers and poked her head inside. She groaned. *For the love of Pete, they're at it again.*

Inside, Lancer and Thena were engaged in their second favorite leisure time activity. Pressed together so closely that they looked fused, the Council Captain and his life-mate were engaged in a terminal case of liplock.

As Juelle watched, Lancer's hands roamed southward over Thena's lush figure, unimpeded by her Greek-style chiton—a garment made for seduction. Rolling her eyes, Juelle thanked providence that she had not caught them in their *most* favorite activity.

She was glad to see her childhood friend and his life-mate so happy, but jeez, it was the middle of the afternoon—work time—and she had an appointment. Noisily, she cleared her throat.

They were so involved they didn't even hear her. Juelle tried coughing. No reaction. She glanced at Seri, Thena's moncat, who sat placidly on the desk grooming herself. The mischievous Delphian moncats, so called because they looked like a cross between a monkey and a cat, were extraordinary creatures. Their empathic abilities enhanced the emotions of the women—the pythias—they chose and enabled them to prophesy.

Thank goodness Seri wasn't enhancing Thena's emotions now—Juelle had no desire to share those kinds of feelings with her two best friends.

Juelle sighed. She'd have to be rude. She entered the room. "Lancer?" No response. Growing impatient, she raised her voice. "Lancer!"

Lancer and Thena broke apart. Thena's cheeks were flushed, and Lancer's eyes were dark with desire as he and Thena shared a secret smile. Their love for each other was obvious—and enviable.

Juelle had never felt that way about anyone and doubted she ever would. She wasn't sure she wanted to, either—not if it was accompanied by the usual pain and agony. Her work as a psychiatrist on Earth had given her more than enough exposure to the seamy side of relationships and just how damaging love could be. No, it wasn't for her. She'd keep her heart whole and free, thank you very much.

Juelle raised her eyebrows, and Thena blushed even deeper while she arranged her mussed clothing. Lancer merely adjusted the fit of his pants and grinned at Juelle, unrepentant.

"I take it you forgot we had an appointment," Juelle said in a dry tone.

Lancer's eyes flicked to Thena. "No, I was just . . . distracted."

Juelle had to admit she could understand why.

Pam McCutcheon

Thena, who was tall with a voluptuous figure and long, honey blonde hair, made Juelle, at five feet three inches tall, feel like a midget. Hell, Juelle felt tiny beside everyone on this planet. Delphi's lighter gravity made the Delphians bigger, taller. Even the teenagers were taller than she was.

Her height, or lack of it, had never bothered her before. On Earth, she was respected for her intelligence and accomplishments. Here, people took one look at her and assumed she was helpless because she was so small. Except for Lancer and Thena. They knew her capabilities and treated her as a professional . . . and a friend.

Lancer seated himself behind the desk and waved Juelle to a chair. Thena, ever graceful, settled herself on a chair next to the desk. "What can we do for you?" Thena asked.

Juelle rubbed her damp palms against the legs of her jumpsuit. "It's been six months and I've pretty much accomplished what I came here for—"

Thena gave her a brilliant smile. "Yes, we know, and words can't express how grateful we are. Thanks to you, my mother has regained her sanity and is well on her way to becoming her normal self."

"I'll second that," Lancer said. "And the methods you've taught us will ensure she never follows her mother into madness. We owe you one."

Good, Juelle thought. *Hold that thought.*

"Well, I'd like to continue my research on the paranormal ability of your pythias. I've done all I can here at Dodona and, now that Rheta no longer needs me, I'd like to continue my research on a wider scale."

Thena and Lancer exchanged a significant glance. Lancer grinned. "We hoped you'd say that."

Startled, Juelle said, "Why?"

14

"You know the Council convenes tomorrow?"

She nodded. The councilmen, representing the four pythian cave-cities and their surrounding villages, were spread throughout Delphi. Lacking speedy transportation, they met only twice a year to conduct business that affected Delphi as a whole. This was one of those times. "How does that affect me?"

"The new councilman from Oasis has requested your assistance in healing one of his pythias. She has the same symptoms Rheta had."

Rheta had been driven mad because she was one of the rare few who remembered her prophecies. If this other pythia had the same symptoms, Juelle could probably treat her successfully. "No problem. You know I'll be glad to help. But there's one thing I'd like to do first. . . ."

"Yes?"

Ever since she'd learned of the Delphians' psi abilities, Juelle had the burning desire to acquire them for herself, to use them in conjunction with her therapy. Having the ability to look deep into people's souls would be a rare and precious gift. She could learn firsthand what was torturing her patients and, perhaps, help them mend their lives. It was a psychiatrist's dream come true.

Unfortunately, she would have to become a pythia first. Twisting her hands together in her lap, Juelle blurted, "I'd like to visit a moncat grove."

Thena smiled. "I'd be happy to take you to one tomorrow."

"Actually, I'd hoped that I could visit one alone . . . at night."

"I'm sorry," Thena said, "but you know the only people permitted to do that are adolescent girls who hope to be chosen by a moncat."

That's exactly why she wanted to go there—it was

15

the accepted way to become a pythia. "Yes, I know."

Thena's gaze turned sober, pitying in her under-standing. "Oh, Juelle, I wish I could let you, but it just isn't done. Only young girls can become py-thias. I'm sorry, but you're too old."

Too old at thirty-two? For a moment, Juelle raged inwardly. She'd expected this answer, but had hoped for another. She looked at Lancer for sup-port, but he just shrugged. He might be Council Captain and ruler of Delphi, but it was only by vir-tue of his life-mating to Thena. He was still a Ter-ran, an outsider like Juelle, and he tried hard to conform to the accepted practices of the Delphian culture. Regrettably, she understood his position.

That didn't mean she had to accept it. "You've only tested women at menarche. Have you ever tried it on someone my age?"

"No. . . ." Thena admitted.

"Then you don't know it won't work. Let me try."

Thena shook her head. "It's too dangerous. Pyth-ias and children aren't in danger, but anyone else who spends the night in a moncat grove risks being attacked and bitten."

Juelle shuddered involuntarily. She'd seen what the bite of an angry moncat had done to Nevan, Thena's former Observer. While he'd deserved it for his unsuccessful coup attempt, he'd been ill for weeks before his banishment. Still, that hadn't stopped him from yelling impotent threats at Juelle for helping to foil his plans.

She didn't want to be bitten like that. But that wasn't the only type of bite. There were three kinds: One incapacitated its victim, one turned a woman into a pythia, and one bonded life-mates together forever. Juelle was only interested in one of them.

"That's what I'm hoping for," Juelle joked. "To be bitten."

Thena rubbed a crescent-shaped scar on her right wrist where Seri had bitten her during her lone vigil in a moncat grove—the bite that had made her into the Golden Pythia, the highest ranking prophetess on the planet. A similar scar on her left wrist denoted the bite that had bonded her and Lancer together forever in a life-mate ceremony.

Juelle wasn't selfish—she didn't want a matching set. All she wanted was the one that would make *her* into a pythia. She didn't care what rank—gold, silver, green, red, or even the lowliest blue—so long as she had the ability.

Lancer frowned. "Thena's right. We can't risk it. Delphians have developed a partial immunity to the poisonous bites over the past two hundred years, but you and I haven't. You could be ill for weeks."

"I'm willing to take that risk," Juelle said softly.

Lancer clasped Thena's hand in his. "We're not."

Juelle sighed. "All right. I expected you'd say that, so I have a backup plan, another proposition."

Lancer raised an eyebrow. "What would that be?"

"I-I think I've synthesized the formula the original colonists used to duplicate the pythian process."

Looking shocked and upset, Thena said, "No! Lancer, you promised."

Lancer frowned. "I swear, I knew nothing about it. Juelle never—"

"He's right," Juelle interrupted. "I researched it on my own. When we visited your ancestors' ship last month, I found Dr. Crowley's notes for the original formula. I've been working on it ever since."

"But why?" Thena asked. "You know why we've kept it a secret. If this gets out, it'll destroy our monopoly on prophesying—the only bargaining chip we have to enter the United Planets Republic on equal terms."

"I know, but—"

"Besides," Thena reminded her, "*you* promised, too."

"I know I did. I promised not to reveal the formula's existence to anyone else and I haven't."

"Then why—"

"I just wanted to see if I could reproduce it using Dr. Crowley's notes. I can. I have."

The empathic moncat fidgeted, a sure indication Thena was upset. Lancer rose and crossed to Thena, resting his hands on her shoulders. "And what do you intend to do with it now that you've made it?"

"I'd like to test it—on Rheta."

"Test it!" Seri's hiss punctuated Thena's exclamation. "Absolutely not. You're not going to try some strange Terran drug on my mother. Why would you even *think* such a thing?"

"I *am* Rheta's therapist," Juelle reminded them. "And she may have regained her sanity, but she's still devastated at the loss of her gift."

"She *can't* prophesy anymore. Her moncat died when she . . . when she . . ."

"Exactly. She can't prophesy the normal way, so I thought I'd try the formula on her." Though why anyone would *prefer* being drugged by flowers and losing consciousness was beyond her. And most pythias couldn't even remember the experience—they had to have an observer write it down for them.

Juelle continued. "According to Dr. Crowley's notes, it was used successfully on your ancestors to help them prophesy *without* the moncats and the flowers, so we know it's not dangerous. If Rheta could use it to regain some of her pythian abilities, I thought it might help her live with the grief."

"It's been more than twenty years—"

"Yes, but she's just now regaining her lucidity. The memories of the loss of her powers and of her

18

moncat are still as fresh in her mind now as they were then. Is that so hard to believe?"

Thena stroked Seri. "I suppose not. But do you think she'd want to?"

Juelle shrugged. "I don't know. I haven't mentioned it to her since you made me promise not to reveal the existence of the formula."

Thena was obviously torn. On one hand, she wanted to make her mother happy. But she also had her planet's welfare at stake.

Lancer's hands tightened on Thena's shoulders as his gaze pierced Juelle. "And what if it works? What then? Do you plan to use it on yourself?"

Despite herself, Juelle blushed. Lancer knew her too well. "Yes, I do."

Thena's mouth dropped open in horror. "No, you can't. You're not a pythia—you couldn't be."

Juelle's mouth twisted into a wry grimace and Thena was immediately contrite. "I'm sorry, I didn't mean . . ."

"It's okay," Juelle reassured her. "I know what you meant. It's just that it would be invaluable to help unlock the secrets of my patients' minds and reduce the amount of time required to cure them. Do you have any idea how frustrating it is to have such a wonderful ability within reach, yet know I can never use it? I'd hoped the formula would help."

Thena's answering look was pitying. "I'm sorry, I didn't realize you felt that way."

"What kept you from trying it already?" Lancer asked in a curious tone.

"My promise. You two are the only ones who know about the formula, and since someone else has to ask the question before I can prophesy, it would have to be one of you. I don't suppose . . . ?"

Thena shook her head vehemently, and Lancer

said, "Not unless Thena agrees. In fact, I don't think we even have the right to make a decision about the formula. If Juelle could duplicate it in the small lab she has on her ship, then anyone else could, too. Don't you think it's time we discussed this with the Council? Let them make the decision?"

Thena sighed. "You're right. Explain it to them tomorrow. And if they agree to try the formula, we can decide whether to offer it to Mother. After all, Father is also a member of the Council."

Juelle nodded and said her goodbyes. It was the best she could hope for—for now.

As she waited for the others to arrive, Juelle glanced around the Council Chambers, brightly lit by the ever-present bioluminescent lightmoss. It was just another cavern in the cave-city of Dodona, but with a difference.

Every item in the room was museum quality, outstanding examples of Delphi's artisans. The focal piece, a beautifully handcrafted table, was made of dark indigenous morlawood, hand-carved and lovingly polished until it shone.

The smooth redstone walls, cut by the original colony ship's digging lasers, were hung with colorful tapestries. One showed the colonists' accidental passage through the transfer point that had thrown them into uncharted space to land here on Delphi more than two hundred years ago. Another gave a pictorial account of the colonists' discovery of their prophetic abilities and their decision to model their society on the Greek legend of Delphi. A third depicted that legend and Apollo's battle with the monster python, from which the pythias took their name. The other tapestries showed more recent historical events. Juelle wondered if they would commission one to portray the Republic's recent discovery of their lost colony.

The drapes curtaining the doorway were suddenly thrust aside. Juelle stood as the members of the Council entered, reminding herself to be decorous and unobtrusive. Most of the councilmen were pretty sensitive about letting people—especially women—attend their precious meetings, and she'd promised Lancer she'd behave.

She knew Lancer and Thena's father, Ketori, the Dodona Councilman, but she'd never met the other three. As the Delphians passed her, giants all, she craned her neck upward to get a good look at them. The two who followed Ketori were older men, like him, one balding with a slight paunch, the other lean and gangly. They were the same height, yet somehow the thin one managed to look taller. That made three, plus Lancer, the Council Captain. Where was the other one?

The councilmen stood behind their chairs and looked expectantly at Lancer. Juelle suppressed a giggle. Lancer wore the traditional male Delphian garb—a gray, thigh-length chiton over a pair of loose trousers, with a white sash around his waist containing one wide gold status band in acknowledgement of his relationship to Thena. He only wore the unfamiliar clothing when he chaired the Council, and he looked as though he felt silly.

Lancer shot her a warning glance and cleared his throat. "By the grace of Apollo, it is my pleasure to introduce our newest councilman. Though we are sad at the retirement of Lina and her life-mate, Homal, we rejoice in the ascension of a new member to the Council. Gentlemen, please join me in welcoming Eron, brother to Silver Pythia Alyssa, and our new Oasis Councilman."

As he finished, Ketori swept the curtain aside and a man entered. He brushed past Juelle to take his post at the table, and Juelle almost gasped aloud. If the other men were giants, this one must surely be a Titan. Fully a head taller than the other councilmen, he towered over Lancer and dwarfed Juelle.

Young and vibrantly alive, he exuded a vital . . . *presence* that was hard to ignore. Unashamed, Juelle whistled under her breath in appreciation. The entire package was primitive . . . and very appealing.

A look of fierce pride sat comfortably on a strong face that seemed carved from rock itself. Long, thick black hair swept away from a high brow and fell to his shoulders. His fawn-colored chiton stretched taut across his broad chest, the sleeve openings revealing tanned, muscled arms.

Disdaining the loose trousers of the other men, Eron wore his chiton tunic long, almost down to his knees, above massive, bare legs. She could only imagine the powerful thighs the chiton covered, and irreverently wondered what sort of underwear he wore—if any.

What a gorgeous hunk of male flesh. He looked . . . he looked like a Greek god. But was there a brain behind all that lovely brawn?

Lancer signaled for them to be seated, and Eron glanced at her, then did a double take, almost as if he recognized her. No, that wasn't possible. She'd definitely remember if she'd met *this* man before.

He frowned and, unintimidated, she merely raised an eyebrow and smiled at him. She knew the type. He was undoubtedly a male chauvinist of the highest order, and was questioning her presence in this bastion of masculine power.

Lancer called the meeting to order. "As the first order of business, I'd like to present Juelle Shanard of Earth. She has a petition to put before the Council, but first, I must invoke the executive session rule. What she has to say could have an enormous impact on Delphi's future, so I must ask you to treat this information with the utmost confidence—it cannot leave this room. Is that understood?"

When everyone nodded in solemn accord, Lancer turned to her. "Juelle?"

Juelle stood and moved to the foot of the table. Eron glowered at her, and she smiled sweetly at him. What was the man's problem, anyway?

"Thank you for hearing me out, gentlemen. First, you are all aware of the log your Council Captain retrieved from the ship that brought your ancestors here?"

They nodded, and Juelle continued, adopting the lecturing tone that had proved useful in convincing skeptical academics on Earth. "In that log, Captain Spencer described a chemical formula that the ship's doctor synthesized. It temporarily duplicates the effects of the floral reagent and the salivary enzyme that produces the oracular results in your pythian rituals."

The men looked blank, and Lancer grinned. "In other words, one injection of this stuff makes any woman into a pythia—once."

Juelle grimaced at his choice of words, but it seemed effective.

Comprehension dawned on the men's faces, and Eron shot to his feet. "Blasphemer!" he shouted in a deep, bass voice. "How dare you mock the gods?"

Lordy, but he was splendid in his anger. She changed her mind. Forget those sissy Greek gods— this man acted more like Thor, the Norse god of thunder. Thank heavens he didn't have a hammer right now or he'd be using it on *her*.

He put his massive hands on his hips and glowered down at her, obviously trying to intimidate her with his size and the sheer force of his considerable personality.

It didn't work—better men than he had tried and failed.

Mocking his stance, Juelle glared right back. "I'm not mocking your gods, I'm merely carrying on the work *your* ancestors started more than two hundred years ago."

He raised one large fist and pointed an accusing finger at her. "You—"

"Enough!" Lancer interrupted. "Sit down, Councilman, and hear her out. You'll have a chance for rebuttal when she's finished."

With obvious reluctance, Eron obeyed. Juelle resisted the urge to send Eron a smug glance and continued her presentation, abandoning the academic tone. "As the Council Captain said, if this gets out, it could be a problem. Since your society is based on your pythias' abilities, it could all come crashing down if, all at once, anyone could foretell the future."

"So why haven't you destroyed this formula yet?" Eron growled.

"It also has the potential to do good, if it's used properly and handled well."

Eron scowled, but Ketori asked, "What good?"

"Rheta may be able to prophesy again," she said softly.

Ketori paled. "Without a moncat?"

"Yes, without a moncat."

The other men frowned in indecision, and Eron addressed Ketori in a surprisingly compassionate tone. "Would she *want* to prophesy without her moncat?"

Ketori sighed. "No. No, I suppose not."

Eron raised a triumphant eyebrow at Juelle and smiled, his even, white teeth gleamed against his tanned face. She nearly keeled over at the force of it. The man could fell a bevy of beauties at thirty paces with that smile—he ought to register it as a lethal weapon.

Juelle smiled back. Two could play at that game. She gazed earnestly into the faces of the other councilmen and launched into an explanation of how the formula worked and how it could benefit Delphi. She concluded, "Don't you all have sisters, cousins, aunts who wanted to be pythias, but were never chosen? Wouldn't they love to have that ability, just once? By distributing this formula with care, you could turn any woman into a temporary prophetess, instantly."

They looked doubtful, so she changed her approach. "Of course, you don't have to let just anyone have access to the formula. You can control it, make it as expensive as you wish. Do whatever you want with it. I only ask that you let me offer it to Rheta." She reiterated the advantages, appealing to their compassion.

When she was finished, Lancer nodded at Eron and the big man rose to pace the room as he spoke. In a booming voice, he called upon Delphi's two centuries of tradition and worship of the gods, decrying her attempt to subvert their society. He pleaded with them to maintain the status quo, to stay with the tried and true.

He glared at the three councilmen. "Don't let this little dab of a woman—this *Terran*—dictate your actions."

Little dab of a woman? How dare he!

Unconscious of Juelle's outrage, Eron continued his tirade. "We must stop this now, before she leads us to our doom. I urge you, fellow councilmen, vote against this blasphemy."

25

Finished, Eron sank back into his chair and nodded to Lancer.

"Does anyone have anything else to add?" Lancer asked. "No? Then, please vote."

Surely these men would be swayed by reason, and not the emotional appeal of that Neanderthal. Juelle watched as each councilman selected a black or white voting marker, concealed it in his hand, then placed it in the covered chest in front of Lancer.

Lancer inspected the contents of the chest, then rose and gave Juelle an apologetic look. "The motion failed."

Juelle's heart sank. She'd just lost a valuable diagnostic tool because of the inability of little minds to grasp its benefits.

She nodded in acknowledgment and, her business done, she rose to leave. Despite herself, she couldn't resist glancing at Eron one more time, just to see his reaction. Surprisingly, there was no triumph in his gaze, merely an odd watchfulness and a strange glint of admiration.

Juelle inclined her head in defeat, but let him see a spark of challenge in her eyes. He had bested her—but not for long.

Chapter Two

Eron watched as Juelle departed the Council Chambers. Despite the fact that she'd lost, she appeared undaunted. That last darting glance she'd given him was a definite challenge.

He grinned in spite of himself. The audacious Terran hadn't balked at taking him on. Grown men had been known to quail at his censorious look, but she'd taken far worse without a quiver. If it weren't for his sister's prophecy, he'd almost find himself admiring her.

The prophecy . . . For once, the oracle had allowed him to remember the experience, had burned the image of the woman in his mind so he'd know her when he saw her. He had no doubt that Juelle was the woman he'd seen in the vision.

It hadn't done her justice. The vision had shown her defiance, but hadn't captured the fire and passion in her voice as she spoke about her healing arts. It hadn't conveyed the keen, mercurial intelligence of her mind. And it certainly hadn't done justice to her beauty.

Slight as a child, she had a fey allure that made her look elfin and mischievous, yet seductively feminine. How in Apollo's name was he supposed to convince this quicksilver bit of a woman to do the right thing and save Delphi?

"Eron? What do you have to say?" Lancer asked, interrupting Eron's musing.

Frowning, Eron said, "Excuse me, would you repeat the question?" Damn the woman—she was distracting him from his duty. He returned his attention to the Council as Lancer asked him for a report on his district.

After Eron summarized the conditions, his attention soon drifted again. As the other councilmen went on at length about crop failures and the relative merits of their pythias, Eron surreptitiously studied Lancer—a Terran, yet their new Council Captain.

Everyone else seemed to trust him completely, but Eron knew better. Months ago, when the first scout from the Republic had landed on Delphi, Eron had sought a prophecy from the Golden Pythia, wanting to know what the man's presence meant to Delphi. Unfortunately, the oracle hadn't allowed him to remember that prophecy, but he kept a copy of her prediction, written on precious parchment paper, close to his heart: "Gaea's discoveries shall bring Apollo to certain ruin."

Cryptic, yes, but he knew what it meant. Earth's technology would destroy Delphi—Gaea would devour Apollo like the black widow spider of legend if the Delphians succumbed to the lure of its trap.

Eron planned to ensure that never happened, which is why he'd accepted the Council position and why he'd continue to fight the Terrans. Why couldn't the others see that? The prophecies were recorded for all to see—why did they ignore this one? Or, perhaps they just didn't see any danger in having a Terran as Council Captain.

Eron watched as Lancer adroitly deflected arguments, making everyone feel their opinion was valuable and bringing discussions to closure without offending anyone. He was very skilled in this aspect of his position—and charming enough to sweet-talk a sandsnake.

". . . final agenda item is Delphi joining the United Planets Republic," Lancer announced.

Eron sat up straighter. Is this where the danger lay? Eron knew little of Lancer beyond the fact that he'd recently been elevated to his present position by becoming life-mated to the Golden Pythia—a position the traitorous Nevan had coveted and schemed to achieve.

Though Eron didn't know the details, he'd heard about the dramatic conclusion to Nevan's kidnapping of Thena. He didn't want to know any more— it was embarrassing enough that a Terran had saved their Golden Pythia from imprisonment at the hands of her own Observer and Councilman. Now the Council appeared so grateful to Lancer that they were oblivious to the potential danger of joining the Republic.

Eron paid close attention as Lancer began to enumerate the advantages. "Already, we've established battery-operated holocams in every querent chamber in Dodona to ensure the prophecies are recorded correctly. . . ."

Eron frowned. That was the job of the observers. What would happen to them?

". . . we're employing our ship's instruments to locate minerals you lack, and we're working on establishing communication among the four pythian enclaves so you won't have to travel as far to conduct vital Council business."

That seemed reasonable, even essential, and if it weren't for the evidence of the prediction the Golden Pythia had given him months ago, Eron might be swayed as well. He toyed with the idea of reminding the rest of the Council of the prophecy, but discarded it. The evidence was leaning heavily toward willful misdirection from Lancer, who, with his glib manner, would probably only discredit Eron's accusations.

Eron focused instead on trying to ferret out Lancer's real scheme. There had to be a negative side to this discussion. Eron would have to watch carefully to find it.

"Unfortunately," Lancer said, "that's all we can do unless the Council votes to join the Republic."

The other councilmen nodded in unison, so caught up in the Terran's spell they couldn't see they were in danger. Eron realized it was up to him to pose the challenge. "Why should we?"

The others looked at him in surprise. Evidently, they'd become so accustomed to his silence on the intervening issues that they'd forgotten he was there.

"Why?" Lancer asked. "Delphi could benefit from the use of modern technology in many ways. For example, the Republic can help us accelerate communication, improve health conditions, increase agricultural yield, assist in mining operations, and much more—in short, it can make Delphi a better place to live for everyone."

Eron could see the covetousness in the eyes of his fellow councilmen. Obviously, only he remembered the prophecy that foretold Delphi's destruction should they reacquire Earth's technology. He had to stop this, now.

But how? He could see the advantages but, according to the prophecy, there had to be disadvantages, too. What was he missing?

Warily, Eron said, "By your standards, we're a backward planet with little to trade. What part of our soul would we have to forfeit to receive these riches?"

Eron congratulated himself. The other councilmen were beginning to look doubtful.

"Our prophecies are a very valuable commodity," Lancer protested. "The ability is unique to Delphi, so once the Republic releases the news of their abilities, our pythias will be in demand throughout the universe—and *we* control the only source."

Lancer was a clever man to include himself as one of them, but not clever enough.

"What does that mean to our pythias? Will they be forced to travel through the vastness of space for years on end, away from home, hawking their wares across the universe?"

"Not unless they want to. People will come to Delphi to seek them out."

"Come here? You mean we are to have an influx of outsiders who don't understand our ways; who may take advantage of our lack of sophistication and exploit our people; who will have access to advanced weaponry we cannot even conceive of; who may steal away our precious resources—*including* our pythias—simply because we don't have the means to protect them? How can that *possibly* help Delphi?"

"The Republic can protect you—"

"So we can live in fear all our lives?" Eron demanded, rising to tower over the Terran to underscore his point.

The others kept still and silent, watching as Eron and Lancer debated the question of Delphi's future.

31

"And the prophecies," Eron continued, pressing his point. "Even they are no longer sacrosanct if anyone can duplicate the formula the healer described."

"True," Lancer conceded reluctantly.

"And if it is, what happens to Delphi then, when any woman can be made into a pythia for an hour? We risk incurring the wrath of the oracle and losing the ability forever. It's sacrilege!"

Lancer looked unconvinced and glanced up with a determined look on his face. "Would a prophecy convince you?"

"Yes, if a prophecy told me it was good for Delphi, I would be convinced." It was an easy concession—there was little likelihood of that happening after the prediction he'd received from the Golden Pythia herself, the most accurate prophetess on Delphi.

Lancer sighed. "Good—we've already had one to that effect."

"And I've had a prediction to the contrary."

Lancer was beginning to look distinctly annoyed. Luckily, Ketori, the former Council Captain, stepped in to add the weight of his experience. "Gentlemen, it appears we are at an impasse. With conflicting prophecies and strongly held convictions, we have no choice but to table this matter for now."

Eron concurred. The longer he could delay their entry into the Republic, the more time he bought for his people—time to find a way to protect Delphi's future.

The Council agreed and Lancer turned to Eron. "You may be under some misapprehension concerning the Republic and its intentions. Perhaps if you were to stick around for a while so I could explain—"

"I think not," Eron interrupted. "I must get back to Oasis, to my people."

"That will take you two weeks. Why don't you spend those extra two weeks here, and I'll take you back to Oasis in my scoutship?"

Eron frowned. Already the Terran was trying to seduce him with the wonders of technology. He couldn't let it sway him or his judgment. "I think not," Eron repeated. "Would you have me play the hypocrite?"

Lancer shook his head, and Eron could feel the man's frustration. He almost felt sorry for him, but he wasn't giving in.

Lancer suddenly grinned and cocked his head. "Would you consider a compromise?"

Eron didn't trust that grin. "What sort of compromise?"

"Well, I'd like you to learn more about the Republic and what it could do for you. You don't have any objection to *hearing* about the Republic, do you?"

"No. . . ." Where was this leading?

"And you'd like to return to Oasis as soon as possible with our healer, right?"

"Right."

"Good, then that's settled," Lancer said in satisfaction.

Confused, Eron asked, "What's settled?"

"We'll combine the two objectives. Juelle will accompany you back to Oasis so she can tell you about the Republic *and* cure your pythia."

"But we need the healer who cured Rheta's madness—Lera has the same symptoms."

Lancer grinned. "Juelle *is* the healer who cured Rheta—the only one who knows how to do it. She's a psychiatrist, a medical specialty Delphi lost centuries ago."

33

Speechless, Eron gave Ketori a questioning look. Ketori nodded to confirm that Juelle was, indeed, the healer who had cured his life-mate.

Eron scowled. Now what could he do? On one hand, he wanted to get Lera the best help possible. On the other, hadn't the Golden Pythia's prophecy foretold Delphi's destruction if they cooperated with the Terrans?

Perhaps not. The other prophecy—his sister's— had shown that Eron was the key to convincing the tiny Terran to choose the correct path for Delphi— away from destruction and ruin. Relief descended upon him. The decision was out of his hands. This was right, destined—his duty.

Eron glanced up at his Council Captain and grinned. "All right, I'll do it." Little did Lancer know that by sending Juelle with Eron, Lancer was giving Eron the ammunition he needed to thwart the Terran's plans and save Delphi.

Lancer grinned back. "Great. Now, if there's no other business . . . ? Then this meeting is adjourned. Come on, let's go break the news to Juelle."

"Break" the news was right. Somehow, Eron didn't think the tiny Terran was going to appreciate his demands.

Juelle glanced at her wristcom as she paced Lancer's office. The Council had been in session for three hours. When would they finish? She'd accepted their verdict—for now—but she wanted to talk to Lancer to get a feel for how adamant they were. Was it just that giant from Oasis who had swayed them? Did she stand a chance of convincing the rest of the Council if she could convince Eron? She had to know.

The curtains parted and Lancer stuck his head

inside the office. "Oh, there you are, Ju. We've been looking all over for you."

Lancer entered the room and Juelle faced him, hands on her hips. "Looking for me? Well, I like that—when I've been waiting for hours—"

She broke off. The Oasis Councilman had followed Lancer into the room and stood there, smiling that killer smile of his, quite different from the scowl he'd given her earlier.

"What is it?" she asked in sudden suspicion. If Eron was grinning, she had a feeling she wasn't going to like what they had to say.

Lancer sat behind his desk and waved them to seats on the opposite side. "We have a little proposition for you. Right, Eron?"

"Right," Eron echoed.

"Oh?"

"We'd like you to go with Eron to treat one of his pythias. . . ."

"Lera," Eron supplied.

Oh, was that all? "No problem, I already agreed to that."

"Good," Eron said.

She nodded. "Okay, my ship is ready to go—"

"No ship," Eron said.

Good grief, this man had been loquacious enough when he'd shot down her ideas in Council. Why did he now sound like a bad actor from the old Tarzan movies Lancer had made her watch? "What you mean, Tarzan, no ship? Me have ship, me take ship to Oasis. Fix Lera good. You come. You help. Savvy?"

Eron frowned at her levity. "What happened to your speech?"

Juelle gave an exaggerated sigh of relief. "Whew, thank goodness. The man can still speak in words

35

of more than one syllable. Now, tell me what you meant by 'no ship'."

"That's what we wanted to talk to you about," Lancer said. "It seems Eron is unconvinced that joining the Republic is the best thing for Delphi."

"Unconvinced? I'm not surprised. He's so progressive and everything. I mean, gee, see how well he responded to *my* simple request?"

Lancer frowned and shook his head at her. Juelle took that to mean she was to cut the sarcasm. She shrugged. May as well; it hadn't put a dent in Tarzan's composure, anyway. "If he's the only holdout, what's the problem? You don't need a unanimous vote to pass it, do you?"

"No, but each councilman represents about one-fourth of the planet's population. It's important that each one agrees this is best for Delphi, or it'll never work—our success will be doomed before it starts."

That made sense. "I assume you have a reason for telling me this?"

Lancer sighed. "Yes. I've tried to convince Eron to remain for a couple of weeks so I can explain the benefits of joining the Republic, but he needs to get back to his people. While you're accompanying him to Oasis, I want you to explain how Delphi would benefit from joining the Republic, okay?"

"Well, sure. Anyone in their right mind . . ."—she shot a skeptical glance at Eron—". . . could see it's in Delphi's best interests. I can do that. But tell me what he meant by 'no ship'."

"He's not exactly crazy about technology—"

"What that means," Eron interrupted, apparently annoyed at being referred to as if he weren't there, "is that you may accompany me, but you are forbidden to bring any items of technology on the journey—nothing of Earth or the Republic—only what's available on Delphi. That means no ship. We'll ride."

How dictatorial. Ignoring his attitude for the moment, Juelle echoed his last word. "Ride? Ride what?"

"Horses."

"You've got to be kidding. I haven't ridden a horse in years."

He gave her a slight smile. "Well, you'll have to learn then, won't you?"

"How long will this take?"

"About two weeks," Eron replied. "Maybe longer if we run into any storms."

Storms? Terrific—she hated storms. She turned to Lancer. "C'mon, this is ridiculous. Why, we could make the trip in two hours instead of two weeks. I could be starting Lera's treatment tomorrow instead of waiting forever."

Lancer shrugged. "I know, Ju. You and I both know the Republic is best for Delphi, but Eron doesn't. And if he's not convinced, his people won't be, either. We can't afford to let Delphi be torn apart by this. Won't you help us?"

She glanced askance at Eron. "Why are you agreeing to this? What do you get out of it?"

"I'm getting your services as a healer."

"I could fly there on my own without you, and you know it. So why did you agree to have me tag along and bend your ear?"

He smiled at her. "Because while you're trying to convince me to join the Republic, I'll be trying to prove we shouldn't."

Juelle's mouth nearly dropped open. Well, well—the last thing she'd expected was the truth.

Lancer chuckled. "I take it by your silence that you agree to go?"

Eron looked at her with a glint in his eye, as if

daring her to say "yes." Well, she never could resist a dare, and she could take anything this barbarian could throw at her. "You betcha. When do we leave?"

Eron stood and headed for the doorway. "Tomorrow morning. Dawn." He paused, then with a lift of his mouth, the glint reappeared and he said, "Me have horses, me take horses to Oasis. You come. Fix Lera good. Savvy?"

Juelle gaped at his retreating back as Lancer broke into guffaws. So, not only was Tarzan drop-dead gorgeous, he was honest and had a sense of humor to boot. Who would've guessed?

Juelle hauled her bags to the stables early the next morning, unsurprised to find Eron already there. He glanced up from where he was fiddling with something on the horse and grunted a greeting. Ah, it appeared Tarzan was not a morning person.

"Good morning," she said cheerily and raised her bags. "Where shall I put these?"

"Drop them for now," Eron said. "I'll get to them in a moment."

Juelle dropped the bags as instructed and was intrigued to see a teenaged boy gawking at her over a horse. "Hi," she said and waggled her fingers at him.

The boy blushed and bobbed his head at her. "Mornin'."

Eron tightened a strap. "Come out here for a minute."

The boy emerged, all gangly arms and legs, with short-cropped dark curly hair and the same intense dark eyes Eron had. He was obviously a relative. Eron's son?

"This is Hermes," Eron said. "Hermes, this is

Juelle, the healer I told you about."

Hermes held out his hand. "Pleased to meet you."

She shook it and gave him a warm smile. "Are you traveling with us?"

The boy appeared tongue-tied, but Eron merely raised an eyebrow. "Yes. My cousin is studying to be an observer. He came here to speak with other observers at our oldest and most progressive cavern—and to give me some companionship on the trip."

Juelle was inexplicably relieved to learn Hermes wasn't Eron's son—and that she and Eron wouldn't be alone on the trip. Tarzan was just too tempting for words, but very straitlaced. Since she didn't want to shock the poor man and ruin Delphi's chance to join the Republic, this boy would do very well as a chaperon.

Boy? Wasn't that the name of Tarzan's son in the movies? Unable to repress a grin, Juelle gave Hermes a warmer smile than she'd intended.

Hermes blushed again and went back to working on the packhorse.

"I see," Juelle said brightly. "You know, it would be faster and safer if we took my ship—"

"No ship."

"Are you sure—"

"No ship."

"You know, you really are beginning to sound repetitive. You ought to work on that—it can be very boring."

"All right, so long as you realize—"

"Yeah, yeah, I know. No ship."

He grinned, and Juelle felt she could almost forgive him for his pigheadedness if he'd smile at her more often.

He knelt down to open her bags. "All right, let's see what you brought."

"Hey," she protested. "What gives you the right to paw through my things?"

He glanced up at her. "I want to ensure you're abiding by our agreement. Nothing technological, remember? Besides, we need to pack these in the saddlebags—makes it easier for the horses to carry."

Juelle crossed her arms and resolved to put up with it. He pulled out several items of carefully folded clothing and laid them aside. "Good—sturdy leather, long sleeves, a hat. You'll need those when we cross the desert."

"Yes, I know. Lancer told me."

He reached in again and drew out a lacy scrap of glittering silver, holding it up for inspection. "What's this?"

What was this guy, a smart aleck? "It's a bra," she said sweetly. "Or haven't you ever seen one before?"

He looked puzzled. "No, I haven't. What is it?"

Oops, that's right. Most women around here went without or wore a breast band. She took it from him. "It holds up my breasts." She demonstrated by putting it on over her sturdy jumpsuit. "See? Like a breast band."

He glowered at her, obviously wondering if she were trying to hoodwink him.

"C'mon, Eron, this isn't exactly high tech, you know. It's just clothing."

He nodded and turned back to her bag as Juelle dropped the bra onto her pile of clothes. He pulled out the matching panties and held them up.

"I don't have to tell you what those are, do I?"

Eron glared at her and dropped the panties, then pulled the rest of her underwear out and added them to the pile. He stuffed them into the saddlebag and turned to her other bag.

"Whoa, wait a minute, buster. Don't mess with

my medkit. There's sensitive stuff in there, and I don't want you accidentally destroying anything."

He gave her a questioning look. "What's in it?"

"Healer stuff. You know, medication, instruments, diagnostic devices, things like that." And a vial of the formula, too, but she wasn't going to mention that.

His face turned hard. "Then it remains here."

"Remains here? What do you mean?"

"You promised—no technology."

"But-but it's my medical kit. I have to take it."

"No, you don't."

"Yes, I *do*." Juelle insisted, feeling distinctly as if she had regressed to kindergarten.

"What's the problem here?" came a soft voice from the doorway.

"Thena, thank goodness," Juelle exclaimed. "This Neanderthal won't let me take my medkit. Talk some sense into him, will you?"

Eron rose at the Golden Pythia's entrance. "It was a condition of the trip. No technology." His tone was respectful, yet firm.

"That's idiotic," Juelle cried. "If I can't take my medkit, there's no sense in my going. I'll just take my ship and meet you there, okay?"

He raised an eyebrow. "And give up the chance to convince me to join the Republic?"

Juelle bit her lip. She *had* promised Lancer. . . .

Thena stepped forward, stroking the moncat who sat on her customary perch on Thena's shoulder. "Please, calm yourselves. You're upsetting Seri. Now, let's see. Will you accept a compromise?" she asked Eron.

He frowned and crossed his arms over his chest. "It appears you and your life-mate are fond of them. Unfortunately, I'm always on the wrong end of them."

Thena smiled. "If I understand correctly, your main concern is that Juelle not use technology on the trip, correct?"

"Yes," he said warily.

"But you have no objection to Juelle using her kit once she reaches Oasis, do you? After all, it's necessary for her to treat Lera."

After a moment of thought, he nodded. "I see that."

"So if you let Juelle take it with her, but she promises not to use it until she gets to Oasis, would that satisfy you?"

He mulled it over. "Yes, but she must use it only to treat Lera."

"Now wait a minute," Juelle protested. "From what I understand, this trip isn't exactly a walk in the park—parts of Delphi are still untamed and dangerous. What if something happens to you and you need my help? What if it's life-threatening and I've got the only cure? What then?"

Eron frowned and considered for a moment. "All right, here's the compromise—take your kit, but you can only use it if I say you may. Do you accept this?"

Juelle glared at him, preparing to tell him exactly where he could put his compromise, but stilled when she saw Thena's pleading look. This was important to Lancer and Thena—and to the Republic.

Hell, it was only two weeks. She could put up with anything for that long. "All right," she said grudgingly. "But remember, you agreed to let me use it when we reach Oasis."

He nodded, then looked startled when her wrist-com beeped.

Here on Delphi, there could be only one person calling her. Pressing the button on the side, she said, "Hello, Lancer. I wondered if you were going to see me off."

His voice came back loud and clear. "Sorry I can't make it down there, Ju. Just wanted to make sure you didn't skip town. Take it easy, and don't give the councilman too hard a time, okay?"

Juelle laughed. "Okay."

"And send my wife back up soon, will you? In her condition, she shouldn't be gallivanting around the stables."

"Will do," she said and terminated the connection. As she looked up, she realized Hermes was staring at her in awe, and Eron was holding his hand out in imperious demand.

"Oh, no," she wailed. "Not my wristcom."

"Yes," he insisted. "That's not part of your medical kit, I assume?"

"No," Juelle said, then could have kicked herself. She should've lied—then she'd be able to contact Lancer in case anything went wrong. Without her wristcom, she'd lose her journal, her watch, her calculator, and her communication. Why, it would be like going . . . naked.

Juelle opened her mouth to argue with him, then closed it with a snap. She wasn't about to beg this barbarian for anything.

"Here," Thena said. "I'll keep it for you."

Reluctantly, Juelle removed the wristcom and handed it to Thena. "But how will we contact you or Lancer if something goes wrong?" Suddenly struck by a thought, Juelle said, "Say, what did Lancer mean? Are you . . ." Juelle's gaze dropped to Thena's stomach.

Thena nodded and blushed. "Yes, I'm going to have a baby—in about seven months."

Juelle hugged her. "That's wonderful! But I shouldn't be leaving you now—you'll need me."

43

"I'll be fine," Thena assured her. "Women have been having babies on Delphi for more than two centuries, and our healers are quite familiar with the process. Besides, you'll be back before the birth."

"You'd better believe it. I wouldn't miss it."

Thena sighed heavily and stroked the moncat's russet fur. "I know you're concerned about keeping in touch without your wristcom, so I want you to take Seri with you."

Take the Golden Pythia's moncat? She couldn't. "But you need her—"

Thena shook her head. "No, I can't perform the prophetic ritual—it would endanger the child. And this pregnancy is bringing my emotions boiling to the surface—one minute I'm euphoric and the next, I'm despondent. Poor Seri doesn't know what to make of it, and has been broadcasting my moodiness right and left."

Juelle nodded slowly. Now that she mentioned it, Juelle recalled seeing some signs of what Thena was talking about.

Thena smiled. "Lancer calls Seri my overload circuit. When my emotions get to be too much, they overload onto Seri and she transmits them to everyone in range." Thena sighed. "It's bad enough that I feel this way, but when everyone else starts feeling my emotions through Seri . . . well, it might be best if she went away for a little while."

Juelle glanced doubtfully at Eron and he nodded, confirming Thena's explanation.

"Besides," Thena said, "she knows and likes you, and if you get into trouble, she could take a message to the nearest pythia."

Thena glanced at Eron. "Does that satisfy your requirement of a nontechnological solution?"

He inclined his head. "Yes, it does. And we'd be

honored to have the Golden Pythia's moncat accompany us." Glancing at the concerned look on Juelle's face, he said, "Don't worry, it's quite common for moncats to visit their kin at times like this, or the whole cavern would suffer. Take my word for it—it's a good compromise." He grinned at her.

She grinned back. "All right, I guess you'd know."

Thena coaxed Seri down from her shoulder and looked deeply into her eyes, communing silently with her. With big, sad eyes, Seri patted Thena's cheek, then reached for Juelle. Juelle took Seri into her arms, and Thena gave the moncat one last, lingering caress before leaving, tears brimming in her eyes.

After being bonded empathically to the moncat for more than fifteen years, sharing every emotion, it must've been very difficult for Thena to give her up, even temporarily. Juelle petted the moncat's furry head, stroking her tufted ears. "Don't worry, Seri, I'll take care of you."

Seri gave her a sad look, but her brow smoothed out as Thena walked away. Juelle realized it must be a relief for the moncat to escape from Thena's emotions for a while.

Suddenly, Juelle threw back her head and laughed.

"What's so funny?" Eron asked.

"Oh, nothing," Juelle said. She could've explained, but he wouldn't understand.

First Tarzan, then Boy, and now . . . Cheetah.

She grinned. It might be fun to play Jane.

Chapter Three

Juelle looked up at the horse, wondering how in the hell she was supposed to get on top of it. Delphi's lighter gravity produced horses much taller and leaner than their Terran counterparts, making the stirrup on this one about level with her chest.

There was no way she was going to be able to get up there without a mounting block. Her gaze scanned the stables. There had to be one here somewhere. . . .

The Oasis Councilman gave her a curious glance from atop his horse. "What are you looking for?"

"A mounting block—you know, something to get me up on this mountain you call a horse."

As she stood, arms akimbo, he swung effortlessly down from his horse and approached her, grinning. "Sorry, I forgot how small you are. Here, let me help."

Grudgingly, Juelle raised her foot, expecting to be boosted into the saddle. Instead, the Delphian giant grabbed her waist and lifted her toward the horse as easily as though she were a sack of potatoes. Yelping in surprise, she struggled in his hold and grabbed the pommel for support. Ignominiously, she ended up bent headfirst over the saddle, flailing one foot to find the stirrup.

Chuckling, Eron grasped her foot and guided it toward the stirrup, then placed his hand under her rump and boosted her into the saddle. Juelle sat there, stunned into silence.

How dare he! She didn't know if she was more shocked by his presumption or by the fact that she could still feel the imprint of his hand on her rear. The warm feeling lingered, spreading a slow heat throughout her.

Unwilling to let the man know how much he affected her, Juelle scowled at him. If looks could kill, he'd be dead.

Eron chuckled and swung back onto his horse. "Sorry, no mounting blocks where we're going. You'll have to make do."

Juelle glanced at her other traveling companions. Hermes was trying hard not to laugh, and Seri was smirking. Juelle glared at the moncat. Seri was supposed to be her friend.

Juelle declined to favor Eron with a reply, but vowed to find her own way up on the horse from now on—even if she had to take up pole-vaulting to do it.

"All right, let's go," Eron said, and led them out into the cool, crisp Delphian morning.

Hermes followed Eron onto the narrow path amid the trees, leading the packhorse that carried Seri behind him. Juelle thankfully took up the rear, trying hard not to bounce in the saddle and show her lack of experience. Anything that barbarian could do, she could, too. She wasn't going to let him see her fail.

Several hours later, she still hadn't caught the knack of riding. She scowled at Eron, envying how he rode so smoothly, as if he were one with the horse. Even Hermes rode like he was born to the saddle. But for the life of her, Juelle couldn't figure out how to emulate them. Seri watched her in concern, obviously feeling some portion of her distress. Unfortunately, the moncat couldn't help.

Right about now, Juelle wished she had a moncat of her own, so it could enhance her emotions and broadcast the pain to the dolts in front of her. Let them see how *they* liked it.

She hadn't had much of a chance these past few months to enjoy the unspoiled natural beauty of Delphi's mountainside because of her preoccupation with Rheta. She couldn't enjoy it now, either—she was too busy worrying about her rear end. Hell, she hadn't even found an opportunity to talk to Eron about joining the Republic because the path was too narrow to ride side by side for long.

Disgruntled and sore, Juelle made herself a promise. If she didn't learn how to ride this damned horse without bobbing up and down, or get a chance to talk to Eron about the Republic by the end of the day, she was going to go home and take her ship to Oasis—regardless of Lancer's wishes. He was a good friend, but not good enough to make this kind of suffering worthwhile.

The horse leaned into a nasty switchback and jolted Juelle out of her reverie. She let out an involuntary exclamation and Hermes looked back in surprise.

He frowned when the horse lurched again and she almost lost her seat. She glared at Hermes, daring him to say anything. His eyes widened and he slowed his horse until they were walking side by side on the widening path.

Giving Eron's unyielding back a tentative glance, Hermes said, "You're not used to this, are you?"

Juelle rolled her eyes in exasperation. That was the understatement of the millennium. "No, I'm not," she said shortly, unwilling to spare what little breath she had left for discussing the obvious.

Lowering his voice, Hermes said, "It's not so tough, really. You need to learn to relax. Grip the horse with your knees and roll with her movements."

When Juelle gave him a doubtful look, he grinned and said, "Try it."

Well, it certainly couldn't hurt any more than it already did. Juelle tightened her knees around the horse and loosened her grip on the reins.

"That's it," Hermes encouraged. "Now just relax and roll with her movements."

Relax? Her rear was bruised and sore, her back was tied up in knots, her thighs felt like raw meat—and he wanted her to *relax?*

Sighing, she tried it, using meditative techniques to loosen the tension in her muscles. Surprisingly, it worked. The horse's gait was no longer so jarring. She relaxed even more, and felt almost comfortable.

"Hey, that's a lot better. Thanks. I owe you one."

Hermes blushed and ducked his head. He mumbled something incoherent, then went back to take his place in line. Eron glanced behind him at Hermes' red face and Juelle's grin, then fell back to ride alongside her.

"Isn't he a little young for you?" he inquired with the supercilious raise of an eyebrow.

Juelle's temper fired, but she controlled it immediately. She'd seen enough manipulators in her life to know exactly how to handle them. She gave him a sweet smile and cooed for his ears only, "Too young? No, I think he's rather sweet, and I like them young and inexperienced. It's so much fun to . . . train them."

Eron stared penetratingly at her, as if searching her very soul. She kept her answering stare open, guileless, and challenging, not giving away a thing.

Finally, he nodded and cocked an assessing eyebrow at her. "Well, when you tire of him, throw him back and I'll show you what a real man is like." Not waiting for her reply, he urged his horse into the lead without even looking back.

Speechless, Juelle stared at his retreating form. Score one for Tarzan. Just when she thought she had him and his responses all figured out, he managed to surprise her. She'd have to reassess her concept of the Delphian male. If Eron were an example, these men didn't behave anything like the men of the Republic.

She grinned. Yeah, research might be fun—just what she needed to make this trip a little more bearable.

By early afternoon, they'd reached the plains and Juelle was heartily sick of the sight and smell of horses. She'd perfected the rolling gait, but it still didn't help her posterior to cope with the unaccustomed stresses. In short, her butt hurt like hell.

A glint off in the distance caught her eye. She urged her horse forward to ride next to the two men and pointed in the direction of the glare. "Look— it's the colony ship."

Eron grunted and nodded, though Hermes turned an eager face in that direction.

If she could get them to stop there, she could fulfill two objectives at once—make Eron realize how his own ancestors had relied on technology, and get off this torture device called a horse.

"Have you been inside it?" Juelle asked, knowing the ship had been opened only recently after two centuries of disuse.

"No."

"Don't you want to?"

Hermes glanced up in eagerness, but the laconic giant shook his head. "No, it's out of our way. If we stop, we'll lose time."

"Lose time?" Juelle echoed. "There's a piece of history sitting a couple of hours away, and you worry about losing a little time? That's the ship your ancestors used—the first people to step foot on Delphi. How can you *not* want to see it?"

He shrugged. "It's not going anywhere. There will be other times."

Exasperated, she said, "What are you, some sort of emotionless rock? How can you ignore the pull of history—of your own people? You need to stretch your mind."

"My mind works well enough as it is," he said, unperturbed by her thinly-veiled accusations.

"But—"

"Besides," he interrupted as if she hadn't spoken, "I am aware my ancestors used technology, but I'm not going to agree to join the Republic just because you point this out to me."

So much for subtlety.

To his credit, he'd said it in a matter-of-fact tone, not at all supercilious or gloating. It seemed she'd misjudged the man again. Score two for Tarzan.

Juelle groaned inwardly. There would be no rest for her aching muscles anytime soon. Of course, if she complained, she was sure Eron would stop, but she was determined not to ask for anything.

She wanted to earn his respect, if only to make him heed her when she spoke of the Republic. Reason wouldn't work—he thought in purely physical terms. So the only way to earn respect was to show him that she was just as tough as he was.

She gritted her teeth and told herself to hold on for a few more hours. Dismissing the pain, she resolved to use this time to her advantage.

"All right," she said. "Since you brought it up, let's talk about the Republic."

At Hermes' questioning look, she said, "Didn't your cousin explain why I'm riding with you?"

Hermes colored. "To . . . heal Lera?"

"That's part of it," she said, ignoring Eron's frown. "But the other half is to try to convince him that it's best for Delphi to join the United Planets Republic. He's the only holdout. Everyone else on the Council is eager to accept the advantages the Republic has to offer—everyone but Eron."

"Oh," Hermes said, giving his cousin a doubtful look.

Eron glanced at her, his expression inscrutable. "I have my reasons."

"Like what?" she challenged.

"Let's hear yours first."

His sudden turnabout was suspicious. "Why?"

"I thought you wanted to convince me this is best for my people. After I hear your arguments, I'd like you to hear mine."

"Aren't you afraid I'll sway your cousin in my favor?"

His answering look held mild contempt. "He can make up his own mind."

She didn't blame him for being sarcastic—it was a petty thing to say. "All right," she said, and launched into a description of how technology could improve everyone's life on Delphi. She described how they could introduce the latest medical practices, educate the children to compete on equal terms with the rest of the Republic, and install the latest communication and transportation equipment.

Hermes' eyes kept getting rounder as he absorbed each wonder she described, and Juelle found herself talking to the boy, responding to his questions and playing to his awed enthusiasm.

When she realized Eron had been silent throughout much of the conversation, she paused and turned to him. "So, what do you think?"

"Are you through?"

"For the moment."

"Then tell me, what happens to the pythias in your grandiose scheme?"

"What do you mean, what happens to them? They'll reap the benefits of technology like everyone else."

"Will they? You've told us our pythias are our primary resource. With our lack of knowledge, it would be easy for your Republic to come in and take advantage of them, to exploit them."

"That won't happen—Lancer won't allow it. He's a true Delphian now. You know that."

"He may not want to let it happen, but he's one man against the entire Republic."

"But that one man is a very effective one. He has the ear of the Republic Cabinet—his father is the Defense Minister. They'll listen to him."

"For now, but what happens when some renegade decides he doesn't want to pay for a prophecy and kidnaps a pythia? Or someone finds a way to duplicate their abilities? How will we compete in your market then? It sounds like a downhill slide into slavery."

"No!" Juelle said in genuine horror. "The Republic would never allow that. Besides, I'm the only one who knows the formula that will make any woman into a temporary pythia."

Hermes gasped. "How is that possible?"

Seri's head came up in surprise as Eron frowned and, for the first time, revealed true anger. Eyes blazing, he turned on Juelle. "That was privileged Council business. You had no right to reveal it to anyone outside the Council."

Oh, Lord, he was right. She gave him a contrite look. "I'm sorry. I got so involved in our discussion, I forgot Hermes was here—it just slipped out." She turned to Hermes. "He's right—I had no right to reveal that to you. Please, forget you ever heard it, okay?"

Hermes' gaze held intense curiosity, but he controlled it and nodded. "Of course."

Juelle sighed in relief and looked toward Eron. "It really was an accident, you know."

He nodded. "I know, but any more accidents like that—"

"There won't be any more, I promise." She hated kowtowing like this, but she was in the wrong, and he was perfectly within his rights to chastise her. How galling.

He nodded. "Good. I think we're all getting tired. Let's continue this discussion later—after we camp for the night."

Juelle had been so intent on their discussion, she hadn't noticed dusk had arrived and, with it, the end of their day's journey. Eron led them to a shaded spot near the shallow river and dismounted.

Juelle gratefully reined in her horse and sat there, content for the moment to enjoy the sensation of being motionless.

Eron stretched his aching muscles, then grinned at the obvious relief in Juelle's sigh. It had been a long day's journey, but a satisfying one. Much to his surprise, the quicksilver Terran had lasted the entire trip without complaint. Maybe he'd misunderstood—she was obviously more accustomed to horses than she had let on.

Hermes dismounted and started unpacking the supplies while Seri bounded down to investigate the campsite. Juelle remained mounted with an odd look on her face.

"I think your horse has carried you enough for one day," Eron drawled. "I'm sure she'd appreciate it if you got down now."

"That makes two of us," Juelle said in a choked voice. "Unfortunately, I can't move."

So that's what her pained expression meant. It seemed she wasn't as experienced as he thought. He went over to help her down. "For Apollo's sake, woman, why didn't you say something?"

She leaned into his outstretched arms and winced. "Would it have done any good?"

"Of course it would." He had to admire her. Here she was, in obvious pain, yet she still found the grit to continue her verbal sparring.

He grasped her around the waist and lifted her off the horse. She weighed next to nothing—no burden at all. Gingerly, he set her on her feet. She wobbled and clutched at his arms.

"Whoa, not so fast there," she said in a shaky voice. "My knees aren't working."

He let her lean into him, surprised at his response. He should have been irritated. Instead, he found himself wanting to protect her, to care for her. Despite himself, he experienced a dawning awareness of her as a woman.

"Eron," Hermes called, interrupting his reverie. "My bed's ready." He gestured at the bedroll laid out on the ground, then blushed. "Juelle can use it until we get hers made up. I'll be glad to help."

In Apollo's name, what am I thinking? She had him as moonstruck as callow Hermes. Eron picked her up, ignoring her cry of protest, and unceremoniously deposited her on the bedroll. "Good idea," he said. "You relax, and we'll make camp."

Juelle closed her eyes and sighed in bliss as she laid back on the bedroll. "I ought to argue with you, but I can't. This feels too good."

Eron's mouth thinned as he caught the adoring look Hermes gave her. She had the boy caught like a lovesick fool in her trap. Then again, who could blame him? Even after riding all day, she was an appealing mix of vulnerability and desirability.

Eron shrugged the thought off. Apollo help him, the last thing he needed was to feel anything for this woman. He reminded himself of his mission— he was to convince her to leave Delphi untouched by technology, not fall under her siren spell. Grimly, he set about making camp and dinner.

When they finished eating and Juelle sighed in repletion, he said, "How are you feeling now?"

"Much better, thanks. But I'd feel even better if I could take a bath." She glanced at the river. "Do you think . . . ?"

He frowned in thought as Hermes gulped and blushed again. Eron was going to have to cure the boy of that habit—his thoughts showed plainly on his red face. Not that he blamed him. . . .

"It's safe to bathe in the river, if that's what you mean. But just in case, I'll guard you."

"I really don't think that's necessary—"

"I do." He rose to fish out a bar of soap from the saddlebags. "There's little danger from the water, but you're so tired, I'm afraid you might lose your balance and fall. If you're not careful, you could be injured or swept away." He tossed the soap and a towel beside her. "It's your choice—I guard you or no bath." At her stubborn look, he raised an eyebrow and added, "I promise not to look."

She glared at him, but picked up the soap and towel anyway. Groaning, she rose on unsteady feet and stood swaying. Ignoring his last comment, she said, "Okay, do what you want. I don't care—I've got to do something to feel human again."

After shooting Hermes a look that promised dire consequences should he leave the fire, Eron took the dishes with him down to the river. Seri scampered after them.

While Eron scrubbed the dishes, he could hear Juelle disrobing in the nearby bushes. The rustling stopped and she called out, "You done there?"

"Yes, I am—just a moment and you can come out."

He set the dishes down on the bank to dry and walked back up to a tree near the water's edge. Leaning one shoulder against its rough bark, he stared out at the distant glow of their fire. "All right," he called.

Soon, he heard Juelle entering the water, then a sharp yelp.

He half turned. "What's wrong?"

"Nothing," she said hurriedly. "Nothing's wrong. The water's a little c-cold, that's all."

Eron smiled and turned back to gaze at the campsite. What did she expect? It was getting close to autumn, after all. "All right. Call me if you need help."

He stood staring into the night, listening to the sounds of Seri exploring the tree above him, presumably to see if it was a suitable resting place for the night. Soon, the moncat settled down and the swish of disturbed limbs gave way to the sounds of Juelle splashing about in the river.

The night grew cooler, but Eron grew warmer as

he thought about what those splashes portended. His imagination roamed, envisioning the soft water lapping against Juelle's torso . . . her languid movements as she rose out of the water to slide the slippery soap across her bare skin. Gradually, Eron allowed himself to slip into the dream and join her in imagination, where he would gently remove the soap from her hand and lave it lovingly across—

CRAAACK! The sound resounded through the still night air. A howl sounded above his head, followed immediately by a thump behind him. He whirled around, seeking the source of the danger, but all he saw was an annoyed Seri sprawled on the ground, glaring accusingly at the broken branch above her.

He laughed in relief, but it caught in his throat as he looked down to the water and saw Juelle, eyes wide open, staring at the moncat. The woman of his dreams stood frozen in the act of reaching for her towel, one foot on the bank and one in the water as her gaze locked with his.

Silvered by the light of the full moon, her exquisite body glowed with a radiant luminescence. Slight though she was, she had a true woman's figure. His gaze skimmed down her feminine curves, from her small, firm breasts, nipples pebbled with the cold, to her narrow waist and gently flared hips, then down into the secret hollow between her legs. He swallowed hard as his gaze caught there, arrested by the sight of water sparkling like glistening dewdrops in the silver curls at the cleft of her thighs.

He stood transfixed, unable to move, his desire rising inexorably as the moment stretched into eternity. Finally, Juelle grabbed the towel and covered herself, releasing him from her spell. She gave him an accusing look, and he gestured helplessly at the moncat in front of him, who was unconcernedly grooming her tail.

Juelle nodded with one curt jerk of her head in understanding. "Enjoy the view?" she asked sarcastically and stepped back into the bushes to dress without waiting for an answer.

He groaned and closed his eyes, then took a running leap and plunged into the icy water, clothes and all. It was the only way to douse the feelings raging inside him.

He took a deep, shuddering breath and came to his senses, realizing how ridiculous he must look, standing there in the river fully clothed, dripping wet. Feeling like an idiot, he peeled off his sodden clothes and tossed them on the bank.

The icy water had solved his problem for the moment, but he wasn't sure how long it would last. He glanced around. Juelle was nowhere in sight. She must have returned to the camp in a huff. Unable to blame her, he decided to take advantage of the situation and cleanse the day's grime from his hide.

When he finished, he climbed out of the water and prepared to put his wet clothes back on, but a towel hit him in the face.

"Here," said Juelle, "use this."

Startled, Eron stood there dumbly as he wiped the water out of his eyes. Juelle half smiled as her gaze wandered over his body as freely as his had roamed hers earlier. When her gaze fell below his waist, her eyebrows lifted.

He glanced downward and quickly wrapped the towel around his waist. "Enjoy the view?" he mimicked.

She tossed him a wicked grin and swiveled to return to the camp, hips swaying provocatively. "Very much," she called back over her shoulder.

Eron groaned. It was going to be a long night.

Chapter Four

Juelle continued her sashay back to camp, knowing Eron was watching. My, my, even after his cold dunk in the river, the man was a splendid specimen of manhood.

She found it difficult not to dwell on his perfection, but it wouldn't serve her purposes to let him know that. He had an entirely too good opinion of himself already.

She reached the campfire and sighed in relief— she could stop pretending for a few minutes. Eron was out of sight back at the river, Seri had found a tree for the night, and Hermes was sound asleep with the resilience of the young, snoring softly.

Groaning, Juelle knelt on her bedroll and grimaced. Her bath in the river had made her cleaner but hadn't much helped her aching body. In fact, the cold water had made her muscles even tighter. She ached to her very bones.

If this kept up, she probably wouldn't be able to

ride tomorrow. What she needed was a good muscle relaxant and painkiller. She leaned over and ran her fingers along the top of her medkit. Maybe . . .

The sound of a snapping twig disturbed her musing as Eron strode up. He must have laid his other clothing out to dry, because he wore nothing but that skimpy towel, leaving very little to the imagination.

The sight of his rugged body brought an immediate surge of feminine awareness. Her intellect catalogued the urge as purely primordial while ages-old instincts screamed that this strong, handsome man would be a good provider and mate. But her intellect wasn't in control, her body was—and it was off in its own little jungle, partying up a storm.

Juelle subdued her libido, reminding herself that mankind had moved far beyond the "Me, Tarzan; You, Jane" type of interpersonal relationships. But oh, her traitorous body did long to be Jane, if only for one night.

Eron looked down at her and scowled. "Is this how you keep your promises?"

Juelle followed his glance down to her medical bag. "I'm not . . . I wasn't . . ." She scowled. Since when did she have to justify her actions to this brute? She struggled painfully to her feet and shoved the bag toward him. "As you can see, I didn't open it. As per our agreement, I was waiting to ask permission."

He weighed the bag thoughtfully. "What do you want from it?"

She'd be damned if she'd admit to any weakness in front of this man. He already thought she couldn't cut it in the real world. "Forget it, I changed my mind," she said and instantly regretted it. Her damned pride was going to make her body suffer all the more.

"Good." He thrust the bag back at her.

The action jolted her sore muscles and she winced.

He frowned. "I'd forgotten how unaccustomed you are to this. Are you hurting?"

Juelle searched his expression. Finding nothing but a detached concern, she decided to admit it. "Yeah, I feel like the horse has been riding *me* all day."

He chuckled. "I remember that sensation. Wait here. I have something that'll help."

He pulled a jar of ointment out of his saddlebags and walked over to hand it to her. "Here. This is gingra salve, which is made from a desert plant. It'll help ease the pain and loosen your muscles."

An herbal remedy, huh? Juelle set her medkit down and opened the jar. The oily lotion inside was a sick shade of green but didn't smell too bad. "You're sure this'll work?"

"Of course." He nodded over at the snoring boy. "I brought it along for Hermes. He needed it at the beginning of the trip, when we first left Oasis."

Juelle glanced doubtfully at Hermes. "Well, he lived. I guess I will, too. Okay, I'll try it."

Eron took the jar from her fingers and gestured toward the bedroll. "All right, take your trousers off and lie down."

Juelle froze. Take her pants off? She glanced at him swiftly, assessing his motives.

He raised one dark, eloquent eyebrow. "Do you think you can apply it alone?"

He had a point. As stiff as she was, she couldn't see bending herself into a knot trying to rub it into her sore spots. She slanted another look at him.

Eron waited patiently. "I'm only offering because

you won't be able to move tomorrow without it. And if *you* don't move, we don't either."

Also true. Hell, he'd already seen her naked, so there was no need for false modesty. She'd just pretend he was a fellow physician, giving her the optimum treatment for her condition. Sighing, she unzipped the one-piece coverall and shrugged it off. Unable to resist teasing him just a little, she let him look his fill as she stood before him dressed in only her lacy bra and underwear, much like the pair he'd been fondling this morning.

Finally, a reaction. Eron's jaw clenched, and she could see his pupils widen as his gaze skimmed her body. So, he was as aware of her as she was of him.

Satisfied that she'd finally gotten a response from him, Juelle suppressed a smile as she lowered herself to the bedroll and laid on her stomach. She had a feeling she was going to enjoy this.

Eron didn't move.

"Well?" Juelle said in a mocking tone. "Are you going to rub it on me, or not?"

She grinned as Eron hissed between his teeth and sank to his knees on the bed beside her. His reaction only added to her anticipation. The skin between her shoulder blades tingled as he took his own sweet time getting started.

"Eron?" she ventured, then yelped as a blob of something cold and slimy landed on the base of her spine.

"Relax," Eron said in a strangely husky voice. "It's only the salve. It'll warm up in a minute."

He gently rubbed the cream into the base of her spine and, just as he promised, it warmed immediately. She relaxed with a pleased murmur as the treatment did its work, and her muscles began to loosen.

His strong fingers continued to caress her skin in

ever-widening circles. Everywhere he stroked, she became languid and yielding. She didn't know if it was the touch of his hand or the healing action of the salve, nor did she care. She only knew it felt good.

He moved on to her legs, smoothing the ointment over her thighs and sweeping slowly down to massage the kinks out of her aching calves, even kneading her feet. Sleepily, she marveled at Eron's gentleness. The big man was full of surprises.

"Feel better?" he rumbled.

"Mmm hmm." But as her muscles relaxed, she became more aware of his strong, callused fingers on her body, of the coarse hair of his legs rubbing against hers as he knelt close, even the pleasant roughness of his towel against her skin.

Preternaturally aware of his every movement, her heart leapt into her throat as his skillful hands swept up her legs again, then lifted the edge of her panties to lavish the lotion on the sensitive skin of her buttocks.

Juelle stifled an intake of breath as a spear of desire shot through her, leaving her aching in an entirely different place. Startled, she gasped and sat bolt upright—right in the circle of his arms. Just where she longed . . . and dreaded . . . to be. Wordlessly, she stared into his dark eyes.

His gaze never wavering from hers, Eron murmured, "I didn't mean to startle you."

The cool night air brushed Juelle's body with its chill fingers, and she shivered. The slight movement brought her knees and breasts into contact with his body, reminding Juelle how small she was against his massive chest. "I . . . it's okay. I thought . . ."

Eron brushed the hair out of her eyes. "I know," he whispered. "I know." A small smile quirked his sensuous mouth. "But I was only trying to apply it where you needed it the most."

Juelle gave a nervous chuckle and licked her lips. "Yes, I suppose I do. I . . . I'm sorry. Shall we try again?"

He nodded, then stopped her when she would have returned to her prone position. "No, I'll do it here."

Fascinated by the strange light in his dark eyes, Juelle nodded and waited to see what he had in mind. Cradling her shoulders in one large arm, he pulled her to his chest and scooped up a generous supply of the gingra, then deftly thumbed aside the elastic of her panties. Juelle held her breath as his hand, warm and slick with the ointment, caressed her buttocks and began massaging in slow circles.

The heat of his body spread throughout hers, and she leaned into him until nothing existed in the entire universe except him, her, and an almost palpable steam of desire rising from their entwined bodies.

She gave in to the moment, pressing herself closer against him, feeling small and vulnerable, yet strong with feminine power as the rock-hard evidence of his need pushed against her abdomen. Slowly, boldly, she stroked her hands across the warm skin of his back and down his ribs as he continued to massage her in sensuous, squeezing whirls of bliss.

When her hands reached the towel at his waist, she looked up, not knowing what she expected to see. Eron stared down at her, his expression full of desire, need, and hesitant anticipation.

The combination was too much to resist. With a sigh, Juelle raised her mouth to his.

Tenderly, he took what she offered and pressed his lips against hers with exquisite gentleness. A deep-seated heat claimed her, and Juelle flicked her tongue against his lips.

Eron groaned and tightened his hold on her, slanting his mouth across hers to give her a rich, wet, satisfying kiss that left her breathless. A thrill arced through her, and the steam enveloping them threatened to hiss into nothingness wherever their bodies touched.

Suddenly, a cough shattered the silence. She and Eron both froze, and the warm mist turned into chill droplets on her skin.

Hermes. They'd forgotten Hermes. She glanced over at his sleeping bag to see him stirring restlessly, still asleep. Lord, what they'd almost done—and with Hermes less than ten feet away! She saw the same realization flicker across Eron's face and knew he could read the uncertainty on hers.

Giving her a lopsided smile, he cradled her head in his large hands and dropped a kiss on her nose. "I know," he whispered in a regretful tone. "Maybe some other time?"

Juelle's heart flip-flopped in her chest as she nodded. "Count on it," she whispered back.

Eron gave her one last lingering kiss before she clambered back into bed, and he strode off into the night.

Juelle sighed. He'd taken care of the physical pain. Now only one small portion of her anatomy still ached—a part that would be eased only by the application of one Eron, Oasis Councilman.

Unfortunately, that was out of the question while Hermes accompanied them. She turned over and tried to sleep.

Suddenly, a loud crack split the night. Juelle sat up in panic. Dear Lord, what was that? A dull thud and a splintering noise echoed across the campfire. But she relaxed, finally recognizing the sounds. It was just Eron. She grinned. Unfulfilled desire caused men to do crazy things, but beating up a tree? That was a little barbaric, even for Tarzan.

The black night echoed the bleakness in Nevan's soul as he sat apart from his men at the campfire and stared into the darkness. He kept a silent vigil, watching to ensure they had not been followed by the villagers.

It was difficult to find provisions for his faithful followers, difficult to provide them with the basics of life—food, shelter, clothing. Only that necessity to provide had brought him to this pass, forced to forage for food like an animal. That, and his exile from Dodona, banished from all he knew and loved . . . and coveted.

His hands clenched in fists of impotent rage. Soon, though, that would be remedied. The oracle had promised him a sign. *Soon, now,* he promised himself, *I will regain the honor and glory stolen from me.*

Eron rose early the next morning, though he wasn't at all rested. His dreams, both waking and asleep, had been full of Juelle—remembering the silken feel of her white skin, the sweet taste of her lips, and the way her passion had flared to life in a quicksilver flash. The embrace had left him wanting more, much more, and he wondered what it would be like to fan that spark into a full-blown blaze.

But that way lay madness. Eron sternly reminded himself to keep his hands off the Terran. She was dangerous, with her lightning-quick intelligence, her technological temptations, and her siren beauty that could drive a man to distraction. No, better to steer clear of her—at least until Delphi's future was assured.

Hermes awoke and fixed their morning meal as Eron packed the horses and resolved to remember that Juelle was the pivot point upon which his planet's destiny turned. Much though he regretted it, he couldn't fall under the spell of her physical charms until he'd accomplished that mission.

His gaze lingered on her as she stirred to wakefulness and crawled out of the sleeping bag, stretching as sinuously as a moncat. The movement made his loins tighten in response as he remembered her parting promise of the night before. Eron wouldn't hold her to it, of course. He'd been less than a gentleman, and he knew it. He'd only meant to soothe her aches, not ignite her desire—and his own.

Her gaze collided with his and his jaw tightened as he strove to keep his face and his body impassive. How would she react? Would she be angry? Indignant? Embarrassed?

Hermes shyly handed her a cup of tea and a biscuit. "Good morning. How're you feeling today?"

"Thank you. Much better than I expected. Eron has a wonderful prescription for saddle sores. Made me forget all about the pain."

Hermes nodded. "Ah, yes, gingra salve."

Juelle flashed Eron a sidelong smile and a saucy wink. "Oh, yes, that too."

He smiled back, barely stifling a guffaw. He should've known he wouldn't be able to predict this woman. So she wasn't at all embarrassed, was she? Ignoring Hermes' puzzled look, Eron said, "Good, then let's eat and get moving."

Juelle looked at her bedroll with longing, but said, "Okay. Lead on, Tarzan."

"Tarzan?"

Juelle grinned crookedly. "Sorry, that just slipped

out. Tarzan is . . . well, let's just say it's someone you remind me of."

Eron shrugged and accepted his breakfast from Hermes. They ate, then resumed cleanup of the camp. Eron surreptitiously watched Juelle as she helped. Even though she still had to be aching and sore, she did her best to pull her own weight, slight though it was. He had to admire that.

Once they had their horses packed, Juelle eyed hers warily, obviously trying to figure out how to mount again. Seri was already perched on the pommel, giving Juelle little chitters of encouragement.

Eron strode over to offer his assistance, hiding a smile. Juelle hadn't seemed to appreciate the way he'd boosted her into the saddle yesterday, and he was positive she wouldn't appreciate his hand on her rear end this morning.

Her wary look shifted from the horse to him, but Eron just grinned and offered her his cupped hands. With a resigned sigh, Juelle placed her foot in his hands and mounted, but not without a wince of pain as her behind hit the saddle.

"Are you all right?" he asked.

Juelle grimaced. "I'll be fine—just so long as you have some of that salve left. I think I'm going to need it."

"And me to rub it in?" Eron murmured, then cursed inwardly as Juelle's gaze locked with his and the rest of the world faded around them for the space of a few heartbeats.

Juelle quirked a sexy smile at him, then glanced curiously at the moncat who was emitting a strange thrumming noise. The moncat purred deep in her throat, reacting to the tension throbbing between them.

Great snakes! Their emotions were so intense that even Seri could feel them. With a startled look,

Eron backed away. He knew moncats could detect the emotions of their pythias' close friends and relatives, but he hadn't realized Juelle was that close to Thena.

"Eron?" Hermes said in a puzzled voice.

"We're ready to go now," Eron said unnecessarily, and mounted his horse. He, too, winced as he hit the saddle and adjusted the fit of his pants. Damn her—she was making him act like a rutting teenager. This wouldn't do. He was accustomed to being in command of his mind and body, but this woman severely jeopardized his control. He had to find a way to get it back—he had to remember his mission.

To do that, he needed support—help from others of his own kind who would assist him in convincing the Terran that Delphi was better off without technology. He smiled to himself—help was close at hand. The village of Riverfork was a hard day's ride away, but there they'd be able to sleep and eat in comfort—and show the Terran what life on Delphi was all about. "All right," he said. "Let's move out."

The morning air was brisk as they headed across the plains toward Oasis, following the river. Eron set a bruising pace, which left little breath for speaking, and even less inclination to do so.

Finally, around midday, Hermes pulled even with him.

"Can't we stop to eat?" Hermes asked plaintively. He glanced back at Juelle. "The horses need rest and water—and so does Juelle. You're pushing her too hard, Eron."

Eron glanced back. Juelle's face was set in determined lines as she doggedly kept up with them, though, from the expression on her face, she had to be in a lot of pain. Hermes was right—the horses and Juelle needed a rest, especially now that the day had turned clear and hot.

Irritated that Hermes had to point this out to him, Eron nodded a curt response. "All right." He pointed with his chin to a stand of trees along the river's edge. "Stop there."

Hermes nodded and slowed, leading the way down to the water where they dismounted to let the horses drink. Juelle eased herself from the saddle and walked stiff-legged over to a flat spot on the bank to lie back with a sigh.

Seri patted Juelle's face anxiously, and Eron grinned. He had to admit the Terran was plucky. She'd borne the hard ride in stoic silence. Only Seri's telltale concern gave her away. Juelle stroked the moncat's fur. Apparently satisfied the woman would live, Seri scampered up a nearby tree.

Eron watched from the bank as Hermes dipped his cup in the river and handed it to Juelle. She grinned her thanks, and Hermes blushed. It was obvious the poor boy was smitten. Although Eron couldn't blame him, he hoped the boy's calf-love wouldn't let him be dazzled by the wonders of Terran technology.

No, he shouldn't worry. Hermes was more sensible than that. Or was he? Frowning, Eron grabbed one of Juelle's shirts and walked over to tower above her and Hermes as they chuckled over Seri's antics in the trees.

Juelle's look was decidedly wary as she squinted up at him against the sun. "What?"

"There's a much more comfortable spot up there—beneath the trees. Shady and cool."

"Sounds wonderful, but I think I'll pass," she said, closing her eyes.

Eron grinned and squatted down beside her. "That's your choice, but your skin is turning pink."

He poked her arm experimentally. "Just like a boiled pig."

Hermes looked horrified, and Juelle's eyes snapped open. "Pig?" she demanded.

"Yes, pig. Of course, if you *want* a bad burn . . ."

She glanced down at her arms and grimaced. "You're right. I need to get out of the sun."

"Here, you'll need this." He dropped the long-sleeved shirt on her chest, and surprisingly, she sat up and slipped it on without demur.

She smiled at Hermes and held out her hand. "Help me up, will you?"

Hermes did so with alacrity, beaming at Juelle in that foolish manner as she stood swaying. She pretended she wasn't in excruciating pain as she nonchalantly brushed off the seat of her trousers. "Where to?"

Eron pointed. "Up that path. Wait, I'll join you." He took some trail rations from the saddlebags and led the way until they came to a large rotted tree that had fallen across the path.

Juelle stopped short, a dismayed look on her face. The log rose to the height of her chest, and it was obvious that her overworked muscles weren't up to the strain of climbing over it.

"Wait, I'll fix it," Eron said.

"That's okay. I'm sure there's a way around."

"Unnecessary." There was no sense in prolonging her agony any further when he could take care of the problem. He handed the supplies to Hermes. "Here—hold these."

With a few hard, swift kicks, Eron demolished the section of the rotten log that covered the path, and strode through the rubble. Realizing no one was following him, he turned with a questioning look. "Coming?"

Juelle glanced down at the disturbed insects

scurrying over the shattered log with a disgusted look on her face and fanned at the residual dust choking the air. "Yeah, I guess."

She stepped through the debris, Hermes hovering solicitously at her elbow. From there it was a short walk to the shaded spot. Eron contented himself with watching as Juelle seated herself, and Hermes handed out the provisions.

As she chewed on the hard journey bread, Juelle looked up at the trees with a curious expression. "These aren't gray like the morla trees near Dodona. The leaves are different, too. What do you call them?"

Eron glanced up. "Arianas."

"Arianas. What a pretty name." She glanced at the moncat who was chewing on the leaves above them. "Seri sure likes them."

"Of course."

"Why 'of course'?"

"Because you always find arianas in a moncat grove."

Juelle sat up straighter and looked around. "This is a moncat grove?"

"Not anymore."

She looked strangely disappointed. "Why not?"

He shrugged. "Who knows why moncats do what they do?"

"But it once was?"

"Probably."

"How can you tell?"

He waved his hand around at the clearing. "There's a space like this in all moncat groves. A shaded bower where hopeful adolescent girls can spend the night in comfort to see if they'll be chosen to serve Apollo as his pythias."

"I thought everyone knew that," Hermes said.

"Obviously not everyone," Juelle reminded him.

"You're aware of it because you grew up here and it's an important part of your culture and environment. On Earth, we learn different things."

Hermes gazed eagerly at Juelle. "Like what? What do you learn?"

"Well, here you learn to rely on brute force—it's what you need to survive. There, we're taught to apply logic to a situation, to think it through to the optimum, efficient solution." She took a moment to dart a glance at Eron. "Take the log for example. A Terran would have used his intellect to find the most efficient way to get around it."

More amused than offended at her blatant dig, Eron said, "My solution was efficient." He was gratified to see Hermes nod in agreement.

"Efficient, perhaps. But optimum? Only if you subscribe to the Genghis Khan system of logic."

Eron raised an eyebrow. "What's that?"

Juelle's smile was sly. "Oh, you know, the one that says it's easier to beat up a tree than admit to your frustrations."

So she'd heard him last night, had she? At Hermes' curious look, Eron felt himself redden. "Genghis Khan was a smart man," he said. Then, before she could plant any more barbed shafts, he said, "We've rested long enough. Let's get going."

Wincing, Juelle rose to her feet. "What's the big hurry?"

Eron nodded at the river. "Downstream, this river joins another, larger one. There's a village there—Riverfork. I thought you'd prefer sleeping in a bed tonight instead of on the ground. We need to hurry if we're to make it there by nightfall."

Juelle looked up, apparently surprised at his consideration. "Sounds good to me."

Eron nodded back. And there, he'd find the support he needed to convince Juelle to keep Delphi safe and free of technology.

Chapter Five

Juelle sighed in relief as she spotted the outlying buildings of Riverfork. It had been a long, hard ride, and she ached all over—which only served to remind her of the previous evening and Eron's remarkably efficacious treatment.

She cast a glance at his uncompromising back. He was definitely avoiding her. His back was the only part of him she'd seen all day and she wondered if he knew he was putting both literal and figurative distance between them.

Because of what had happened between them—or for some other reason? She hesitated to ascribe conventional motives to Eron. Seat-of-the-pants psychological diagnoses were seldom accurate, especially with this man. Only one thing was certain. With his current attitude, she'd have to apply the gingra salve to her own backside tonight. Too bad.

In resignation, Juelle looked around at her surroundings. The buildings were more numerous now, and even nightfall couldn't hide the unexpected size of the village. Judging by the number of stone buildings spread out over the rolling countryside, there were several thousand people living here—all apparently home for the evening. Smoke curled from chimneys all over town, and the delicious aroma of real food wafted toward them on the evening breeze.

Juelle's stomach growled, demanding attention. She frowned at her body's lack of manners, and Hermes grinned.

"I'm hungry, too," he confided. "And the food here is great."

Juelle returned his smile. The way she felt right now, she'd be grateful for anything, so long as it wasn't trail rations.

As they rode farther into the town at a slow gait, a young boy, who looked only a couple years younger than Hermes, spotted them and dashed up. "You'll be wanting the lieutenant, sir?"

Eron gave him an indulgent smile. "That's right, son. Let him know we're here, will you?"

"Can I tell him who's coming?"

Offended they hadn't been recognized, Hermes stared down at the lad with a grand assumption of dignity. "Tell him he has the honor of hosting Eron, the Oasis Councilman—*your* councilman."

Juelle found it hard to hold back a chuckle as the boy's eyes grew round with astonishment. He darted off, shouting the news of their arrival.

Visitors must be rare, for the townspeople stuck their heads outside and stared, or called greetings. Hermes sat erect, staring straight ahead with an aloof look on his face that defied anyone to challenge his importance. Eron, on the other hand, relaxed his cold mask and responded to everyone they met with warmth and courtesy.

The townspeople beckoned them toward a large open area, evidently the communal gathering place. It was covered with a thatched roof supported by sturdy poles, and huge trestle tables and benches lined the edges, leaving a clear area in the center. A large smoldering pit lay off to the side—for community cooking, Juelle supposed.

As they approached, people streamed out of the houses, bringing food and piling it on the tables.

"How'd they know we were coming?" Juelle wondered aloud.

"They didn't," Eron said. "Having visitors is always an occasion in a remote village like this—"

"Especially when that visitor is their councilman," Hermes interrupted.

"There's that, too, but it's a special occasion no matter who visits. So when a guest arrives, everyone brings whatever they have on the stove to share with everyone else."

Juelle glanced around. Everyone's faces were expectant, as if they were attending an impromptu party. "Should we have brought something?"

Eron chuckled. "No, but don't worry. We'll more than pay for our supper."

"Pay?"

An explanation would have to wait, for they'd reached their destination. They halted, and several respectful young boys came running up to take their horses and urge them into the town common. Juelle gladly dismounted and, taking the curious moncat into her arms, followed Eron with a stiff-legged gait into the circle of townspeople.

A dignified older man slipped through the crowd, smiling. "Welcome, Councilman. I'm Ferrin, Riverfork's lieutenant. What's ours is yours," he said with an expansive gesture. "Won't you share in our bounty?"

77

Eron half bowed in acknowledgment. "We thank you and would be most happy to share with you."

Beaming, Ferrin escorted them to a table heaped with food. Finally! Juelle grinned at Hermes, and he smiled back, momentarily dropping his supercilious manner.

A couple of young girls approached Juelle, asking, "Please, may we feed the moncat?"

Unsure of the protocol in the situation, Juelle gave Eron a questioning look. When he nodded, she placed Seri on the ground, encouraging the moncat to go along with the girls.

Seri sniffed in disdain, but condescended to retire to a quiet spot where she was pampered and spoiled like a queen. Hermes, who hadn't been invited to sit at the head table with the adults, muttered something about keeping an eye on the children and followed Seri.

As Juelle seated herself, she realized that here in the villages, women had no status. Being a guest, she sat at the table of honor, but she was the only female to do so. The other women waited upon the head table or sat apart, seeing to the children.

Though the men treated both of their guests with deference, it was Eron to whom Ferrin turned for news of Dodona and Oasis, ignoring Juelle. She did her best to tolerate it. She was in their world, and subject to their customs. Now was not the time for a lecture on equality.

She concentrated instead on filling her stomach and studying the village and its people. She was pleasantly surprised. For a people with so little technology, they were remarkably healthy, appearing fit and well-fed. The common areas were meticulously clean, what she'd seen of them, and she suspected the interiors of the houses were as well.

78

All in all, it was rather impressive.

It would be nice to sleep in a real building again, too. Juelle understood the pythias had to reside near their caroline-covered querent caverns, but living and sleeping in a cave became very old after awhile.

As they finished dinner, Ferrin and his men ran out of questions. The women cleared away the remains of the feast and brought them each a cup of a hot, alcoholic brew.

Juelle sipped in appreciation. The drink had a sweet, smooth taste, almost like a chocolate liqueur, but with a slightly smoky flavor.

Eron took a large swig of his and closed his eyes, then let out his breath in an appreciative sigh. "Wonderful."

The villagers beamed their gratitude and Eron leaned forward to cup his hands around the drink. "We thank you for your hospitality and the delicious meal. Is there anything we may do for you in return?"

This was obviously not a rhetorical question. By his phrasing, and the way the villagers received it, it seemed more like an established ritual.

Ferrin darted glances at the other men and laced his fingers together, twisting them in agitation. "Yes, there is. Some of our outlying shepherds are having problems with bandits—"

"Bandits? What sort of bandits?"

"We don't know. They come by night, steal our sheep and any food or drink left lying around, and vanish. Lately, they've become more bold, raiding our fields. No one's been harmed yet, but we fear it's only a matter of time."

Eron frowned. "This is the first I've heard of bandits in the area. Do you know who they are? Where they live?"

Ferrin shook his head. "No, they're very clever. They leave no traces, and no one has ever seen them. If it weren't for the missing sheep and crops, we wouldn't even know they exist."

"What would you like me to do?"

"I know it's a great deal to ask, but could the honorable pythia provide a prophecy to advise us?" Ferrin glanced expectantly at Juelle.

Her mouth dropped open as realization dawned. For heaven's sake, he thought *she* was a pythia. Then again, it was an honest mistake. She'd arrived with a tame moncat in the company of a councilman, and her long sleeves hid her wrists, so they wouldn't be able to see she was missing the telltale scar of a pythia's moncat bite.

Eron chuckled. "I can see how you'd make that mistake, but Juelle isn't a pythia."

"But the moncat—"

"Belongs to our Golden Pythia," Eron explained. "She sent the moncat to accompany her friend on our journey."

Ferrin looked at Juelle in awe. "You are indeed fortunate to have such a friend."

Juelle smiled. "That I am." But why wasn't Eron explaining her purpose here? "And I'm even more fortunate to visit Riverfork—the first village I've seen on Delphi."

Ferrin's eyebrows rose and he turned to Eron for an explanation. "First . . . ?"

Eron scowled at her, but gave Ferrin a polite smile. "Perhaps you've heard of the healer from Earth who cured a pythia's madness?"

"Yes, we have. Is this . . . ?"

Eron grunted an affirmative, and Ferrin turned to her with a delighted smile. "How wonderful to have you here."

Juelle wished she hadn't mentioned it. There was

a mixture of awe, fear, and avid curiosity on everyone's face—all now directed at her. It made her distinctly uneasy.

Seri must have felt it, too, for she scrambled over to sit in Juelle's lap and stare in defiance at the villagers. The moncat's obvious championing seemed to ease their fear, but also started them talking all at once—asking questions about Earth, the Golden Pythia, the ship, her cure, and hundreds of other things Juelle didn't quite catch.

Overwhelmed, she didn't know who to answer first—especially since she couldn't get a word in edgewise. Seri grew more tense and Juelle feared the moncat would become so agitated that she'd bite some overzealous fool. That was *not* the way to repay their hospitality. Doggedly, Juelle tried to answer some of the questions, but only generated more.

Suddenly, Eron rose and yelled, "Quiet!"

His roar thundered over the noise of the crowd, and everyone quieted. After taking a deep breath, he said, "Thank you. Juelle would be more than happy to answer your questions, but we need to take them one at a time. First, though, I want you to understand why she's here."

Uh-oh. He was trying to sabotage her before she even opened her mouth. She stood, too, trying to put herself on an equal basis with him. That was futile next to this giant, but it made her feel better. Quickly, she said, "I'm here to convince Eron to let Earth's technology bring you into the twenty-fourth century."

"And I'm here to prove we don't need Earth's help," Eron replied. A murmur of agreement ran through the crowd, and he slanted her a grin.

His smile was smug, but so infuriatingly sexy that her pulse leaped in response and she found herself

81

reliving the night before. Damn him. If he weren't so pigheaded on this one subject, she could grow to like him. A lot.

Eron gestured in a wide arc. "Look around you. Isn't the village flourishing? Aren't the people hale and hearty? Aren't they prosperous?"

Abruptly recalled to their debate, Juelle said, "Why, yes—"

"Then why do they need your fancy technology?"

"I'll tell you why." She turned to the crowd and searched for a friendly face. Pointing at a young man, she called out, "You there. What's your name?"

He reddened and bobbed his head. "Jarel, ma'am."

"I'm pleased to meet you, Jarel. What do you do?"

"I work in the fields, ma'am. You know, plowin', plantin', harvestin'."

Good. At least one person was listening to her. Maybe the rest would, too. "That's a pretty tough job, isn't it?"

Jarel squared his shoulders, flexing his muscles. "It ain't so bad."

"Of course, you're strong, you can take it. But what about some of the older men? Don't you think it might be a little rough on them?"

He cast a considering glance around at the crowd. "Maybe."

"Well, what would you say if I told you there was a machine, a . . . a device that would make it ten times easier to plow, plant, and harvest your crops?"

Jarel grinned and his face brightened. "I'd say bring it on!"

The crowd laughed, but before Juelle could pursue her advantage, Eron interrupted. "And what would you do with all that extra time, Jarel?"

The young man scratched his head. "I dunno. Plant more fields, maybe?"

Everyone laughed again, and Juelle seized the advantage. "That's right, you could plant a lot more fields and feed a lot more people."

She turned around to point at one of the bolder women. "And you. What would you say if I told you there's a way to make cooking a lot easier, and to keep food fresh for weeks?"

The woman looked pleased to be singled out. Hope lit her face. "How?"

"And you," Juelle said, pointing to a shepherd. "How would you like to know the location of every sheep in your flock, to know when they go astray—and where?"

The man looked startled, then thoughtful. Juelle continued firing questions, explaining how the wonders of technology could help with every aspect of their lives to make them easier and more satisfying.

Finally, when she had everyone's attention, she said, "All of these things I described are available on Earth. If Delphi decides to join the United Planets Republic, these wonders can be yours, too."

Excited babble erupted, but Eron held up a hand and said in a ringing voice, "Wait. Think about this a moment. The Terran promises that all these things are available. But ask her—how will you pay for them? What do they want in return?"

Everyone's face, including Hermes', turned toward Juelle.

She smiled. "You need only trade for them, if Delphi joins the Republic."

Eron glared at her. "And there's the rub. They want us to join their Republic, to corrupt us with their technology, then trade away the only thing that will let us compete on an equal level with the other planets—our pythias."

Grumbles sounded through the throng and Juelle cried, "That's not true. Your Council would control all trade with Earth."

Eron scowled. "And who runs the Council? The Council Captain. A *Terran*."

Indignant, Juelle turned to face Eron. "Lancer has Delphi's best interests at heart. Do *you?*"

"Of course I do. I'm a councilman."

"So you're above reproach, but Lancer's not? The man the Golden Pythia chose as her life-mate?"

At the mention of her pythia, Seri bristled.

"That's not what I meant—"

"It's what you said. You're implying—"

"Children, children," Ferrin interrupted. "Please, no more shouting. You're disturbing the moncat."

Juelle glanced down at Seri, who was jittery with the effects of all the emotions roiling around her. Repentant, Juelle stroked the moncat and glanced up to see Hermes chewing his lower lip in agitation, his gaze darting back and forth between her and Eron. The moncat wasn't the only one who was disturbed.

She murmured an apology and looked to Eron, but his face was set in uncompromising lines. Logic didn't work with this man—the only thing that got through to him was physical violence. Maybe if she beat it into him . . .

No, she didn't work that way. But, oh, she was tempted. She turned back to the townspeople. "Obviously, we disagree," she said with a wry twist of her mouth.

The tension dissipated, and everyone chuckled. Even Eron looked relieved that she'd defused the situation.

Juelle continued. "But make your own decision. I say the Republic has your best interests at heart, and only wants to provide you with the latest technology so you can join them on an equal basis."

Eron opened his mouth, but Juelle forestalled him. "On the other hand, Eron here says we're greedy and corrupt, out to trick you in order to take away your culture and to subjugate you into slavery. Right, Eron?"

The Oasis Councilman nodded grimly.

"Then you decide—"

"How about the bandits?" a voice yelled out from the back. "Will you get rid of them?"

Eron frowned. "As your councilman, that's my duty. I promise it will be done."

"How?" came the voice again.

"When I get to Oasis, I'll gather a group of men to hunt these thieves down, force them out of hiding, and ensure they never bother you again."

The villagers cheered, seeming suitably impressed by Eron's fierce demeanor.

Juelle grimaced. Physical force—Eron's answer to every problem. Driven by the desire to goad the stoic councilman, she said, "You know, you could do this a lot quicker using logic and technol—"

Eron grabbed her arm and whispered in an exasperated tone, "Don't you think we've quarreled enough for one evening?"

Juelle thought about it for perhaps a millisecond. "No, not nearly enough. Why—" She broke off at the sight of Hermes' and Seri's anxious faces.

"All right," she conceded. "That's enough . . . for now. But I haven't given up, you know. I'll convince you yet." She glared pointedly at his hand, which still held her arm in a firm grip.

Eron released his hold and gave her a grim smile. "Sure. When a Terran becomes a pythia."

* * *

Their brief stay at the village hadn't gone at all like Eron planned. Rather than rallying to his side, the townspeople had split into two factions. Some, mostly the older people, had supported him, but the younger men and women saw only the chance to get out of a little work, and had hung on Juelle's every word. Neither he nor she had budged one iota, so the whole argument had been futile. He was glad when they'd left early the next morning.

His pleasure didn't last long. Juelle obviously had taken him on as a challenge. Her words came flowing out as if a dam had been blasted open, flooding him with argument after argument, wearing away at his resistance. Grimly, he withstood it like a boulder, letting her words flow over and past him, hoping the deluge would soon slow to a trickle. Unfortunately, it never did.

Oddly enough, Seri bore up fairly well under Juelle's intensity, but Hermes didn't. The poor lad seemed torn between his respect for his councilman and his worship of the Terran. Not knowing how to reconcile the two, he tended to agonize in silence. Eron wished he could do something to help the lad, but he knew of nothing that would help, except to agree with Juelle—or gag her.

The former was impossible, and while the latter was tempting, he knew Hermes would never go for it. But it had been four days since they'd left the village, and there was still no sign of letup.

Worse, his libido was suffering. A nagging woman should be wearying. Instead, he felt challenged and stimulated by her intellect, and he admired her determination and stamina. Nothing slowed her down. They'd passed from the plains into the extreme temperatures and unforgiving landscape of the black desert two days ago, and she still gamely kept up with them.

She was quite a woman, this Terran, not to mention provocative and seductive. And she made no secret of the fact that she wanted him just as much as he wanted her. If it weren't for Hermes' presence, Eron would've found a more personal—and satisfactory—way to stop that mouth of hers long ago.

Unfortunately, it was still moving.

". . . and another thing—"

"Let's make camp," Eron said, interrupting her diatribe.

Hermes' face brightened, and he made a quick dismount near a stand of scraggly trees, scarce in the desert.

Thankfully, Juelle's monologue ceased while they all pitched in to make camp. Once the essentials were set up, she muttered something and headed off toward the bushes.

Eron strapped on his knife and called out, "Watch out for—"

"I know, I know," she said and waved an impatient hand at him. "Watch out for blood-sucking plants, watch out for poisonous sandsnakes, watch out for biting insects, don't go too far, don't burn your tush, don't . . ."

Her voice faded to a mutter as she stalked off, and Eron grinned.

Hermes gave him an earnest look. "Don't you think you're a little hard on her?"

"Hard? I don't think so. If anything, it's the other way around." He gestured at the moncat, still asleep on the packhorse. "See, she's even worn Seri out. This woman has been talking nonstop for four days, and all I did was warn her about a few hazards of the desert."

"Yes, but you warn her every time we stop."

"Great snakes, boy—it's the only time I can get a word in!" Besides, the more he needled her, the longer she stayed away from camp and the more blessed silence he earned.

Hermes compressed his lips into a thin line. "Well, I still think you're too hard on her. Can you let up, just for tonight?"

Eron sighed. It wasn't Juelle this was hard on, it was Hermes. "All right, I'll try."

Juelle returned and pirouetted for his inspection. "See, no bites, no burn, no wounds, no problem."

If he didn't respond, they couldn't argue. Eron grunted noncommittally and continued stirring the stew as Hermes laid out the beds.

Juelle cocked her head. "You don't believe me? I'll strip right here, if you'd like. Prove it to you."

"I believe you," he said curtly.

"Sure you do."

Carefully, he placed his spoon down and rose to tower over her. "Are you *trying* to force an argument?"

Arms akimbo, she said, "No, you big oaf. I'm just trying to get you to respond. For four days—"

He cut her off with an angry gesture. "For four days, you've done nothing but talk. Even if I wanted to respond, you haven't slowed down long enough to listen."

"That's not tru—"

"And when I do, you treat me with contempt, as if I'm some dumb animal who doesn't have the brains to understand your technology." Despite his best intentions, his voice rose until he was bellowing.

She glared right back. "I do *not*—"

Hermes stood, his fists clenched in the fabric of the bedroll. "Stop it—just stop it. I can't stand it anymore." He threw the bedroll down and darted off—away from the camp and their angry voices.

Eron frowned. Should he go after the boy?

Juelle shoved him in the chest. Hard. "Now see what you've done?"

He captured her hand. "What *I've* done? You're the one who drove him off with your constant bickering."

"No, I—" She tried to wrench her hand free, but he held fast so she couldn't push him again.

She hit him with her other hand. "Let me go!"

He grabbed that hand as well and held them both clutched against his chest. "Not until you promise to stop beating on me. Who's the one resorting to physical force now?" he jeered.

Juelle quit fighting him, and a look of dismay crossed her features. "You're right. I'm sorry."

Sorry? That's it? Her apology and its directness caught him off guard, and he didn't know how to react for a moment. Hesitantly, he freed her hands and stared down into her serene, beautiful, *quiet* face.

She left her hands where he'd released them and gazed back at him, a question in her eyes. Now a different kind of tension crackled in the cold night air, leaving him very aware of her proximity, the fragile lines of her body, her ethereal beauty.

"I—"

Eron placed a finger over her mouth. "Shh."

She lowered her eyes, but didn't move away. Captivated by this bewitching new side of Juelle, Eron experimentally rubbed his thumb over the soft curve of her lips.

She nudged into his hand like a little monkit seeking a caress. He obliged her by cupping her delicate head in his large hand. Dear Apollo, it had been so long. . . .

Juelle rested her head against his chest and put her arms around him in a gesture of trust that struck to his very soul. He held her like that for a few moments. But he couldn't hold her and not react to the sensation of her body against his, remembering how her soft, warm skin had felt beneath his hands.

All too soon, his very predictable reaction began to impinge upon his awareness—and against her belly. Rather than being embarrassed or offended, Juelle just smiled and stretched up to snake her arms around his neck, raising her lips to his.

Groaning, Eron drew her close and bent his head to kiss her with all the pent-up frustration of four days of unfulfilled desire. To hell with gentleness. This time he was taking what he wanted, what he needed. His kiss was savage, but she met him on equal terms—giving as good as she got until he almost burst with sweet agony.

He pulled back to look at her. Her lips were bruised and dark with desire. Eron longed to explore further, to let his hands roam her delectable body. Did he dare with Hermes so close by?

The decision was taken from him as Juelle tugged at his large hand with her small one and placed it upon her breast.

Eron inhaled sharply, only to be brought up short as a terror-filled scream rent the night air.

Hermes!

Chapter Six

Eron bolted into the darkening night toward the source of the scream, never pausing as he forced his way through brush thickets and leapt over small obstacles. He was vaguely aware of Juelle following him, muttering imprecations as she encountered each hurdle.

His heart pounded in fear, not knowing what he would find. What had happened to the boy? Abruptly, Eron stopped.

Hermes lay unconscious about twenty feet away . . . with a deadly sandsnake coiled at his feet. Thick terror seized Eron as the reptile crept its way up his cousin's legs. Dear Apollo, the snake was black as the night and huge—at least sixteen feet long and as big around as his thigh.

Juelle slammed into him from behind, and Eron seized her in a restraining grip. "Quiet," he whispered fiercely. "Don't startle the snake."

"Oh, my God. . . ." Juelle covered her mouth as

she stared in horror at the reptile, whose head had turned in their direction, hissing.

The sandsnake's first bite had incapacitated Hermes, leaving him delirious—and giving the snake time to devour its helpless prey at its leisure. It appeared to be hungry, for it slithered its way up Hermes' body, tongue flickering in and out as its eyes fixed on the tender skin of his exposed throat.

Eron leaned down to whisper in Juelle's ear. "Stay here. When I get on the other side, make a little movement, just enough to distract it. Then, when I give you the sign, shout, scream—do anything to get its attention. Do you understand?"

Juelle nodded and squeezed his arm. He pulled out his knife and circled slowly around to the other side. Her instant acceptance and approval calmed him, making him feel ready to take on the world. Shame followed immediately. If he hadn't been so distracted by her, Hermes wouldn't have felt the need to go rushing off into the night—they wouldn't be in this predicament.

Eron shook his head. He'd worry about that later. Right now, each passing second was agony as his body urged him to action. His hands itched to tackle the repulsive creature head on and wrestle it away from Hermes, but the snake was much too fast. He'd probably only get bitten himself, leaving two unconscious bodies and a deadly snake for Juelle to contend with. Lost in the desert, with no way to call for help, she'd die, too. No, patience was the key. That, and a lot of luck.

As he approached the opposite side of the tableau, Juelle rustled in the bushes, right on time. The snake's head rose, swinging toward the source of the sound, its tongue flickering even faster.

Eron locked gazes with Juelle and nodded. She yelled, rushing toward the snake. It oriented on the movement and reared its head to strike. She was a perfect target.

Too perfect.

Terrified, Eron took aim and stabbed, piercing the snake through the base of its head, sprawling over Hermes to pin the writhing snake to the ground. He hung on and averted his head to avoid the deadly fangs and slashing teeth as it bucked and jerked in its death throes.

A small furry body flew by, attaching itself to the thrashing snake. Seri—where had she come from? The determined moncat added her bit to the fight as she sank her teeth into the reptile's thick hide and hung on fast. Neither one of them let go until the snake finally stopped twitching and lay upon the ground, dead.

Eron released his grip and drew a shaky breath, willing his heartbeat to stop thumping in his ears. Seri relaxed her hold as well, then gave her conquered foe a triumphant hiss—for all the world as if she'd killed the thing all by herself. Eron smiled in spite of himself, and turned to seek Juelle. She was just getting up from the ground where she'd evidently been bowled over by the snake.

"You all right?" he asked.

She nodded and rushed to Hermes' side, taking his pulse as Seri chittered anxiously over the fallen boy. Juelle's head snapped up. "He's alive, but his pulse is sluggish. Was he bitten?"

Eron untangled himself from the snake. "Probably." He gave the boy's unconscious body a quick once-over. Both hands were folded over his right side, as if he'd been clutching it. Eron pulled Hermes' tunic free of his trousers. There, right below his ribs, was the telltale double-fanged mark of a sandsnake bite, already red and swollen.

Heartsick, Eron said, "Yes, he was bitten." There

93

wasn't much he could do, but he could at least make his cousin comfortable. He gathered the boy up in his arms to take him back to the warm comfort of the fire.

Juelle's eyes were troubled. "How do you cure it?"

Eron frowned. "You don't—the venom is already in his blood. You treat it with jetoba juice to counteract the poison and hope he lives. That's his only hope."

Juelle's answer was a grim tightening of her lips. She grabbed the knife, which still pinned the snake to the ground, and yanked it out. She began hacking at the snake's neck, egged on by the excited moncat.

He gave Juelle a pitying look. "Taking your frustrations out on the snake isn't going to help Hermes."

Her answering look was exasperated. "Don't be ridiculous. I'm retrieving the venom sacs."

Baffled, Eron said, "What for?"

She continued sawing at the carcass. "I have a machine in my medkit that can analyze the poison and formulate an antidote."

"No."

Her grisly job done, Juelle glanced up with a surprised look. "What do you mean, no?"

"You promised not to use technology, unless I agreed. I don't."

Juelle stood then, with her hands on her hips. "You mean you'd let Hermes die, just to satisfy some silly principles?"

He wouldn't let Hermes die, but principles and honor were what made a man, couldn't she see that? If he gave in now, it would be so much easier to continue giving in, to let technology get an insidious toehold on his world. To eventually ruin Delphi as foretold in his vision. No, he couldn't let that happen.

Eron gave her an uncompromising stare. Hermes was young and strong. The odds were great that he'd live through this. In fact, the odds were much better for him than they were for Delphi if Eron capitulated.

If the boy took a turn for the worse, Eron would consider using Juelle's technology. But there was no need to tell her that, and no need to make the decision until the situation arose. Until then, he was adamant. "He *won't* die. So, no technology."

He turned on his heel and headed back to camp with Hermes in his arms. Once, he glanced back to see Juelle following him with Seri on her shoulder, lugging the knife and bloody head along with her like some sort of ghastly trophy. He tightened his mouth in a grim line. The woman was stubborn as hell.

Juelle fumed as she followed Eron back to camp. If Tarzan thought the argument was over, he'd bet ter think again. No way was she going to let an innocent boy die just to satisfy Eron's Neanderthal prejudices.

As Eron laid Hermes down on the bedroll, the boy moaned and clutched at his side. In an instant, Juelle dropped her burdens and knelt on the bedroll, gently pulling the boy's hand away from the wound in his side and laying her hand against his forehead.

Seri patted Hermes' face anxiously as Juelle glared up at Eron. "He's burning up. He needs medical help—help I can give him with my kit."

The man's face stayed in uncompromising lines. "No. You promised—no technology. Jetoba juice should get his fever down."

Frustrated, Juelle spat out, "But we don't have any, do we?"

"No, but I know where to get it."

"Where?"

"The jetoba is a desert plant—those gray ones you asked about this afternoon."

Oh, yes, the fleshy ones that looked like shark fins haphazardly stuck together. "That'll cure him?"

Eron grimaced as he bent to retrieve the knife. "No, but it'll take his fever down and help him rest. Then it's in the hands of Apollo."

Juelle said nothing, trying to figure out how she could keep her promise to Eron, yet ensure Hermes remained alive. Her thoughts must have shown on her face, for Eron looked pointedly at the medical kit. "Remember your promise, Terran."

Juelle just glared at him.

He waited for a few moments, but when she didn't reply, he said, "I remember seeing jetobas about a half hour away. Stay here and watch over Hermes. Keep him still, give him lots of water, and *don't* open your medical kit. Do you understand?"

Juelle refused to make any further promises. Instead, she changed the subject. "What about the bandits?"

Eron's mouth twisted into a wry smile. "Don't worry about them. They won't come scrounging in the desert, not when they have villages to raid. The only thing you have to worry about are the animals of the desert. So long as you keep the fire going, you won't have to worry about them, either."

He sheathed the knife and turned away from the camp.

"Aren't you taking a horse?" she asked.

"No—too dark. I'll be able to spot the plants better on foot than from atop a horse." He glanced back at her, concern for Hermes etched on his face.

"I'll be back as soon as I can."

Juelle nodded and watched in frustrated silence as Eron strode off into the night. Damn. How could one man be so pigheaded—especially when it came to his cousin's life?

Juelle bit her lip and glanced down at Hermes. He looked worse. His face was pale and still, so unlike the cheerful, adoring teenager she'd come to know. As she watched, a sudden shiver racked his body and he moaned and grimaced, scrabbling at the wound on his side.

Seri sat on her haunches above his head, glancing up at Juelle with a worried look that seemed to entreat her to do something. Indecision warred within her. She'd promised Eron she wouldn't use the medkit without his permission—but did that supersede her hippocratic oath?

What would the repercussions be? If Eron caught her using the kit, she'd just confirm his suspicions of Terrans as honorless brutes who'd take whatever they wanted without regard to his planet's wishes—he'd never agree to join the Republic. Then again, if she did nothing and Hermes died, she'd have his death on her conscience.

Damn. At times like this, she really wished she was a pythia so she could petition the oracle for a quick peek at the future—and her patient's chances of survival.

Seri looked up at her in solemn entreaty, as if the moncat knew Juelle had the solution at hand. She sighed. The safety of one human life overrode any future negative consequences for the Republic. They were only possibilities—Hermes' need was unmistakable and immediate. She had the capability to save his life and she had to use it.

Besides, if she was quick enough, she could get it over and done with before Eron came back, and he'd never be the wiser. Let him think his native juice cured Hermes. What did she care, so long as the boy lived? Her decision made, Juelle tugged her medkit next to Hermes and opened it without a further qualm.

Extracting a scalpel, she turned to the snake head and examined it. If the venom was in the protruding fangs, then she need only follow one back to the . . . there it was—the venom gland. Carefully, she cut out the sac and prayed there was still enough liquid in it to analyze. She spread it open and found perhaps an ounce left.

Sighing in relief, she poured half the poison into the portable analyzer and pressed the appropriate buttons, setting it carefully on the ground. It would take the unit about twenty minutes to generate an antidote. That should be plenty of time before Eron came back.

Seri looked up at her anxiously, and Juelle stroked the moncat, murmuring reassurances. Seri seemed to understand, for her worried look subsided. Juelle's mouth twisted into a wry grimace. At least the moncat trusted her.

Her anxiety relieved, Seri turned her attention to the snake head still lying next to the medkit. She hissed in distaste, her fur bristling.

"Okay, I get the message," Juelle said in amusement. Seri had a point. If there were scavengers in the Delphian desert, this wasn't the best place to leave the head. It was like shouting, "Here's dinner—come and get it." Juelle picked up the bloody thing, and walked to the edge of the camp, then threw it as far as she could into the night. *There— that ought to do it.*

Now all she had to do was keep Hermes safe, wait for the analyzer to finish, and wait for Eron to return. She hoped it would be in that order.

The minutes ticked by slowly as Juelle knelt next to Hermes. She did her best to scrub some of the blood and grit off her jumpsuit, but to no avail. She could sure use a bath. A bath . . .

Her mind wandered as she remembered the river with longing. Even those icy waters were appealing right now. Ah, and the aftermath—she wouldn't mind reliving that either, not if she caught another glimpse of Eron's splendid body.

She chastised herself. This was hardly the time or place for that sort of thinking. What was the matter with her, anyway? She generally considered herself a cerebral, logical sort of person, but when she was near Eron, all her thinking went fuzzy and she found herself responding to him at the deepest level of her femininity. She yearned to touch him, to make love to him, to have him make love to her.

Her medical training helped her recognize the feeling as a mild obsession—but what was the cure? Unfortunately, the analyzer couldn't come up with an antidote for the Oasis Councilman. No, the recommended treatment was to give in to her need, and satisfy it. It was the only way to get the man out of her system.

And if it wasn't for their continual disagreements about what was best for the future of Delphi—not to mention Hermes' interruptions—that need would have been satisfied by now.

Juelle gave the boy a guilty glance. Of course, she shouldn't blame him for this last interruption. He hadn't *wanted* to get bitten by a sandsnake, though she couldn't help but wonder what might've happened if he hadn't—

BEEP . . . BEEP . . . BEEP. Her analyzer's alarm went off, startling her and Seri so that they both jumped. Juelle grabbed it and turned it off, checking the readout.

99

It was yellow. She suppressed a delighted whoop. Not bad—that meant the unit had been able to synthesize an antidote, but it wouldn't be as fast acting as she'd hoped. Instead, it would take a day or two to take full effect. That was just as well. That way Eron wouldn't get suspicious—he'd simply ascribe Hermes' cure to the jetoba juice.

She hadn't heard any indications of Eron's return, so she still had time to give Hermes the antidote. She decanted the serum into a sterile injector and placed it against the boy's side, driving it home. Good. It was done and she had fulfilled her promise as a healer. Seri gave her an approving look, and Juelle ruffled the little moncat's fur.

Suddenly, she heard a noise out in the darkness. Startled, she dropped the injector and froze. What was it?

"Juelle? It's just me."

Eron! Damn, he was back early. She tossed the analyzer into the medkit and put it back where it had been when he left, then scooted back to sit next to Hermes.

Eron entered the camp, sweating and winded, and carrying several large, fleshy gray leaves.

"Did you find them?"

Eron nodded, then knelt down next to Juelle. "I didn't find very many, but this should get his fever down for the rest of the night. We can look for more tomorrow."

He sliced open a leaf and poured its liquid into Hermes' water cup, then squeezed the leaf until it gave up its last drop of moisture, filling half the cup.

Juelle and Seri scooted closer, watching. "I never would have believed a desert plant could hold that much liquid."

He repeated the procedure with another leaf, saying, "The desert has many dangers, but it also has

100

many cures, if you know where to look. All right, help me here."

He handed the cup to Juelle and leaned down to raise Hermes in his arms. Hermes struggled fitfully, but Eron held him steady so Juelle could pour the juice into his mouth. When they finally persuaded Hermes to swallow most of it, Eron laid him back on the bed. "That's all we can do for now."

He leaned back on his haunches and Juelle could see he was exhausted. He must have run as fast as he could to get back to camp and Hermes. Eron glanced up at her, and their gazes locked briefly before he looked away.

Puzzled, Juelle reached out to touch his arm. "Eron?"

He pulled away, still avoiding her gaze. "You might as well get some sleep," he muttered. "I'll watch over Hermes. Then, in the morning, if he's better, I'll ride back to Riverfork to get help."

"And if he's not?" she asked, goading him. "Will you let your principles overcome your need to save your cousin's life?"

Eron stayed motionless, though Juelle could almost see the doubts and emotions seething inside him. "I don't know," he said in an agonized tone. "I'll make that decision in the morning."

Feeling a little ashamed and wanting to comfort him, Juelle rose to her feet and walked around Hermes to give Eron a hug. "Everything will be all right." And it would; she'd taken care of that.

His body was stiff and unyielding. "Relax," she murmured.

Eron stiffened even more and reached up to peel her arms away in one swift motion. He rose to tower over her, his face shrouded in darkness as he looked down at her. "This is not an answer. This mustn't be."

Shocked, she said, "I was only trying to comfort you."

"That is the way it always starts with you—so innocent, yet you touch me and my body burns like fire."

"So what's wrong with that?"

He looked away, his expression hard. "Nothing . . . and everything."

She rose to her feet. "Whoa, bud. You're going to have to explain that one to me."

His answering gaze was fierce, almost angry. "If you were a Delphian woman, it would be normal, natural. But you are not."

"Of course I'm not. But I *am* human—just as human as you, with the same needs and wants." Stronger needs and wants than she'd ever felt before, but the same nonetheless.

"And look what they have driven us to."

Incredulous, Juelle said, "What? We haven't done anything yet."

"No, but we almost did, and because of my . . . distraction, Hermes lies wounded and perhaps dying."

So that was it—Eron had a case of guilt weighing on his shoulders. Wanting to touch him but knowing it was a bad idea, Juelle kept her hands to herself. "This isn't your fault, you know. You didn't force him to go running off into the desert. He did that on his own."

"But he did it because we argued. And because of our . . . inattention, he was attacked."

"Okay, so it's my fault, too."

"No—I didn't mean that. It's my responsibility. My duty to keep him safe."

And Eron obviously felt as though he had failed in that duty.

"No, Eron," she said softly. "It's not your fault he

102

ran off. It's not your fault he was bitten. And what happened between us was perfectly natural. You're human, too, you know."

"Perhaps, but it won't happen again."

Juelle sighed, knowing when to give up . . . for the moment. She'd tackle him again in the morning when Hermes was better.

She glanced back at the boy, relieved to see the moncat hadn't budged from her station near his head. "Come on, let's both get some sleep. Seri will let us know if his condition changes."

As he seemed rooted in indecision, Juelle said, "You've got to get some sleep, too, or you won't be able to ride in the morning."

His shoulders slumped. "All right. Let me pull him a little closer to the fire. The nights get chilly here in the desert." He went to move the boy, but stilled in the act of raising him, his gaze locked on the ground. A low hiss sounded from between his teeth.

"What is it?"

He placed Hermes back on the bed, picked up an object from the ground, and rose to display it on his open palm. Oh, no—her injector.

"What is this?" he asked in a calm, menacing tone.

Hell, there was no way she could lie about it. The plastic and metal casing screamed its origin. "I think you know." She grabbed it and placed it back in her medkit.

"Why, Juelle? Why did you break your promise?"

She jerked around to face him. "To save Hermes' life!"

"But your promise—does honor mean nothing to you?"

"My oath as a healer takes precedence over my promise to you. I couldn't stand by and watch him die when I had the means to save him."

Eron's voice rose in anger. "How do you know he would have died?"

Juelle's voice rose in equal volume. "How do you know he wouldn't? You may have been willing to take that chance, but I wasn't."

"So you took matters into your own hands. You, alone, made the decision whether Hermes should live or die? That is for the gods to decide."

"Well, how do you know the gods didn't tell me—"

"Enough. Now I understand the prophecy. If this is the sort of help the Republic provides, I don't want any part of it. We will make our own decisions, not let you decide what is best for us."

He strode to his horse and began saddling it.

"What are you doing?"

"Going for help," he snarled.

"But I thought you were going to wait until morning."

"There's no reason for that now. Thanks to your technology," he almost spat the words, "we know he'll recover—but he won't be able to ride. I'm going to Riverfork for help."

"But—"

"Enough, woman. You stay here and take care of Hermes. You have enough food and water here for several days. I should be back in three with help."

He finished saddling, then mounted and turned the horse in a tight circle so he could look down at her. "The trees should shelter you from the heat, and the fire should keep away the snakes. Do not leave this spot."

Without waiting to hear her reply, he turned and kicked his horse into a gallop. Belatedly, one of his phrases demanded her attention. "What prophecy?" she called after him, but there was no response.

Juelle turned to stare down at Hermes and his faithful nurse, Seri. "What prophecy?" she muttered again.

Chapter Seven

At the edge of the desert, outside the ruins of an abandoned pythian cave-city, Nevan stared into the fire. He sat surrounded by his supporters, with his father, Shogril, and cousin Orgon at his side.

The wind howled, whipping black sand into their eyes and stirring the fire into a frenzy as he glanced up into the murky night sky. Apollo had provided once more. The sandstorm had bypassed them, leaving them protected to do Apollo's will.

Though Nevan was grateful, he found himself becoming more and more impatient. Where was the sign the pythia had promised?

One of the new recruits, a young man named Ivar, darted nervous glances into the surrounding darkness, then came to sit near the fire. "Should we be out here?" he whispered in a harsh voice.

Nevan fixed him with a supercilious stare. "Why should we not?"

"I just thought . . . you know, being bandits and all—"

Nevan rose to tower over the lout and glare down at him. "Do not believe what the villagers say of us. We are not common bandits. We serve a higher purpose."

Ivar shrank back. "Oh, of course. I didn't mean—" He gulped, then dredged up some shreds of bravery from the depths of his petty soul. "But . . . why are we out in the open where everyone can see us? Why don't we stay in the caves?"

Nevan's lip curled. Hide? No, though he had been banished, he wouldn't hide. Instead, he would turn this abandoned wreck of a city into the new ruling power of Delphi. If necessary, he would destroy Dodona and all its inhabitants to regain his family's honor. "Would you have us cower like grass hares, afraid of our own shadow?"

"N-no, but we're so . . . visible like this. We've raided four or five villages in the area. What if the villagers come looking for us?"

Nevan gave him an amused look. If Ivar chose to think of it as raiding, so be it. Nevan knew he was merely claiming his due. "What if they do?"

The man gulped again. "Aren't you worried?"

Shogril rose and stood by Nevan's side. "What does my son have to worry about?"

The whole camp turned silent as heads turned in their direction. Ivar's gaze darted around the camp, looking for support. "Well, the banishment—"

"Is irrelevant," Shogril snapped. "The Council Captainship was wrested from my son's hands by a corrupt, unscrupulous Terran with no sense of honor or tradition. We wait only for the opportunity to redress this injustice."

"But what are we waiting *for?*"

Nevan merely watched as Shogril handled the upstart.

"We wait for the sign foretold by the prophecy."

Ivar's face brightened and everyone else's attention fixed upon the threesome by the fire.

Nevan remained silent, leaving the explanations up to Shogril. His men had been questioning the months of inactivity. It would do them good to be reminded of what they were waiting for.

"Yes," Shogril said, playing to his audience. "Carina foretold that my son need only wait here, in this godforsaken place, and that if he were patient, help would come to him."

Murmurs rose amongst the men and Nevan felt their tension ease. Good—the prophecy had reassured them.

Unfortunately, it hadn't done the same for him. *When* would his patience be rewarded? He had waited six long months. Had Apollo deserted him? Surely Nevan and his followers had proven their devotion by now. Where was the sign he'd been promised? He sent an urgent, demanding prayer heavenward.

Suddenly, a light appeared in the heavens and streaked toward them. Even through the muddy turbulence left by the sandstorm's passage, he could see the light grow bigger, stronger, as it came ever nearer. Just when he thought it would pass over them, it fell to the west with a ground-jarring thump.

Ivar stared in fear and awe. "Is that the sign?"

Concealing his sudden surge of hope, Nevan murmured, "Perhaps." Snatching up a firebrand, he strode rapidly toward the object. Never before had Apollo answered him in such a clear and immediate manner. Could this be it?

He halted at a ridge overlooking the object and scowled as he recognized it. It was one of those scoutships the Terrans had brought to pollute Delphi with its stench and waste of precious metal. His mouth tightened in disappointment. This was no sign.

Or was it?

There were only two people on Delphi who could command such a ship—Lancer and Juelle. Had Apollo dropped one of the offenders into Nevan's lap? Between the two of them, the Terrans had managed to ruin his plan to restore his family and their honor to their rightful power on Delphi. He owed them both—and he intended to pay.

The other men joined him and stared down at the ship in rising awe. Nevan came to a quick decision. This had to be it—why would the ship land *here* if not to further Nevan's plans? He smiled. Even if it weren't the sign, he was certain he could turn it to his benefit.

He raised his arms, letting his torch cast light upon the ship's opening. His followers stilled. "This is the sign," Nevan intoned. "Orgon, Shogril, come with me. The rest of you wait here."

He made his way down the short slope to the ship, wondering why no one had yet made an appearance. Could it be they were afraid of him? Schemes flitted through his mind as he sought for the best way to turn this situation to his advantage. First, though, they had to open the ship. Apollo would provide. His god would surely not bring them this far only to be thwarted by such a small thing as an unopened door.

As they approached, an entrance appeared in the side of the ship and Nevan smiled to himself. Holy purpose rose within him and he strode to the ramp that appeared before them. Who would it be . . . Lancer or Juelle? He stopped at the foot of the ramp and handed the torch to Shogril.

A figure appeared at the opening and stepped into the light. Taken aback for a moment, Nevan realized the man was a total stranger. Slender and a little below average height, he wore one of the one-piece garments the Terrans favored.

As the man caught sight of Nevan and his followers, he stepped forward and offered them an insincere smile. "Hello, gentlemen. I'm Alexander Morgan, Terran ambassador to Delphi. Whom do I have the pleasure of addressing?"

"Sweet Apollo," Shogril blurted out.

"Apollo?" the Terran asked, his eyebrows raised.

His mind racing, Nevan stepped forward and inclined his head. If this man wanted to believe him Apollo, then so be it.

His mind worked fast. Alexander must be related to Lancer Morgan, the upstart Council Captain. If so, it would be prudent for Nevan to keep his identity hidden until he could learn how best to use this man.

"Well . . . Apollo," Alexander said, "would you like to come aboard?"

"Blasphemer," Orgon muttered. "Shall I kill him?"

Nevan shushed him, whispering, "No. Wait. He doesn't know who we are. Let's see what happens."

Nevan stepped forward into the light and smiled, spreading his arms. "Thank you for your kind invitation." What did Apollo intend for him to do with this vehicle? Nothing good had come of contact with Terrans and their technology, yet. Unless . . . perhaps he could use it against them.

Nevan motioned for Orgon to accompany him, leaving Shogril to keep the others subdued outside.

Once inside, Nevan's gaze darted around the interior, cataloging the unfamiliar furnishings as best he could. His ancestors had brought a much larger ship across the stars—surely he and his men would be able to figure out how to work this small one.

A good leader understood his enemy and used that understanding against them. Terran technology was no different. Nevan glanced covetously about the interior. What could he do with this at his beck and call? And how could he wrest its secrets from the Terran?

With a flourish, Alexander took them on a tour of the tiny ship, but provided little information other than naming the various rooms and their functions. Once Alexander pointed them out, Nevan could recognize the bathroom, the kitchen, and the sleeping areas. He memorized how each one worked as Alexander demonstrated them.

Feeling more confident and jubilant with each moment, Nevan reentered the forward cabin and studied the control panel. "Could you show us how it flies?"

Alexander grimaced. "I'm afraid not. I lost my way trying to find Dodona and accidentally flew through a sandstorm. It clogged my filters and forced me to land—I won't be able to lift off until they're cleaned."

Plans began to coalesce in Nevan's mind. "And how long will that take?"

Alexander shrugged. "It depends on how much sand got into them. But I'm afraid it's a tedious job—it'll take a few days, at least." He cocked his head and gave them a speculative look. "Unless some of your people might be willing to help?"

Nevan granted him a cool smile, trying to hide his elation. "Yes, of course." It was all coming together. Here, at last, was the chance he'd been waiting for.

Juelle bathed Hermes' brow once more as Seri watched anxiously. It had been two days since Eron left, and the boy's fever had finally broken. He was coherent now, though the venom had sapped a lot of the life out of him. The heat didn't help much either, and it was a constant struggle to keep him cool and to ward off the drying effects of the desert sun.

Luckily, that was the only hazard they faced. Eron had chosen their campsite well. They were shaded by the nearby trees and, though she had seen signs that scavengers had enjoyed the snake carcass, nothing had tried to bother them. Even the storm had moved to the east, bypassing them entirely.

Thank heavens. That was one hazard she did *not* want to deal with. Juelle watched the approach of nightfall gratefully. With night came coolness—and relief for Hermes.

His eyes fluttered open and he glanced up at her, then struggled to rise.

"No, don't get up," Juelle cautioned. "You're still too weak. Tell me what you need."

Hermes let his head flop back against his makeshift bed. "I'm thirsty."

Juelle gave him some of their precious water and watched as he swallowed it. "Sleep now," she said.

He shook his head. "I'm tired of just lying here. I want to *do* something."

Juelle frowned. Active adolescents always found sickbeds difficult. On Earth, she would have distracted him with vids or books but, here, she had nothing but her wits.

For the hundredth time, she cursed Eron for making her leave her wristcom at Dodona. If he hadn't, she could've called Lancer to come pick them up, and Hermes would be in the House of Healing by now, well on his way to renewed health.

Hell, if Eron hadn't been so stubborn about not letting them use the ship in the first place, this never would've happened. But there was no use speculating about might-have-beens. "What do you want to do?" she asked.

Hermes formed his sleeping bag into a pillow, then propped himself up and looked at Juelle. "Let's talk," he said shyly. "Why don't you tell me about yourself . . . and Earth."

Juelle eyed him askance. While the boy had been sick, he'd forgotten his crush on her. Now that he was recovering, he'd apparently rediscovered it.

She sighed. She didn't want to encourage him, but she didn't want to hurt his feelings either. "I'm not sure that's such a good idea," she said. "Me arguing about Earth with Eron is what got you into this situation to begin with."

He grimaced. "No—it was my own stupidity. If I'd been looking where I was going, I wouldn't have blundered into that sandsnake and—"

"Nonsense. It was our argument that sent you running off in the first place. You were upset, so you weren't watching where you were going."

"But—"

Juelle held up a restraining hand. "No buts. And there's no use in assigning blame. It's over and done with. Let's move on to something more productive, okay?"

Hermes nodded with obvious reluctance and plucked at the sleeping bag. "All right. But I wish you two wouldn't fight. Why do you dislike him so much?"

Juelle sighed. She didn't dislike Eron. In fact, she liked him entirely too much for her peace of mind.

"I don't dislike him—I think he's a fine man. He's just . . ." *stupidly pigheaded,* ". . . stubborn."

She gave Hermes an exasperated look. "The man is obviously intelligent. Why does he attack everything with brute force? He's smarter than that."

Hermes shrugged, but Juelle questioned him until a picture emerged. It appeared strength was more prized than wits in the village where they grew up. It made sense. In the villages, they were more concerned with the source of their next meal. Only in the pythian cave-cities did they have the luxury of logical thinking.

It wasn't until Alyssa, Eron's sister, became a pythia that they were given the opportunity to work in the caves as observers. And once Alyssa became the ranking pythia in Oasis, Eron had taken his place as councilman. So Eron *was* learning to think—he just hadn't had enough practice.

"Why is he so adamant against technology?"

Hermes squirmed. "I'm not sure, exactly. It has to do with a couple of prophecies he received."

That's right. Eron had blurted out something about a prophecy right before he left. That had to be the key. "What did they say?"

Hermes grimaced. "He said the first prophecy foretold technology would ruin Delphi and—" He broke off, looking sheepish.

"And what?"

He shook his head, obviously unwilling to say more.

Juelle fixed him with her best glare. "How am I going to learn how to get along with him if you won't tell me everything I need to know?"

Hermes squirmed some more, then blurted out, "The second one said you were the key to saving or destroying Delphi."

"Me?" Juelle rocked back on her heels in surprise. No wonder Eron had agreed to go with her on this trip, if he felt she held the key to saving his planet. "Did he say *how?*"

"No, just that the oracle showed him he might be able to influence you for our benefit."

Juelle nodded. That tracked. "But I know Delphi will benefit by Earth's technology, and Eron is equally certain it will destroy your planet. How can he be so certain *he's* correct?"

"Because the first prophecy said so."

"What exactly does it say?"

Hermes sighed. "I don't know that either. All I know is that he thinks it means technology will destroy us."

Exasperated, Juelle said, "Then why didn't he tell the Council this?"

"I-I think he did, but the Council Captain said there was a prediction to the contrary."

That figured. Only on Delphi would people put their *entire* hopes and dreams on the garbled sayings of a drugged soothsayer, rather than relying on something less subject to interpretation.

"So, how can I convince your councilman that technology is good for Delphi?"

Hermes gave her a pitying look. "I don't think you can. At least, not unless there's another prophecy that confirms it."

More obscure predictions? Great. Just what they needed. She opened her mouth to persuade Hermes she was right, but saw his eyelids drooping. Now was not the time. He was still recovering from the poison. "Enough talking for now. You need to rest."

He didn't argue, so she helped him arrange his bedclothes comfortably and watched as he fell into a deep, healing sleep. She, too, settled down for the night, lying near him so she could hear if he stirred during the night.

Seri made her bed in the trees above them, and Juelle forced her racing mind to sleep. Tomorrow would bring with it a new perspective.

She woke refreshed the next morning, glad to see Hermes had passed a peaceful night. As she went about the business of cooking their morning meal, she thought about what she could do to convince Eron that Earth's discoveries could help Delphi and its people achieve their true potential.

"Hermes, do you feel up to answering some questions?"

"Of course. What do you want to talk about?"

"You know, the more I think about it, the more I'm convinced Eron is just being pigheaded. The other councilmen can see the benefits of technology—hell, even the villagers can—but not Eron. How can I convince him otherwise?"

Hermes shrugged. "I doubt you can."

"Why not? The Republic is doing its best to keep Delphi a secret, but sooner or later the word will leak out about the pythias. Once Delphi is discovered by the masses of humanity, you'll be overrun by people seeking instant answers to all their problems."

"Is that bad?"

"Very bad. Without technology, the people of Delphi will have no way of keeping those hordes at bay—or of preventing them from taking over with their superior weapons and technology. That will destroy Delphi more surely than anything else I can imagine."

"Have you told Eron this?"

"Yes, but he's not convinced. How can I make him understand that Delphi is in more danger *without* technology?"

"There's only one thing that'll make him listen—"

"I know, I know. A prophecy." Juelle sighed. "Unfortunately, I'm fresh out of pythias at the moment."

"There are pythias at Oasis," Hermes reminded her.

"Yes, but who knows when—or if—we'll make it there? Besides, Eron is so angry at me, I'm not sure I can wait until then."

And it took too damned long for an idea to percolate through that thick skull of his. Unless she took direct action to beat some sense into him, she didn't think she'd ever be able to persuade him that she was right.

But brute force was *his* way, not hers. She needed to find a different method.

Ideas flitted through her mind. She discarded most of them as being too impractical or unworkable. Damn. If only *she* were a pythia, she could contact the oracle directly and ask how to convince Eron of the rightness of her cause.

Wait. She *could* be a pythia . . . with the formula. She glanced at her medkit in speculation. Did she dare?

No, Eron would kill her for sure. But he was already angry at her. Could he get any angrier? She doubted it. Maybe . . .

"Hermes?"

The boy looked up from stroking the purring moncat. "Yes?"

Juelle knelt beside him, trying to figure out how to broach the subject. "You remember the formula we talked about? The one that makes any woman into a pythia?"

"Yes," he said with a wary look on his face. "But I thought we weren't supposed to talk about that."

"True, true. I'm not supposed to talk about that

117

with anyone else because it's a secret—but you already know about it."

"I don't think—"

She put her hand out to forestall him. "I'd like to use it, and I need your help."

Alarm dawned on his face. It must have transmitted itself to Seri, for the moncat began to fidget, then turned a concerned gaze on Juelle.

Hermes' eyes widened. "Didn't you promise not to?"

"No, I promised not to reveal its existence. I never said I wouldn't use it—and I have some with me."

"But, but—" he sputtered.

"What, Hermes? I propose to use it on myself, not you."

"Isn't it . . . dangerous?"

"Not according to Dr. Crowley's notes."

"But there's no cave, no carolines, no pythia."

Juelle patted his hand. "While Thena was on Earth, I did a lot of research on her prophetic abilities in order to learn exactly how the prophetic process works. What I found is that the primary ingredients are the carolines and the enzyme in the moncat's saliva."

At his puzzled look, she explained, "The bite that makes a woman into a pythia."

He nodded, appearing relieved. "So you can't use the formula unless you're a pythia?"

"No, the formula Dr. Crowley prepared duplicates the effects of both the flowers and the enzyme. Once I inject it into my bloodstream, it should make me into a pythia for as long as the formula is still in my body."

Distaste was written plainly on Hermes' face. "That's, that's . . ."

Suspecting the reason for his unease, Juelle supplied the word. "Sacrilege?"

"Yes!"

"If the gods allowed it to be made and allow me to use it, how can it be sacrilege?"

Her arguments weren't very logical, but neither was Hermes' reasoning. He frowned but didn't answer.

"And we won't know if it really works until we test it. How can the Council ban something they don't understand—when they don't even know how it works?"

"You might be right, but . . . I don't think I should help you."

"If this is to do any good, I have to have your help."

"Why?"

"Because I assume it works just like the regular ritual. Once I utter the prophecy, I probably won't be able to remember a single word. I'll need you to write it down for me—to be my observer. Isn't that what you're training for?"

"Yes, but . . ." It was obvious Hermes was torn. On one hand, he wanted to do what was right according to his society's mores, yet he also wanted to be forward-thinking and help Juelle.

She pressed him further. After all, she was doing this for the good of his planet. "If you're worried about what Eron will think, I'll take full responsibility."

His face relaxed a little, though he still looked doubtful.

Juelle played her trump card. "I'm going to do this with or without you, Hermes. Without you, I can only hope I'll remember. With you, I know at least you'll remember. And if anything goes wrong, you'll be there to help me."

Indecision twisted the boy's face, and Juelle felt a momentary remorse. The poor kid was recovering from illness himself. Was this too much to ask of him?

No. According to Dr. Crowley's notes, the formula was perfectly safe. Nothing would go wrong.

He looked up at her and nodded. "All right. I'll do it—but only because I want to make sure nothing happens to you."

Juelle gave him an impulsive hug. "Thanks, kid. You're the best."

The tips of his ears turned red and he muttered something unintelligible. He glanced up to give her a questioning look. "When do you want to do this?"

Juelle thought for a moment. "How about this afternoon after we eat? That way we won't have to worry about hunger or feeding the horses." And she could get it done before Eron returned this evening.

Hermes nodded. Juelle spent the rest of the morning trying to convince herself she was doing the right thing. She examined and re-examined her motives and, each time, persuaded herself they truly were altruistic. She was doing this to learn what was best for Delphi.

Satisfied that her reasoning was sound, she worked on the wording of the question until she got it just the way she wanted it, then wrote it down for Hermes.

They finished their midday meal. Although they both lingered over the food, Juelle forced herself to ignore her apprehension. She set her dishes aside and asked, "Are you ready?"

Hermes sighed. "I guess so. Are you sure you want to do this?"

"Yes, I am. Let me just set the stage."

She retrieved the formula from her medkit and filled an injector, then sat next to Hermes. Knowing he'd feel more comfortable with a few familiar trappings, she arranged the bedclothes to look like the pythian cushions and coaxed Seri into her lap.

The moncat came reluctantly. It must have been obvious that something was up, and it appeared Seri wasn't sure she cared for it. Juelle stroked the moncat soothingly, gaining some comfort from the motion herself.

Taking a deep breath, she handed a slip of paper and a pen to the apprehensive Hermes, "Here. This is the question I'd like you to ask—and you can record the answer underneath it."

He took it reluctantly. "How will I know when to ask it?"

Juelle frowned. She hadn't thought about that. "Well, once I inject myself with the formula, things should proceed rapidly. I assume it will work the same way as any other prophecy—the oracle will speak through me to tell you when to ask the question. Okay?"

Hermes shook his head with a worried look as he gazed down at the paper.

Juelle squeezed his hand. "It'll be okay. You'll see. Ready?"

He nodded, and she seated herself on the cushion. Despite the boy's misgivings and her own rising doubts, she lifted the injector and, taking a deep breath, drove it into her arm.

As Hermes and Seri watched, wide-eyed, Juelle felt no sensation at first. Then slowly, her senses began to spin. Anxiety clutched at her until she remembered this was how the carolines always affected her. The formula must be working correctly.

Her tension eased, but the dizziness intensified, drawing her deep into a vortex of her own imagination. Down she went, faster and faster, spinning out of control. She cast about for something, anything to hold onto, but there was nothing. Nothing but her own fears and rising panic.

Hastily, she drew upon the strength of her training and years of experience, somehow keeping the terrors at bay. She held onto that lifeline with all her might until she finally reached the terminus and was thrust into the void.

There, calm descended upon her, and she took a shuddering breath. The transition from total tumult to absolute stillness was shattering, and she needed a moment to still the frantic beating of her heart.

She waited, floating in the void for what seemed like an eternity, until she finally felt a presence. She turned toward it expectantly. It rushed toward her, seizing control of her body to speak the traditional words of the ritual. "State your question."

As if from a great distance in time and space, she heard Hermes stutter over the question. "H-How can Eron be persuaded to let Delphi join the Republic?"

Juelle felt the oracle's elation as it seized on the question and searched for the querent's mind. Frustrated at not finding it, the oracle chose the only option left to it—exploring Juelle's subconscious.

Bright light flashed in the void, then dimmed and pulsed as it hovered, poised, at the beginning of myriad paths. It hung in indecision for a moment, then the light split in two and sped down two paths at once.

Juelle cried out in anguish. It was too much. She couldn't follow both at the same time, yet she had to—she had no choice. Quickly, urgently, the searing, painful lights sped to the end of both shining paths to provide the answers she sought.

The first answer tumbled painfully from her lips. "There is nothing Gaia can do to convince Apollo."

The second was even more excruciating. Feeling

as though she'd been hauled up in front of the ultimate court and found wanting, Juelle uttered the oracle's second pronouncement, "If the Terran uses the false elixir to willingly prophesy again, Delphi's gift will be lost forever."

The last thing she heard before she lost consciousness was an anguished, deep voice crying out, "No!"

Chapter Eight

Eron rode as fast as he could toward the camp where he'd left Juelle and Hermes. He'd pushed hard to get to Riverfork and back, knowing they were alone, defenseless, in the desert.

Guilt racked him—he had just assumed Juelle's treatment would be effective and had left Hermes. Eron cursed himself. He'd fallen into the very trap he'd warned his people of—succumbing to the seductive lure of technology, assuming it could solve everything.

What if her treatment was wrong? What if he'd been wrong to leave? What if Hermes lay dying because Eron had made a fatal mistake?

Frustration ate at him. Doubts were useless. He was *doing* everything he could. He'd convinced a healer and two strong lads at Riverfork to return with him. Even now, they labored behind him, trying valiantly to keep up.

Unfortunately, he didn't know if it would be

enough to save his young cousin. And Eron had all too much time during this hurried trek to think . . . think about what had brought them to this point.

His own selfish desires had brought him to this. If he hadn't been so wrapped up in the siren call of the Terran, none of this would have happened. Around her, he acted like an adolescent boy, controlled by his hormones and lured by her femininity.

Well, no more. He'd just have to ignore the temptation Juelle represented. After all, if *he* couldn't ignore the temptations of technology and the Terran way of life, how could he expect his people to?

This was undoubtedly a test sent by Apollo. Eron shook his head in bitter memory. He'd failed it, and Hermes had been bitten as a result. He wouldn't fail the others.

The terrain began to take on a familiar aspect. Eron's heart leapt as he surged even farther ahead of the others. Juelle and Hermes should be beneath those trees—if the stubborn Terran had followed orders and stayed where he'd told her.

He pulled into camp and stopped short. Juelle sat across from Hermes, the moncat in her lap, swaying as if entranced. She spoke in a deep voice totally unlike her own, ". . . willingly prophesy again, Delphi's gift will be lost forever."

"No!" he cried as Juelle toppled over.

Dear Apollo, what had she done? He dismounted and ran toward her. He froze and stared down at the scene, seeing the same type of device Juelle had used on Hermes, and a worried look on Seri's face.

Eron glanced at the boy. Fierce relief at Hermes' apparent recovery was supplanted by concern for his world. Eron blurted out, "What happened?"

Hermes turned ashen. "She . . . took the formula."

Eron swore under his breath, then grabbed the device and tossed it aside, hiding it in the folds of a blanket. Giving Hermes a stern look, he whispered, "Not a word of this to anyone."

Hermes nodded and shoved a piece of paper into his shirt.

Exasperated, Eron snapped, "How could you let her do this?"

With an incredulous look, Hermes answered, "How could I stop her?"

Good point—no one could stop that feisty Terran when she had the bit between her teeth. Eron shook his head in disgust as the others came riding into camp.

He turned to glance at Hermes and saw a look of horror on the boy's face. Following his gaze, he saw Juelle convulsing in spasms on the ground, the moncat frantic with worry.

Fear leapt within him at the sight of the independent Terran so helpless. He grabbed her, wedged a stick between her jaws so she wouldn't bite her tongue, then held her steady. He'd seen this before. If he didn't restrain her, she might hurt herself.

The healer jumped off his horse and ran over to give assistance. "Good thinking," he told Eron. "Keep holding her."

The man rummaged through his saddlebags and came up with an elixir. By now, Juelle's convulsions had weakened until her muscles were no longer spasming. He tugged the stick out of her mouth, then poured the liquid down her throat with Eron's help.

Seri chittered away, making distressed sounds as she watched Juelle with anxious eyes.

Juelle swallowed, then relaxed, her head falling to one side. The healer said, "There. That should help her rest." He rose to stare down at Juelle. "What caused this?"

Eron threw Hermes a warning glance. "She must be allergic to something. Did she eat anything different, Hermes?"

The boy swallowed hard, then said, "She, uh, tasted my jetoba juice to see if it was too hot."

The healer nodded. "That might account for it. Now, how about you, young man? I understand you had an encounter with a sandsnake."

As the healer examined Hermes, Eron's thoughts turned to Juelle. She looked so defenseless and vulnerable . . . like a frail child. Eron's protective instincts screamed to the fore, colliding with his ire.

Damn, but she was brave—*and* foolhardy. How dare she take the formula without permission? It was dangerous—couldn't she see that?

Of course she could— she was no fool. She just wouldn't acknowledge how destructive technology could be. Well, if and when she awoke, he'd ensure she saw how her stubbornness—and the technology she'd been forbidden to use—had jeopardized not only her life, but Delphi's future.

Luckily, her prophecy would reinforce that. He'd heard only the last portion, but he knew it had unequivocally stated that she should never prophesy again. If she did, Delphi would suffer. Would she accept that?

Should *he?* The prophecy hadn't been obtained in the normal way. Was it valid?

Eron thought about it for a minute. It was probably valid—otherwise, the Golden Pythia and her mate wouldn't be at such pains to keep the formula from public knowledge. That meant it was accurate, or at least as accurate as any neophyte pythia's prophecy. In either case, he'd have to treat it as such—he had no other choice. He'd do his utmost to ensure she never prophesied again.

Was this the role the oracle had foretold for him? To keep the Terran from prophesying in order to ensure Delphi's preservation? Yes, that had to be it. He didn't relish the duty, but he'd perform it nonetheless.

Sighing, Eron began to pack up the camp with the help of the Riverfork men and constructed litters for Juelle and Hermes. Though Hermes was much better, he was still too weak to ride any distance—and Juelle hadn't regained consciousness.

The healer said her condition was stable, and Seri seemed to concur. Though she hovered over Juelle's limp body, the moncat seemed far less anxious than earlier.

Eron's fears eased. If anyone knew about possible repercussions from this travesty of a prophetic ritual, it would be the Golden Pythia's moncat. Satisfied he'd done all he could, Eron led the way back to Riverfork.

The two days it took to get there were two of the longest he'd ever spent. The only bright spot in the trip was Hermes' obvious recovery. In fact, the healer expressed surprise at how rapidly the boy was healing.

Eron wasn't surprised. He could've told the man that Terran technology was responsible, but he didn't want to say or do anything that would add to the mystique or glamour of Earth, or encourage the acceptance of technology in one of his villages.

Though he no longer needed to worry about Hermes, he was concerned about Juelle, still unconscious and pale as death.

Juelle woke and stared groggily about. What was going on? She took stock of her surroundings and gradually realized she was bound to a litter. But what was all that jostling? As she came further awake, she realized the litter was being dragged by a horse.

She tried to lift a hand to her aching head, but her arms and legs were tied down. She turned her head, the only part of her body that would move, and immediately regretted it. Dizziness and nausea washed through her, threatening to overpower the pounding in her head.

She painfully opened her eyes and saw Hermes staring back at her from another litter.

"Juelle?" he asked.

She gave him a weak smile.

"Eron," Hermes shouted. "Juelle's awake."

The horses stopped, and the jolting blessedly ceased. She heard a thump and a couple of firm strides, then saw Eron's dark face bending over her, scowling.

Great—just what she needed. An angry councilman.

She closed her eyes against the anger in his expression. She certainly wasn't up to dealing with him when she felt this way—especially if Hermes had told him what she'd done.

"Juelle?" Eron asked, the concern in his voice at odds with his scowl.

"What?" she managed to say.

"How do you feel?"

"Like I've swallowed two buckets of sand," she gritted out.

Eron chuckled with what sounded like relief, then grabbed a watersack and held it to her lips. "Here. Drink."

Juelle opened her eyes and drank then laid back down, exhausted. "What happened?" The last thing she remembered was giving herself the injection. After that, everything was a blur.

Eron's face froze into an impenetrable mask. He bent down to whisper in her ear. "You used the formula, didn't you?"

Her spirits sank. Hermes *had* told him. Unwilling to argue, she kept her mouth shut.

"And the oracle warned you never to do so again," he said in a clipped tone, though he kept his voice low.

"What do you mean?"

"Shh," he cautioned as another man dismounted and approached them. "Don't breathe a word of this to anyone. We told them you were allergic to jetoba juice."

Though she was filled with curiosity, Juelle decided discretion was in order, considering Eron's black mood and her own weakness. She glanced up at the man who bent over her.

"Hello," he said in a pleasant tone. "I'm a healer. How do you feel?"

As she answered his questions and endured his probing, she surreptitiously watched Eron. The councilman was not happy. More specifically, he was not happy with *her*. That boded ill for her wish to convince him to convert to Earth's technology. How could she convince him otherwise?

Good question—and that's exactly what she'd asked the oracle. But just as Juelle had expected, she couldn't remember the prophecy. She glanced at Hermes. If the boy had done his job, he'd have the answer written down. She trusted that much more than Eron's biased assumption about what had happened.

Unfortunately, there was no way to ask the boy without going against Eron's edicts, and it wasn't exactly smart to do that right now. She laid back down and closed her eyes, hoping she'd get a chance to corner Hermes soon. She'd need all the help she could get.

They reached the village by mid-afternoon, and Juelle finally escaped the jolting of the primitive litter. She felt even better when the villagers led her to a room in the Healing House, where she could lie down and recover her faculties in peace, quiet, and blessed stillness.

She slept, then woke at twilight. Feeling much refreshed, Juelle rose to check out her surroundings. Seri stirred as well, and Juelle stroked the attentive moncat.

Poor Seri—she was probably as confused as everyone else with the odd ritual Juelle had just gone through. But the loyal moncat had stayed by her side and supported her, which is more than she could say of the Oasis Councilman. Where was that pigheaded man, anyway?

She pushed through the doorway and saw Hermes lying on another bed in the corner. He gave her a shy smile. Good. Now was her chance to find out what had happened during the prophecy.

She knelt next to his bed and put her hand against his forehead. It looked like her antidote had done the trick. The fever appeared to be gone. "How are you feeling?" she asked.

Hermes shrugged, obviously uncomfortable at being the focus of her attention. "Fine. How about you?"

"Oh, I'm okay. But I don't remember much of what happened." She raised an inquiring eyebrow at him, hoping he'd take the hint.

He avoided her gaze. "Neither do I. It happened so fast."

"What happened?"

"Oh, you know. First the prophecies, then you passed out and Eron arrived."

131

"Prophecies?" she repeated. "More than one?"

Hermes squirmed and still wouldn't meet her eyes.

"Come on, Hermes. Tell me what happened. You did write them down, didn't you?"

He nodded.

"Well, what did they say?"

"Eron told me not to tell anyone—"

"He didn't mean *me*, did he?"

"I-I'm not sure."

"Look," Juelle said in a reasonable tone, lowering her voice to a conspiratorial whisper. "I understand why Eron told you not to tell anyone. He doesn't want them to know the formula exists, right?"

Hermes nodded.

"But I already know, so you won't be telling me anything you shouldn't. I just want to know what the oracle said. They're my prophecies. Don't I deserve to know what came out of my mouth? Especially after I went through all that pain and agony?"

"I guess so," he said in a reluctant tone.

"Okay, then. How many prophecies were there?"

He hesitated for a moment, then said, "Two."

Good grief, this was worse than extracting cube roots. "And what did the first one say?"

He hung his head. "It said there's nothing you can do to convince Eron that Delphi should join the Republic."

That rocked her back on her heels. "Nothing?" Eron must be more stubborn and opinionated than she'd thought. Well, then, she'd just have to find some other way to convert him—or convince the Council not to listen to his tales of woe.

Wait . . . "What was the second prophecy?"

Hermes fidgeted and shook his head.

"Come on, Hermes, it can't be that difficult to remember. What did the second prophecy say?"

"Can't you leave the boy alone?" asked a deep voice from the doorway.

Damn. It was Eron, back too soon . . . again. Juelle scrambled to her feet. "I'm not hurting him."

"No? He's still recovering, remember? You shouldn't do anything to stress him."

A quick glance at the boy showed his head averted while he stroked the moncat.

Juelle crossed her arms over her chest. "I know he's recovering. It's because of my antidote, remember?"

He scowled. "Which you administered without my permission."

"I told you before—a doctor's oath takes precedence over any petty concerns of some . . . some . . ."

"Some what?"

She placed her hands on her hips and glared at him. "Some barbarian who wouldn't know a good thing if it reared up and bit him!"

Rather than the anger she'd expected, Eron just chuckled and raised an amused eyebrow at her. "Reverting to childish insults now?"

Exasperated, Juelle knew he was correct. Damn him—what right did he have to act so superior? Realizing anger would get her nowhere, she tried the force of calm reason. "Look, all I want to know is what the second prophecy is."

When he merely frowned at her, she persisted. "Don't you normally tell pythias what their prophecies are?"

"Yes, but you're no pythia."

He was right, but did he have to be so blunt? "Still, I think I deserve to know what the prophecy said. If you don't mind, I'd like Hermes to read it to me."

133

She said it in a sarcastic tone, but Eron took her question seriously.

He nodded. "All right. But you don't need Hermes—I heard it, too." He frowned down at her as if considering, then said, "The oracle said if you ever prophesied again, every pythia would lose the ability forever."

Juelle stared at him, open-mouthed. "That can't be true." She turned to Hermes. "Can it?"

Hermes nodded, and Eron turned toward the doorway. "Believe it. I have to go now to attend a village meeting on what to do about the bandits. When I get back, we'll talk." With that, he strode out the door.

Juelle stared at Hermes in disbelief. "Did it really say that?"

Hermes nodded. "I don't remember the whole thing, but I do know Eron left out a word—the prophecy said it would happen only if you *willingly* prophesied again."

Terrific. Now all she had to do was find someone to force her and she'd be all set.

She grimaced and spent a moment wishing for the impossible. Imagine the good she could do if she could delve deep into her patients' minds with the help of the oracle. It would be the biggest boon to psychiatry since mind-body melding. She slumped. Unfortunately, now there was no chance of that ever happening.

Hermes clutched her arm and stared up at her with pleading eyes. "Please, promise me you'll never prophesy again."

"All right, I promise I won't do anything to jeopardize Delphi." She paused and ventured a joke. "Unless I can talk you into forcing me to prophesy?"

Hermes frowned. "I don't want to make Eron angry again—"

Juelle jerked away from him. "To hell with Eron. I'm tired of watching everyone around here kowtow to him as if he were some sort of god. He's not, you know—he's only human. Only a councilman."

Hermes froze and glared at her for the first time since she'd known him. "He's *my* councilman . . . my liege. And you owe him your life."

The moncat became agitated by the emotions in the room, but Juelle found it difficult to control hers. "My life? Ha! If he hadn't been so damned stubborn, we wouldn't be making this trip in the first place. None of this would've even happened. I could've flown to Oasis and back by now. At this rate, we'll never get there."

Hermes stiffened. "He was right."

"What do you mean?"

"He did as he saw right—for the good of Delphi. Can you say the same?" The look on Hermes' face was stubborn, full of defense for his cousin and councilman.

That hurt. She had nothing but their best interests at heart. Couldn't he see that? "Yes. Yes, I can," she said softly. "In the six months I've lived here, I've come to know and appreciate what a unique and wonderful society you have. I wouldn't do anything to jeopardize that, no matter what your *councilman* says."

He gave her an uncertain look, but Juelle turned away and walked out the door. Her methods had been questioned often enough, but never her motives. How could they doubt her? Later, she'd sort that out. For now, though, the hurt was too raw, too new.

Seri scampered after her, and Juelle paused to pick her up. The moncat patted her face and gazed with concern into Juelle's eyes. Sighing, Juelle stroked Seri's soft fur. At least someone still understood her.

Wanting solitude, Juelle wandered aimlessly, avoiding the people. She soon reached the boundaries of the village and paused. The moon was bright, but was it safe out there in the darkness?

Seri leapt down and scurried forward into the night, looking back at Juelle as if encouraging her to follow. Juelle shrugged. She might as well. Seri would know if it was dangerous or not, and she couldn't get lost with the moncat around.

She followed Seri, who seemed intent on leading her in a specific direction. Juelle paused a couple of times, uncertain, but each time the moncat urged her on. Feeling better now that she was away from Eron's depressing visage and the anxiety that beset the village, Juelle was content to follow.

The night was cool, but the lack of a breeze made it bearable as they walked past the outbuildings and a moon-washed meadow, coming to a stand of trees. Seri entered them but Juelle hesitated. The trees looked ominous, bending over her in the moonlight like silent sentinels . . . harbingers of doom.

Seri urged her in, and Juelle scoffed at herself for her fears. They were nothing but trees, not some demented Rorschach test of her imagination. Shaking her head, Juelle followed the moncat into the trees, down the moonlit path.

Once inside the grove, she felt safe, warm, and secure. She smiled at her earlier foolishness. Seri had brought her to just the place she needed.

Soon they came to a clearing and Seri paused. Needing rest, Juelle sat on the soft grass and soon found herself lying down, looking up the stars. Exhaustion overtook her as she wondered when she'd get back to Earth—if ever—and if Delphi would ever take its rightful place in the Republic. Slowly, stroking Seri, she fell asleep.

Nevan watched in satisfaction as his men opened the side of the ship and began working on the filters again. The coming of the sign—the Terran's ship— had raised their spirits once they were convinced the metallic monstrosity was necessary for Nevan's plan.

He'd given Ivar and his crew orders to delay the cleaning of the filters and they were doing a good job of it, if the Terran's frustration was any gauge. Now, with each hour that passed, they learned more about the ship.

Alexander gave him a tight smile as he surveyed their handiwork. "I appreciate all your men have done to help with the filters, but I can take it from here."

"Oh, no, I wouldn't think of it," Nevan said with an expansive smile.

"But you've done more than enough already," Alexander gritted out.

"Nonsense. We're more than happy to do this for our new ambassador."

Nevan watched the war of emotions on Alexander's face. He could tell the Terran was frustrated with the lack of progress, but didn't want to say so for fear of insulting them.

Nevan steered Alexander into the ship. "They've learned a great deal, don't you think?" Mostly they'd learned how to give the appearance of working without doing anything at all.

Shogril and Orgon joined them as Alexander said, "Oh, sure, sure. But do you think they're . . . suited for such a complicated job?"

Shogril bristled. "These are our brightest young men."

"Oh. Of course. But do you think perhaps the young man supervising them could be a little more . . . conscientious?"

"What do you mean?" Shogril demanded.

"Well, the cover was left open last night, and more sand blew into the filters."

Shogril scowled. "Because you didn't show them how to close it."

It was a blatant lie, and Nevan could see the Terran wanted to say so but was too polite. It was all Nevan could do to keep from laughing out loud. He patted the so-called ambassador on the back. "We'll ensure it doesn't happen again. Perhaps if we understood more about how the ship works . . . ?"

Alexander sighed heavily. "All right. What would you like to know?"

Nevan had been maneuvering toward this moment for hours, but chose to underplay it so as not to arouse Alexander's suspicions. "How does Delphi look from up there?" he asked, gesturing vaguely above his head.

"Well, if the ship were working, I could show you first hand," the Terran said, revealing exasperation in his voice.

Nevan ignored it. "Don't you have maps or something similar?"

"No, your planet hasn't been charted yet, but I have some vids."

"Vids?"

"Yes, a recording of how your planet looks from space."

Ah, now they were getting somewhere. Nevan allowed a look of curiosity to cross his face. "May we see them?"

"Sure."

Alexander fiddled with some buttons and levers, and a vision suddenly appeared on the wall. Having seen one of Lancer's holofilms, Nevan was somewhat familiar with the medium, though he allowed his expression to appear awestruck. "Is that Delphi?"

"Yes, that's how your planet looks from space."

Nevan took a moment to appreciate it. Soon this beautiful world would be his. "Do you have any closer views?" He wanted to know if he could identify landmarks from the air. "Perhaps we could help you find the place you were looking for."

It was a blatant hint. Would the Terran pick up on it?

Alexander's eyes lit up. "Good idea. I was trying to find Dodona. Do you know it?"

Good—he took the bait. "Yes, it's our capital city."

"Maybe you can help me find it then. I want to surprise my little brother."

Nevan played dumb. "Brother?"

"Yes. Your Council Captain, Lancer Morgan, is my brother."

"Oh, I see. And you want to . . . surprise him?"

"Yes, he doesn't know I'm here yet—or that I've been named ambassador. I want to see his face when he realizes that it's me."

Ah, that cleared up one mystery. Nevan had wondered why Alexander hadn't been in touch with Lancer on their communicators. Well, if the ambassador wanted to surprise the upstart Council Captain, Nevan would be more than happy to oblige—though perhaps not in the manner he expected.

Nevan smiled. "Let's see if we can spot Dodona."

Alexander explained how to interpret the signs from the air. Nevan caught on quickly, and he could see Orgon did as well. As he watched, he realized

139

the Terran had passed over Dodona on his way here.

The second time through, Nevan said, "Stop. That's it."

"That's Dodona?"

"Yes."

Alexander slapped his forehead. "Of course. I was expecting a large city. I forgot most of Dodona is underground, in the caves."

"So you can find your way there . . . from here?" Nevan asked in a nonchalant voice.

"Sure, no problem."

Nevan plastered a bewildered look on his face. "But how?"

"The coordinates are listed in the upper right hand side of the picture. See?"

Nevan nodded.

"Well, I just punch the coordinates in like this"— he demonstrated for them—"and the autopilot is set."

"Autopilot?"

"It means automatic pilot—the ship will automatically take you there if you type in the right code."

"Code? You mean the coordinates?"

"No—a word or two that describes the place. Like this." Alexander punched more buttons. "Okay, now all I have to do is type in 'Dodona,' press this red key, and the autopilot will take us there."

Elation rose within Nevan as he committed the information to memory. Could it be that easy? "That's all there is to it?"

"Well, not quite. The filters have to be clean, or the ship won't take off, and I didn't set the landing sequence, so I'll have to take it off autopilot to land or it'll crash into Dodona. But that's pretty much all you have to do, yes."

Nevan smiled. Delphi was once more within his grasp.

Chapter Nine

Eron left the village meeting satisfied he'd learned all he could of the bandits. There was little to go on, but enough for him to delegate a couple of men to contact the other villages in his domain. They would put them on alert and find volunteers for a scouting expedition. After he delivered Juelle to Oasis, he'd come back to take care of the bandits threatening his people.

The sooner, the better. She was an unwelcome distraction—and a potent one. He'd already demonstrated his shameful lack of willpower around her.

It was much easier when she was unconscious. Then all he had to deal with were his feelings of protectiveness, of concern for her well-being. But now that she was awake, more feelings—unwanted feelings—came into play.

He couldn't listen to that sassy mouth of hers without wanting to stop it with a kiss, couldn't endure her stubbornness without wanting to drag her against him and feel her go soft and yielding in his arms. He grimaced. Couldn't keep his feelings from interfering with Council business.

Eron shook his head to clear it and strode toward the Healing House. If he were to deal with Juelle in a rational manner, he needed to have all his wits about him.

He would have preferred to avoid her entirely, but that was impossible. He'd promised to speak with her after the meeting, and speak with her he would—if only to ensure she understood the prophecy and what it portended for Delphi.

Pausing outside the Healing House, Eron took a deep breath, then mocked himself. He'd faced a sandsnake without this much trepidation. What was this Terran woman doing to him? Fortified by self-disgust, he stepped into the hut and glanced around.

He didn't see Juelle, but Hermes raised onto one elbow and called out a greeting. Eron waved and headed toward Juelle's room.

"She's not there," Hermes said.

Eron paused. Trust the stubborn woman not to stay where she was told. "Where is she?"

Hermes sat up in bed, looking worried. "I don't know. She left a couple of hours ago, right after you did."

"Where'd she go?"

"I thought she was with you. She was so mad. . . ."

So she'd gone off angry, had she? No telling where she was. But she didn't know the dangers of leaving the village after nightfall. He had to find the woman before she ran into a night predator, or worse—was discovered by the bandits. He scowled. "We'd better find her."

143

Hermes nodded and rose. "I'll help."

"No—you stay here. We don't need two ill people wandering around the village."

"I'm better now—I can walk. And if I feel tired, I'll come back and lie down."

"I don't think—"

Hermes' face turned stubborn. "It's my fault she's out there. She left because of . . . because of something I said."

Eron sighed. Guilt. He knew just how that felt, and the boy wouldn't be able to live with it unless he did something about it. "All right. But come back here as soon as you tire—understand?"

Hermes nodded, and Eron led the way out the door to question everyone in sight. The small Terran stood out in this small village, and many remembered having seen her pass through with the Golden Pythia's moncat. Slowly, a picture of her movements emerged, and one woman recalled seeing Juelle depart toward the north fork.

Eron sighed in exasperation. Being alone after dark in this country was not as safe as it seemed. Bandits weren't the only predators who roamed the night, and though lobcats tended to avoid human habitations—and humans—they'd been known to attack lone stragglers. He had to find her.

By this time, his search had gathered a crowd of curiosity-seekers, as well as those who were concerned about Juelle. He picked out a couple of older men who looked sensible and asked them to grab their weapons and torches, then dismissed the rest of the villagers.

Eron glanced at Hermes, prepared to send him back to bed, but the stubborn look on the boy's face made the words freeze on his lips. He knew exactly how Hermes felt. "Ready?" he asked.

Hermes and the villagers nodded, and Eron led

the way out of the village.

The taller of the two men halted and pointed down at the path Juelle had taken. "Wait. Look."

They knelt to look and, in the light cast by the torch, they could see the tracks where the moncat had passed . . . and the distinctive prints left by Juelle's Terran shoes. "Good work," Eron said. Keeping their torches low, they followed the prints.

Eron's hopes rose as the prints led him down a well-worn path. If she'd kept to it the whole time, it would be easy to track her down. As time passed and they still hadn't seen any recent prints other than hers, he became more confident they would find her unharmed.

Forty minutes out of the village, they came to a stand of trees. The path continued through them, but the village men barred his passage. "Don't go in there."

Why not? He glanced up at the trees around him in sudden realization. Arianas.

Fear rose to choke him. Dear Apollo, she'd stumbled into a moncat grove . . . at night. Only adolescent girls who hoped to be chosen as pythias were allowed into moncat groves after dark. Anyone else who dared enter the sacred bower was bitten, suffering the effects of the moncat's poison for weeks afterward.

At least that's how Delphians were affected. How would a moncat bite affect a Terran? It probably would be worse. Much worse. He couldn't let that happen to Juelle; she'd suffered enough this trip. She didn't deserve to be bitten. She didn't know!

Damn the consequences. He took another step into the grove, ready to barge in and take her out by force if need be.

"No," Hermes cried out, taking a step forward as if to stop him.

The other two grabbed Eron's arms. "No, sir," exclaimed one. "Can't you see? It's a moncat grove."

Eron tugged against their restraint. "I know, but—"

"You can't help her till morning."

"But she'll be bitten."

"Yes, but if you're bitten, too, you won't be able to help her. You must wait for daylight."

Eron ceased his struggles and hung his head in despair. The man was right.

Hermes turned to him with a thoughtful look on his face. "Maybe she won't be bitten."

Eron looked up in disbelief and hope. "What?"

"Maybe they won't bite her," Hermes repeated.

Irritation surged through Eron. "She's trespassed in a sacred moncat grove," he explained. "The only way she won't be harmed is if they choose her as a pythia." And there was no likelihood of that happening.

"But Seri was with her. Won't the moncat protect her?"

Relief supplanted the irritation. "Perhaps . . . I hope you're right." He relaxed and addressed the village men. "It's all right. You can let go of me now."

The men released him with obvious reluctance, but Eron ignored them. He found a soft spot on the grass off the path and did the only thing he could. He settled down to wait for dawn.

Juelle woke, coming to in the midst of darkness lit by an eerie violet glow. Feeling strangely lethargic, she blinked, a long, slow shuttering of her eyelids that did nothing to make sense of her surroundings. Her rational mind tried to catalog what was going on, though it moved sluggishly, as if mired in weary emotion.

146

She glanced vaguely around and identified the source of the familiar light. Hundreds of flowers spread throughout the clearing and climbed the trees, their five spiky white petals shading to purple in the center and crowned by a circlet of golden filaments. Carolines. The light emanated from the caroline flowers.

How odd, she found herself thinking. She hadn't noticed them when she stumbled into the grove earlier and had thought they existed only in caves. But these were definitely carolines. And since the moon was hidden by the clouds, the flowers had unfurled their seductive petals in the darkness that was their element, shining their hypnotic violet glow, and emitting a drugging fragrance that kept Juelle in thrall.

Knowing the reason for her lethargy didn't give her the ability—or the strength—to combat it. Instead, Juelle found herself looking about in a detached way, able to think and rationalize yet unable to move, to do anything about it.

With that realization came acceptance. So be it. The carolines wouldn't harm her, and they would close come sunrise, shut against the bright light of dawn, their potency disguised once more. Juelle closed her eyes. She need only stay here until then—sleep—and she could leave in the morning, unharmed.

She felt something graze her face. Recognizing the familiar touch of Seri's small hand, Juelle opened her eyes to look at the moncat. Seri stared back, her yellow eyes bright and luminous. Juelle merely watched, unable to voice a query.

Seri patted her face again, then looked up into the trees, glancing around full circle, chittering in soft tones. Juelle gazed upward, too, and blinked. What were those yellow lights? She blinked again.

147

Those weren't lights . . . they were eyes.

Dozens of bright yellow eyes stared at her from the trees. The carolines didn't allow her to feel fear, but a slight uneasiness possessed her until her vision adjusted. Then, she saw that the eyes belonged to moncats—moncats just like Seri—all of whom stared fixedly at Juelle.

Seri backed away, behind Juelle and out of sight. The other moncats crept down out of the trees to the ground, pausing to form a ring around Juelle where she lay on the grass, their eyes unblinking.

Juelle stared back. Their surreal presence made the whole thing feel like a dream.

A dream. That was it. This was just a dream.

She smiled and relaxed. In the morning, she would laugh about it. Her analytical side kicked in, and Juelle realized this must be one of those wish-fulfillment dreams. Her subconscious must've decided the clearing was a moncat grove and populated it with intelligent, sophisticated moncats. Ones who would see beyond the narrow, restricted definition the Delphians had for pythias and know that Juelle was exactly what they were looking for.

Juelle closed her eyes and willed the dream to change. She didn't need wish fulfillment, nor did she want to wake in disappointment to find it had been only a fantasy. Fantasy . . .

Eron. Now *there* was something to dream about. A softer, gentler Eron who lacked the stubbornness of the real one—yet just as sexy, just as desirable. She opened her eyes, expecting to see his dark eyes gazing into hers. Instead, dozens of yellow eyes stared back.

Awareness spiked through her. *This is no dream.*

The carolines calmed her, yet she was still aware of a distinct sense of unease. She must be trespassing in a sacred moncat grove. Would she be bitten? Would Seri protect her? How would the bite affect her, a Terran, who hadn't developed the same immunities the Delphians had over the last two centuries?

With caroline-induced resignation and a strange acceptance, Juelle awaited her fate. As if her acceptance were some sort of signal, one of the moncats left the circle to approach her. By the white on his muzzle and his air of quiet dignity, Juelle assumed he was one of their revered elders. *Well*, she thought irreverently, *at least I'll be bitten by only the best*.

The elderly moncat approached, pausing to stand at her feet. Two others joined him, forming a triangle around her body. *What's this? A moncat tribunal?*

Curiosity filled her as she watched the triumvirate squat to stare at her. A strange sound filled the grove, and Juelle realized it emanated from the herd of moncats in the trees. No, that wasn't right. Moncats didn't come in herds, they came in ... mischiefs. Yes, that was it. The mischief of moncats hummed, and the buzzing sound filled her ears as the carolines filled her senses.

The elderly moncat's eyes whirled, capturing her attention. The other two emulated him, their eyes whirling faster and faster until the sensory overload dragged her spinning, down into the unknown.

There, in a void deep in her subconscious, something, she knew not what, bombarded her. It sought answers, measuring her in ways she could not comprehend. She found herself unable to refuse it anything, and soon her entire life and psyche were laid out for inspection as clearly as a star chart.

The veil of confusion thinned and she could sense three beings about her in the formless void. They regarded her gravely, studying her with a searing intensity that defied explanation. She could deny them nothing as they probed the darkest corners of her subconscious, dredging up memories long forgotten.

Nothing was scared. Happy moments and crowning achievements shared the limelight equally with small embarrassments and shameful episodes she would rather have forgotten. The torture went on for what seemed like forever until they had reviewed every moment of her life and laid it open to dispassionate scrutiny. Then, finally, they released her.

Juelle's senses snapped back to semiawareness and she opened her eyes to find herself back in the grove, still watched by the moncats and feeling humbled by the entire experience. She'd been judged and found . . . what? Wanting or worthy?

The trio of judges, for that's how she saw them now, regarded her steadily, not revealing a thing. Slowly, the elderly one turned and faced the mischief. His two adjuncts faded into the crowd, and the older one opened his arms in a questioning gesture that looked like an appeal.

They stirred, and one moncat after another melted back into the trees. Soon there were only two moncats left besides the elderly statesman—a young male and an older female.

Juelle could almost feel their communication as the older moncat regarded the other two. The male was brash, arrogant with the confidence of the young, and withstood his scrutiny with an air of defiance while the female stood calmly, waiting his pleasure.

The older moncat turned back to Juelle and made a gesture as if to present the two for her approval. Puzzled, Juelle surveyed them. The female moncat, with her air of dignity and reserve, reminded Juelle unnervingly of her grandmother. The male was much more intriguing, Juelle decided, as she locked gazes with his impudent stare.

The elderly male nodded once, then backed off, as did the female. They, too, melted into the trees until there was no one left but Juelle—and the impudent moncat. She felt a sharp spear of pleasure from his direction, then he scrambled toward her and bent down to her arm.

Pain! He'd bitten her. Fear stabbed through her and the moncat's whirling eyes regarded her with excitement and triumph as her wrist throbbed. Her wrist . . . he'd bitten her on the wrist. Fear segued into excitement and hope. That's where moncats bit their chosen pythias. Did that mean . . . ?

Red-hot spikes of pain suddenly shot from her wrist and tore through her veins. She gasped. Molten lava ran through her, burning, changing everything it touched. Dear Lord, what was happening to her?

As the moncat watched avidly, Juelle lost consciousness.

She woke sometime before dawn and sat up, touching her hand gingerly to her head. What a night. Had she dreamed it, or . . . ? She darted a glance at her right wrist. Yes, there it was. A moncat bite.

She felt fine, except for a slight hangover from the carolines. They were just now folding their petals at the onset of the sun. Hope leapt within her. Was she a pythia now?

She vaguely remembered dreaming of her life intertwining with that of one mischievous, marvelous moncat whose mind meshed in perfect unison with her own.

The moncat of her dreams came scurrying out of

a nearby tree and made a dash down the trunk, then executed a dramatic back flip and landed light-footed in front of her. He cocked his head and posed for a moment, as if awaiting her accolade.

He *wasn't* a dream. So . . . she must be a pythia. Filled with relief and exultation, Juelle laughed and applauded. "Bravo, little one. What other tricks can you do?"

Little one? That wouldn't do—her moncat had to have a name. What should it be? The Delphians seemed to favor giving moncats short names ending in *i*. And with this imp, she had just the name.

"Loki," she said. "I think I'll name you Loki, for the Norse god of mischief."

Okay, so it didn't fit with the Greek theme around here. Who cared? He was her moncat, wasn't he? "Is that okay with you?"

A serious look crossed his comical little face as he appeared to consider her question. Wait—maybe he *was* considering her question. Juelle had never asked Thena about the limits of her communication with Seri. Most of it appeared to be emotional, or mental projection with pictures. Maybe . . .

"Loki?" she ventured again, trying to project the mystical, mischievous, larger-than-life feeling the name evoked for her.

The moncat wriggled, and a distinct feeling of acceptance washed over her from his direction. Juelle grinned. Apparently, they had bonded some-time during the night and now shared their emotions. "Then Loki it is."

She looked up in delight as he bounded toward her, then leapt onto her shoulder. She chuckled and rubbed his head as he snuggled into her neck and sighed.

What a sweet little guy. Juelle smiled. Well, if she

was going to spend the rest of her life with a moncat, she was glad it would be Loki. It appeared she'd
made the right choice. A staid, proper moncat
wouldn't have suited her at all.

Seri regarded her gravely from a few feet away.
Juelle smiled. "Thanks, Seri," she said softly.
"Thanks for bringing me here."

It was a little more difficult to communicate with
Seri since they weren't bonded, but Juelle put all
her gratitude and thankfulness into her thoughts
and projected them at the moncat. Seri accepted
them with a mild blink of her eyes, then turned to
look at Loki, as if giving the newcomer a critical
once-over.

Loki leapt down from Juelle's shoulder and
swaggered over to Seri. Seri looked down her nose
at him and Juelle grinned at the sight of her friend's
moncat, surely more sober now than Juelle had
ever seen her, playing at being the grande dame.

Seri's russet fur was complemented by Loki's
slightly darker shade. He had lighter rings of fur
around his eyes and on the tufts of his pointed ears,
making him look somewhat like a comical raccoon.
They looked good together.

Loki must have thought so, too, for he turned a
beguiling gaze on Seri and flipped around to lovingly entwine his tail with hers.

With an indignant look on her face, Seri leapt to
one side, away from the impertinent young moncat. She gave him an altogether human look of affronted dignity, then began preening her tail.

Loki's lovesick look made Juelle laugh, and before the rejected suitor could make any further ad-
vances, Juelle called him over. "That's all right," she
whispered. "You'll have plenty of time to press your
suit. Besides, I have a feeling Seri isn't as indiffer-
ent as she pretends."

Loki cast a forlorn look at Seri, then settled down next to Juelle, content for the moment to have her stroke his silky ears. Juelle smiled. Everything was right with the world.

"Don't touch him," a deep male voice boomed out.

Juelle frozen as Eron, Hermes, and two other men stepped into the clearing.

"Get away from that moncat," he ordered. "Now."

Chapter Ten

Eron froze. Juelle hadn't moved. Didn't she realize the danger? Quickly, he formulated and rejected several rescue schemes.

"It's okay. He's my moncat," Juelle said.

Eron gaped at the scene before him, trying to make sense of it. Juelle remained calm, unconcerned, and apparently unharmed. His gaze moved to the moncat. The animal didn't move either—he just watched Eron with an unblinking stare.

Eron relaxed a little when it appeared there was no immediate threat. "*Your* moncat? Impossible."

"Yes, mine," she said, a hint of pride in her voice. She raised her right wrist to display a small wound that looked remarkably like a moncat bite. "See?"

Comprehension dawned, mixed with horror. "No," he breathed. "Impossible."

"Impossible?" Juelle echoed. She got to her feet and stood glaring at him, hands on her hips. "Why do you keep saying that?"

He gestured helplessly. "No adult has survived a night in a moncat grove without being bitten."

Her eyebrows rose. "I *was* bitten. On the right wrist," she said, enunciating each word as if he were too dense to understand.

Hermes voiced the concern Eron had been afraid to put into words. "But . . . that would make you a . . . a pythia."

"Bingo! Give the boy a gold star." Juelle folded her arms across her chest with a belligerent look.

The village men exchanged incredulous glances as Eron stood, too stunned to say anything.

"Impossible," one of the men uttered.

Juelle rolled her eyes. "You guys *really* need to find a new line."

They just stared in incomprehension.

Juelle sighed. "Okay, *why* is it impossible?"

"You're too old," one blurted out, then blushed and ducked his head in chagrin as his friend elbowed him in the ribs.

"Too old? I'm only thirty-two."

The men appeared embarrassed but kept their mouths shut. Eron shook his head dazedly. It was time he came out of shock and said something. After all, he was the councilman here.

He cleared his throat and all eyes turned to him. Their expressions varied widely—Hermes looked confused; the villagers, relieved; and Juelle, challenging. Even the two moncats gave him assessing stares.

"Traditionally, only young girls—adolescents—are pythias." Eron's voice rose despite himself.

Juelle snorted inelegantly. "Well, that's obviously not the case here."

"But—"

"Look, I'm a pythia now. Deal with it."

He couldn't. "Dammit, it just is not *done*," Eron thundered.

Unmoved by his display of temper, Juelle merely raised her wrist, showing him the evidence once again. The feisty young male moncat beside her bristled, glaring at Eron and hissing.

Sickening realization swept over him. Sweet Apollo, if the moncat's defense was any indication, Juelle really *was* a pythia. A maelstrom of emotions jumbled through him, but he didn't have the time or inclination to sort them out. All he knew was that the whole time he'd agonized over her safety, she'd been having a grand old time becoming a pythia.

Frustrated, Eron burned with the need to *do* something, to put his feelings into action. Shoving a hand through his hair, he said, "Let's return to the village."

"Why?" Juelle demanded.

"Because . . ." He floundered, looking for an excuse to break up this uncomfortable tableau and *move*. ". . . they're worried about you. We've been looking for you all night. And when we followed your tracks to the grove, we thought—"

Understanding and remorse flickered across Juelle's face. "I'm sorry. I had no idea."

He nodded curtly. "Let's go."

The short trek back to the village was silent, filled with unspoken words and sidelong glances. Unfortunately, that gave Eron plenty of time to think, and wonder. Why was he so upset about this new turn of events? It was unprecedented, true, but the moncats *had* chosen her . . . and they'd never been wrong before. So, why?

He calmed himself and tried to list the reasons. First, Juelle was Terran—not of his world. No, that wasn't true anymore. Becoming a pythia definitely put her in his world, giving her immediate credibility with any Delphian so she could tout her damned technology.

Wasn't that reason enough to be upset? Yes, but there was more.

It wasn't just the fact that she was Terran, it was Juelle herself—he was too attracted to her for his peace of mind. It had been easier to be aloof when she was obviously off-limits. But now she was a pythia. And that meant he could view her as a possible mate . . . even a life-mate.

The thought was exhilarating and frightening at the same time. Despite himself, Eron began to wonder what it would be like to have such a woman as life-mate . . . until he realized one thing hadn't changed. Juelle still couldn't prophesy.

His anger and frustration turned to pity. She probably hadn't realized it yet, and it would devastate her when she did. But now was not the time to tell her—he'd wait until they were alone. Until then, he'd let her have her brief moment in the limelight, since it would be the last time she would be able to enjoy the privileges of a real pythia.

He frowned and cast her a concerned glance. Though he didn't care for the thought of her being a pythia, he wouldn't wish that kind of pain on anyone. But perhaps if he could convince the others to keep their mouths shut about what had happened, she might never have to go through that agony.

Eron glanced at his companions and groaned inwardly. Between Juelle's pride and belligerence, and the villagers' obvious desire to tell everyone what they'd seen, it would be impossible to keep this a secret. He'd just have to make the best of the situation and give her his full support.

When they arrived at the village, his suspicions were confirmed. People rushed out to check on the health of the petite Terran and drew back in awe when they saw her carrying two moncats.

The young one rode proudly, defiantly, on her shoulder, daring anyone to say anything. Eron's lips quirked in amusement. Now there was a perfect mesh of personalities if he'd ever seen one—you couldn't find a better match for the feisty Terran.

He glanced at her as she fielded questions from the villagers. If the tight expression on her face was any indication, he'd better rescue her—and fast—before her irritation got the better of her.

He shouldered his way through the crowd. He held his hands up until an expectant silence fell. "Yes," he confirmed. "The moncats have chosen Juelle."

The crowd exchanged uneasy looks, and a voice in the back called out a question. "Isn't she too old to be a pythia?"

Juelle's mouth tightened again. Eron started to say she wasn't as old as she looked, then thought better of it. That wasn't exactly the best way to get in her good graces. Besides, she'd blurted out her age to the villagers, so it wouldn't work anyway.

He stood next to her and whispered, "Let me handle this."

She grimaced but nodded, apparently realizing she was out of her depth.

Eron smiled with a wry twist of his mouth and placed a hand on her shoulder. "Too old? Apparently the moncats don't think so."

"But she's . . . Terran," another voice protested.

"So were your ancestors—and the first pythias," Eron reminded them. "We are all descended from Terrans."

There were a lot of frowns and a few nods, but most still appeared uncomfortable with the whole idea. One woman ventured, "Does that mean other

159

women—older women—can become pythias?"

There was a collective gasp—of realization, hope, or disapproval, Eron wasn't sure. All eyes turned toward him for the answer. Luckily, Juelle kept quiet as Eron tried to appear wise and learned. He searched for an answer, then realized only the oracle would know the correct response to that question.

"That remains to be seen. This situation is without precedent. It would be remiss of me to make a pronouncement without consulting the Council . . . and the oracle."

Relief appeared on many faces, and most of the crowd nodded. Eron relaxed and said, "I will consult the oracle when I return and let you know its determination."

The tension lifted and the villagers turned with expectant faces to Juelle, obviously prepared to bombard her with questions again. To forestall them, Eron said, "I'm sorry, but she's just had a very busy night and is still recuperating from her illness. Please, let her rest."

There were a few grumbles, but they were basically decent people, so they withdrew to give Juelle the rest she needed. The crowd started to disperse until one woman asked, "What about the celebration?"

"Celebration?" Juelle repeated and glanced up at Eron in inquiry.

Ferrin stepped forward. "Of course. There must be a feast to honor your selection as a pythia." The lieutenant smiled and bowed his head. "It is a tradition to fete the lucky ones who are chosen to serve the oracle. You bring great distinction to our village by your selection in our moncat grove, and we would deem it an honor if you would allow us to celebrate with you."

Juelle looked questioningly to Eron. He nodded. The lieutenant's sentiments were correct and the village would find it odd if the celebration were omitted.

Juelle gave the man a beaming smile. "I would be honored," she said and stroked the smug-looking moncat.

"Thank you, Juelle," Ferrin said. "And might we inquire as to the name of your new companion?"

"Loki," Juelle replied.

"A fine name," Ferrin responded. The silly little moncat preened himself and Ferrin bowed again. "The celebration will begin with the evening meal."

Eron nodded and led Juelle away from the crowd, back to the Healing House. As Hermes was about to follow them into the building, Eron forestalled him. "Perhaps it would be better if you were to circulate among the villagers, allay their fears."

Hermes nodded, though there was a flash of excitement in his expression. "Do you think there might be . . . trouble?"

"I'm not sure," Eron hedged. It would do the boy good to have some responsibility, but he didn't want him overextending himself and perhaps getting hurt. "But subtlety's the key, mind you. Keep it light, honest, and aboveboard. Do you think you can do that?"

"Sure."

"Good. Then go, and report back to me a half hour before the celebration. Take Seri with you to remind these folks who you represent."

Hermes took a willing Seri into his arms, grinned, then dashed off. Eron opened his mouth to remonstrate with the boy, but Hermes apparently remembered the seriousness of his mission, for he slowed his pace and sauntered toward the nearest villagers.

Eron grinned and turned to Juelle, gesturing her into the deserted Healing House.

After he followed her inside, she said, "That was nice of you."

Taken aback, Eron could only repeat, "Nice?"

"Yes, to give Hermes something to do—a mission."

Eron shrugged in embarrassment. He didn't want to accept praise for something that seemed natural—especially since he had an ulterior motive. "It won't hurt, and he will enjoy it. Besides," he admitted, "I want to talk to you in private and I didn't want to hurt his feelings—or upset him."

Juelle raised an eyebrow as she sat cross-legged on a nearby bed. "Upset him? I see. You plan to say something to me that would upset Hermes?"

"No, no. I just want to talk to you about"—he gestured at the moncat and her wrist—"this."

"This," Juelle repeated in a flat tone. "You mean the fact that I'm now a pythia?"

"Yes." Wasn't it obvious? Eron paced the room, which suddenly seemed a great deal smaller than it had when they'd come in—and Juelle a great deal closer than was comfortable.

She rose to plant herself in his path and stare up at him. "What about it?"

"Huh?"

"Look, this has been bugging you since the moment you learned that a Terran—and an *old* biddy at that—broke all the traditions of your precious society and was chosen as a pythia. So, tell me how you feel."

Eron gave her a sharp glance. "Why?" He wasn't used to sharing his thoughts and emotions with anyone and wasn't sure he wanted to start.

Juelle sighed in exasperation. "Look, you know I'm a doctor, right? A healer?"

"Right."

"A healer of the mind?"

He nodded.

"Okay, so trust me when I say it's good for you to get your emotions out on the table so we can discuss them."

Eron glanced doubtfully at the table next to them.

Juelle rolled her eyes. "Not *literally*. I mean, express them, tell me how you feel. It'll help. I promise."

The feelings he'd suppressed earlier rose to roil within him once more. Perhaps she was right. Perhaps if he named them, they would have less power over him.

"Besides," Juelle said, "How can you allay the villagers' fears and concerns if you don't understand your own?"

She had a point—and perhaps letting her play mind healer would make it easier to break the bad news to her. "How do I start?"

"First, get comfortable." She glanced around. "These beds are too small," she muttered, and gestured him into her room. "Lie down."

He darted her a wary glance.

"It's okay," she assured him in a sarcastic tone. "I'm not going to ravish you or anything."

Eron groaned to himself at the images she'd conjured up and tried to force his body—and his wayward thoughts—back into some semblance of control. He laid down. "All right. Now what?"

"Close your eyes and focus on your emotion."

He closed his eyes. "There's more than one."

He heard Juelle settle in a chair next to the bed. "That's okay," she said in a soothing tone. "That's to be expected. Let's just take one at a time. What's the first thing that pops into your mind?"

Eron concentrated on the roiling emotions baying through his body and settled on the most prominent one. "Desire," he said without thinking, then covered his face and groaned in disbelief at his own stupidity. He should have kept that to himself.

When Juelle didn't say anything, he peered out through his fingers to see her grinning at him, a mischievous glint in her eye. "We'll deal with that later, but for now, let's concentrate on some of your other emotions, okay?"

The primary one ruling him now was embarrassment, but since she probably already knew that, he searched for another. "Shock."

"Shock?"

"Yes. Shock . . . and surprise." He regarded her warily. "It *is* unusual, you know, for you to be chosen as a pythia."

"I know. But dammit—it shouldn't be." She sighed. "I'm sorry. Please continue. What else?"

Loki settled down next to her and regarded Eron steadily, as if trying to see into his thoughts. Eron smiled. The moncat might be young and brash, but he appeared to be taking his new duties very seriously. Eron searched within himself for another of those emotions. "Pride."

The surprised expression on her face was almost comical. "I-I don't understand."

He gave her a half smile, glad to see he'd caught the normally unflappable Terran off-balance. It surprised him, too. "I am proud of you," he said with far more confidence. Expressing these emotions was getting easier with each utterance.

"Me?" Juelle said in an uncharacteristically small voice. "Why?"

"Because you are . . . you. You're unique. I don't know of anyone else who would have the courage to cross the world with a total stranger, not knowing what's in store for her, just to do what she thought was right." He continued. "Few others would brave those dangers, face down a sandsnake, or guard an ill adolescent alone in the perilous desert."

She shrugged, but said nothing.

"And all without complaint. No wonder you were chosen as a pythia."

She smiled and covered his hand with hers. "Thank you."

Her gratitude was premature, as she'd soon find out. "I have another emotion."

"What's that?"

"Fear."

"Of what?"

"Of your new status."

He could see her bristle. Oh, she tried to hide it, but Loki's indignant reaction revealed much. "Why is that?"

He sat up on the bed to look her in the eyes. "Remember your own prophecy?" he asked gently.

Her gaze slid away from his and she rubbed her arms. "Yeah. I remember." She glanced up at him then, a troubled expression on her face. "I won't be able to prophesy, will I?"

He sighed in relief. She understood. "No, not willingly."

She cast him a sad smile. "Then I don't suppose you'd consider forcing me, would you?"

He grinned. "Sorry, I draw the line at coercing women."

"So, I'm a pythia who can't . . . pyth."

He chuckled. Nothing could subdue this woman for long. "I never heard it expressed that way before, but yes, that's true." There was no sense in holding out false hope.

"So what do I do?"

Pam McCutcheon

He shrugged. "I'm not sure. This isn't exactly your normal case."

"So what would you do in a normal situation— you know, if I wasn't old, wasn't Terran"—her mouth twisted in a wry smile—"wasn't the doom of Delphi?"

"We would take you to the nearest caverns for testing—to see what your rank is—then enroll you in the training program so you could take your place as a practicing pythia."

"Damn. Do you have any idea how useful this ability would be in therapy? No, of course you don't." She slammed a fist down on the bed. "And now that I've finally got it, I can't even *use* it."

Frustration was evident in her voice and her emotions were strong enough to leak over onto her moncat, who was making little sounds of distress. Hating to see her like this, Eron gathered her into his arms and held her close, wanting nothing more than to hold her, comfort her.

The tiny Terran clutched at him as if he were her lifeline, hugging him in a tight grip. Though no words were spoken, Eron could feel her pain, her frustration, her need. He just held her in his lap, absorbing her pain and offering wordless comfort in the form of his large body. Loki hovered around them, obviously upset, yet not knowing what to do.

Eron held Juelle for a long time until her grip eased and she shifted within his embrace. With that slight movement of her body, the comforting embrace turned into something more. Something . . . intimate.

Juelle rested her head against his chest and put her arm around him, stroking his chest in tentative exploration. Eron found himself returning the favor, rubbing his hands over her back and the sweet feminine glide of her waist and hip, enjoying the way she felt in his arms, unable to stop touching her.

Juelle gazed up at him, desire plain in her eyes, and whispered, "Remember that first emotion you felt? Why don't we explore that now?"

Eron smiled and cradled her head in one hand to search her face. Loki purred, a deep thrum that proved Juelle really did feel the same way Eron did.

Gathering her close, he kissed her. Tentatively at first, then harder, more demanding as she responded. Juelle shifted to come more fully into his arms. He cradled her gently, not wanting to hurt this fragile yet strangely strong woman who had wormed her way into his affections.

The world narrowed to just the two of them as they explored each other's mouths with mounting eagerness. Could they . . . ?

Eron heard a sudden gasp from the doorway and looked up to see Hermes, wide-eyed, staring at them in shock. As Eron watched, the boy turned bright red and stumbled back out the door.

Eron gave Juelle an agonized look. She sighed and patted him on the back, slipping off his lap. "You'd better go to him."

Good—she understood. He pressed a swift promissory kiss on her forehead and followed Hermes out the door.

Nevan grimaced when he heard Alexander call out behind him. He'd been trying to avoid the Terran all day and had been successful so far, but his luck had finally turned.

Though Nevan and his men had learned how to operate the ship's weapon systems, there was still much they didn't know, and Alexander was slow to teach them. Worse, he was becoming more vexed about the lack of progress on the filters, which was undoubtedly what he wanted to talk about now.

Nevan composed his face into a pleasant mask and turned to greet Alexander. Shogril did the same beside him.

Alexander held out his hand. "I'm glad I caught you."

Nevan used the political smile that had served him so well in the past and shook his hand. "So am I."

The Terran raised an eyebrow in disbelief but was obviously too polite to contradict him. "Good. About those filters—"

"They're coming along quite well, don't you think?"

"Oh, certainly, but when do you think they'll be done?"

They'd be done when Nevan learned everything he needed to know about the Terran's ship. "Oh, soon. Soon."

"How soon?" Though Alexander was still polite, he was becoming more insistent.

Nevan gritted his teeth. The Terran had turned cagey, and had started answering their questions about the workings of the ship with vague, uninformative answers. Well, two could play at that game. "Right after the festival," he replied.

Alexander's expression turned wary. "What festival?"

Nevan's mind churned. "Didn't I tell you about the festival?"

"No. No, you didn't," Alexander said in a flat tone. "What about it?"

"It's a nationwide holiday."

"Celebrating what?"

Shogril rescued him. "Celebrating the anniversary of the first pythia," he said, his voice matter-of-fact.

"That's right," Nevan said, and elaborated, improvising as he went along. "It's the annual . . . Caroline Festival, to honor our esteemed pythias."

"And when is this festival?"

Nevan smiled. "Why, it's tomorrow."

"And I suppose it's a nonworking holiday, too, huh?" Alexander asked.

"Of course."

"That figures. Well, I guess I'll just have to finish the job myself."

Nevan couldn't have that. "I'm afraid not."

"Why not?"

"No one works during the Caroline Festival."

"But—"

"No one," Shogril repeated and scowled. "Or you'll offend the gods."

The Terran sighed heavily. Nevan could almost sympathize with his frustration. The man had a remarkable store of patience, and they'd taxed it to the limit.

"Well," Alexander said, "I certainly don't want to offend your gods."

"Good," Nevan said and took him by the arm. "Now, while Shogril prepares for the festival, why don't you and I have a discussion, Ambassador Morgan?"

Shogril gave him a nod and hurried off, presumably to cobble together a suitable festival on such short notice.

Alexander gave him a tight smile. "Sure. What would you like to talk about?"

"About this ship . . ."

Chapter Eleven

Eron caught up to Hermes just inside the village common area and grabbed the boy's shoulder. "Wait."

Hermes stopped, but wouldn't look at him. Shrugging off Eron's restraining hand, he remained motionless, staring into the distance as he tried to keep his face impassive.

It didn't work. The hurt showed in his expression, and Seri gave the boy a concerned look.

Eron glanced around at the curious stares of the villagers. They didn't need an audience for this. "Come," he said. "Let's go somewhere we can talk."

Hermes nodded and followed Eron to a secluded spot under a tree. The boy flopped down on the soft grass, his face hidden as he stroked Seri.

"Hermes . . ." Eron paused, not knowing what to say to him.

"I thought you hated her," Hermes mumbled.

"Hated her? No, I never hated her," Eron said,

"though I dislike what she stands for."

Hermes flashed a look of pain and accusation at him. "Why'd you kiss her, then?"

The boy deserved an honest explanation. "Because I couldn't help myself."

Hermes dashed a tear out of his eye. "Did you force yourself on her?"

"Did it look like she was struggling?"

"No, but . . ."

"But what?" When Hermes didn't answer, Eron continued. "Juelle's a very desirable woman, you know."

"I know."

"And with the close proximity of this trip, being near her day and night, I can't help thinking about her." *Wanting her.*

Hermes' sigh was heartfelt. "I know what you mean."

Gently, Eron said, "And it appears she feels the same way about me."

Hermes stiffened, then relaxed gradually. "I guess she does," he muttered.

Eron squeezed the boy's shoulder. "Is that all right with you?"

"Does it matter?" he asked, a tinge of bitterness in his voice.

"Yes, it does. I don't want you to have any hard feelings over this."

Hermes shrugged. "I don't. It's just that—" He stopped abruptly.

"I know. You rather fancied her yourself."

Hermes reddened, but nodded as he lowered his head to pet the moncat again. "Stupid, huh?"

Eron chuckled. "No more so than me. That woman could frustrate the hell out of any man."

The boy agreed with an expressive roll of his eyes. "So, what do you do about it?"

171

"I beat up trees."

"You beat up . . . ?"

Eron grinned. "That's right. It's a bit hard on the tree, but helps get rid of the excess tension. Want to try it?"

Hermes laughed. "Sure."

"There's a likely one right behind you." Eron rose to give the tree a considering look, and prepared to show Hermes the time-honored method that Delphian men used to get women out of their systems.

Once he and Hermes had taken their frustrations out on the unsuspecting vegetation, Eron returned to escort Juelle to the festivities as promised.

Entering the Healing House, he stopped and stood stock-still at the sight of her. During his absence, someone had provided her with the traditional clothing for this sort of celebration—a pythia's floor-length chiton.

"Isn't it lovely?" Juelle asked. "The villagers gave it to me."

Eron could only nod. The silky white fabric hung from her shoulders to dip low over her breasts, the sleeve openings providing tantalizing glimpses of her bare arms. Delicate sandals graced her feet, and a wreath of fragrant ariana leaves sat becomingly on her silver-blonde hair.

But the rank sash was his undoing. Blue in deference to her novice status, it criss-crossed under her breasts, emphasizing her soft contours. His gaze lingered there and her nipples hardened to taut peaks under his scrutiny.

Eron caught his breath as his own desire swelled in response, surprising him with its intensity. A simple pythian robe had never affected him this way before.

Hermes entered behind him and took one look at

her, then blushed bright red, muttering, "Sweet Apollo."

Juelle laughed. "That's the reaction I wanted." She moved over to clasp Eron's arm and glanced up at him with a mischievous glint in her eye. "Yours was flattering, too—that poleaxed look suits you."

Eron smiled faintly as he tried to control his breathing. If it weren't for Hermes' presence, he'd untie that blue sash and let it fall to the floor, then see where her clever mouth took her.

Silently, he raked her with his gaze, promising a closer inspection later. Juelle smiled, an answering acceptance in her expression.

Hermes cleared his throat in the doorway. "Uh, they're waiting for you."

Eron glanced down at her. "Ready?"

"Almost. Where's Loki?"

He glanced around the room for the moncat. When he finally spotted Loki, Eron grinned. He didn't know if it was the spillover of Juelle's emotion, or if the young moncat was naturally amorous, but Loki had backed Seri into a corner and was nuzzling up to her, trying hard to entwine his tail with hers.

Eron chuckled. Seri seemed indecisive, not knowing whether to be offended or flattered, whether to push him away or draw him near.

"Loki," Juelle called, "leave Seri alone. Come on, let's go."

The young moncat gave Seri one last, longing look, then scurried over to leap onto Juelle's shoulder.

"Really," Juelle muttered. "You'd think one of us would have some sense."

Loki just huffed, then assumed a dignified expression as they walked out the door toward the celebration.

Ferrin and the village elders greeted them, and gave a pretty speech about how honored Riverfork was to have been the site of Juelle's selection as a pythia. Kindly, they avoided mention of her age and her origin. In return, she was gracious as she thanked them for their hospitality.

The festivities began, and the food and wine flowed freely as every man in town vied to be the new pythia's dance partner. A local group of musicians provided the music. Though it was slightly off-key, it didn't deter the villagers from enjoying the dancing with great enthusiasm. Eron watched from the sidelines as Juelle partnered everyone who asked her.

Hermes sat next to him and followed Eron's line of vision to see Juelle laughing up at her partner as she missed a step in one of the more intricate dances. To punctuate her merriment, Loki performed a standing back flip, delighting the crowd. Even Seri seemed amused.

Hermes grinned. "It's too bad she'll never be a real pythia."

"Why is that?"

"She's a natural. She's what everyone assumes a pythia is—smart, gracious, pretty, and wise—without even trying." Hermes snorted. "She's what all those silly girls in the caverns are trying to be."

Eron agreed. But her inability to prophesy would pain her. "You didn't mention that to anyone else, did you?"

"No, of course not. I wouldn't spoil her fun—it may be the last time she'll be able to enjoy the privileges of a pythia."

"True." Eron sighed and changed the subject.

"So, did you learn anything today in your wanderings?"

"Yes, I'm afraid I did."

Eron didn't like the sound of that. "Oh? What? Are they upset because of Juelle's age? Or her origin?"

"Both, but for the most part they're dealing with it." Hermes shrugged. "Since you're their councilman and *you* accept it, they really can't do anything else."

"So what is their problem, then?"

"I'm not sure. . . . It's more of a feeling than what anyone's actually *said*."

"That's all right. It's called gut instinct, and you should learn to rely on it. I do—and it's seldom wrong."

"Really?"

"Really. So, what does your gut tell you?"

"I-I think there's going to be trouble in the village when you leave."

"Trouble? Why?"

"Well, some of the women have been looking at Juelle with envy."

"That's only natural—"

"I know, but this is different. It's envy . . . and something more. Like hope."

Eron felt a sinking sensation in his gut as he gestured for Hermes to continue.

"They look at Juelle, then glance toward the moncat grove as if wondering what their chances are."

Eron's mouth firmed into a thin line.

"And when the men see that, they look like you."

"Like me?"

"Yes—you know, all forbidding and angry."

Eron nodded. He'd been afraid of this. "You've done well. It appears we need to do something about it before it tears this village apart. What do you suggest?"

"M-Me?"

"Yes, you. You're training to be an observer. That entails a great deal more than just watching prophecies and writing them down, you know. Observers are the most powerful men on the planet. From them, councilmen are chosen. If you aspire to that position, you need to learn how to make decisions that will help your people."

Hermes gulped and nodded.

"So, what is your recommendation?" At the boy's apprehensive look, Eron said, "It's all right. Just take your time and think about it."

Hermes glanced at Juelle. "Well, they're not going to forget about it just because she leaves. We have to do something now."

"That makes sense. What do you suggest?"

"I think you, as councilman, need to explain how unusual this is—perhaps say that the only reason she was chosen at her age is because she's a Terran."

"Good, good. That's believable enough, and might keep them wondering so the women won't risk themselves in the moncat grove after dark. I'll drop a word in Ferrin's ear before we go. What else?"

"Then you and Juelle leave for Oasis and ask the oracle what to do. I-I'll stay here until you come back."

It was the right thing to do, but Eron raised his eyebrows in question, wanting to hear Hermes' rationale.

"I figure leaving me here will help enforce your authority."

"You're right—just your presence and the knowledge I'll be back might make some of the more foolhardy women delay trying their chances in the grove." He clapped the boy on the back. "It's a good plan."

Hermes glowed with the praise.

Eron rose and glanced around for Juelle, spotting her on the dance floor. The tiny Terran looked flushed and tired from the dance that had just ended. When he signaled her, she came over and sat down, casting him a grateful look.

Grinning, Eron said, "We need to get an early start in the morning. Are you ready to call it a night?"

"More than ready. I'm dead tired."

"Then let's get some sleep, shall we?" He hadn't forgotten his earlier promise, but now was not the time. They'd have plenty of opportunity during the rest of the trip to get to know each other better. Much better.

Juelle blinked sleepily at the villagers who'd come to see them off. The party the night before had been exhausting. She hadn't gotten nearly enough sleep, especially since Eron had rousted her out so early this morning.

Eron thanked Ferrin for their hospitality, and the lieutenant frowned. "There have been a number of sandstorms reported in the desert lately, and more are anticipated. With the dangers there, do you think it wise . . . ?"

Eron nodded. "I know. That's why I already decided to skirt the desert."

Juelle shot him a questioning glance.

"It adds a few extra days," he explained, "but it's a lot safer—especially since there are only two of us."

Eron had explained why Hermes wasn't accompanying them. She approved. The boy was still recovering from a snake bite, after all. And anything that allowed them to avoid a storm met with her full approval.

Ferrin looked relieved. "Good. May Apollo bless you and keep you on your journey."

Eron smiled and thanked him, and they were soon on their way. Loki rode with Juelle and Seri rode with Eron, pointedly keeping her face averted from the attention-seeking antics of the male moncat.

As they headed away from the rivers, the vegetation density decreased dramatically. The climate was harsh here on the edge of the desert, but nowhere near as bad as the desert itself, for which Juelle was grateful.

Eron took it easy this time and she was able to keep up with little effort. She didn't know what had happened to mellow him, but she rather liked the change she'd seen in him recently. He'd even stopped behaving like Tarzan and started thinking and reacting like a real person.

Wondering how far his sudden affability extended, she decided to test it. "Eron?"

"Yes?"

"About the Republic . . ."

And the fight was on.

By the time night fell, Juelle had grown tired of arguing. The man was incredibly stubborn and opinionated, unwilling to budge an inch.

Oh, he admitted that the Republic and its technology could benefit Delphi, but he was adamant that the prophecy had said it would ruin the planet. He couldn't say how, or even postulate a reasonable explanation why—he just took it on blind faith. That was impossible to argue with, so Juelle stopped trying.

When he called a halt for the night, she gratefully

dismounted. Unfortunately, her backside hadn't quite gotten used to riding yet, and it still hurt. But at least she wasn't as stiff and sore as she'd been at the start of the trip.

She helped Eron with the now familiar routine of setting up camp and cooked dinner while he fed and watered the horses. To entertain herself, she watched the moncats.

Loki hadn't given up on his courtship yet, though Seri constantly rebuffed him. Even now, he bounded over to offer her a few leaves with an earnest, supplicating expression. Seri sniffed at his offering, then with an upturned nose, accepted them and nibbled at one.

Loki stared at her with lovesick eyes and Seri sighed, seemingly with her entire little body. She handed him a leaf, and Loki took it with an expression that looked remarkably like a triumphant grin, then whipped around to sit next to her.

Seri suffered the brash male's closeness, but kept a wary eye on his tail. It appeared to twitch too close to hers for Seri's peace of mind.

Juelle heard a deep chuckle behind her and turned to see Eron watching the moncats as well. Hiding her amusement, Juelle offered him a bowl of stew, trying to emulate Loki's earnest expression. "I'm sorry it's not leaves, but . . ."

Eron laughed and Juelle's heart flopped in her chest. There was that smile again—the one that could melt any woman's heart. Hell, it could melt the polar ice caps, given half a chance.

Eron joined her on one of the bedrolls and accepted the stew. "This'll do." He took a bite. "Mmm. Good."

They ate in silence for awhile, watching the progress of Loki's courtship. Or rather, lack of progress. His eagerness overcame his good sense, and

Pam McCutcheon

he couldn't seem to keep his tail under control. He let it stray once too often to Seri's backside, and she let him have it, with a furious hiss and a smack on the ear.

Eron and Juelle both chuckled as the subdued moncat came slinking back to Juelle for commiseration.

Even as she stroked Loki's soft fur, Juelle chided, "Don't come to me for comfort. You got what you deserved."

The moncat nestled closer, providing some welcome body heat. Now that it was dark, it was starting to turn cool. They finished eating and cleaned up, then returned to their former spots on the bedrolls next to the fire.

As Juelle stared into the dancing flames, her mind wandered back to the shattering events of the previous day. "Eron?" she asked idly.

"Yes?"

"What are you going to do with me?"

"What do you mean?"

"What are you going to do with me when we get to Oasis? People will wonder if I don't take my place with the other pythias, but it's obvious I can't. So, what do you plan to do?"

"I don't know. I'll leave that up to the oracle."

The oracle? That's who had gotten them into this mess in the first place. "If only . . ." She trailed off, unwilling to put her yearning into words.

Eron glanced down at her and hugged her to him with one arm. "I know. I, too, wish you and Loki could take your place in the pythia caverns. But it is not to be. The oracle has spoken."

Juelle nodded and snuggled into his warmth. At the moment, she didn't care. Her skin tingled where it came into contact with his body and she felt warmed clear through. Right now, all she could think about was Eron, and his closeness.

A rush of desire washed over her, then surged again, stronger, more demanding. Shocked by the intensity of it, Juelle realized the second sensation had come from outside herself. She looked down at Loki, who purred deep in his chest as he picked up on her emotions and fed them back to her, amplified threefold.

"What are you doing, you little scamp?" she whispered. "Go away." She tried to shoo him away, but he appeared so disconsolate that Juelle didn't have the heart to be the second one to reject him tonight.

But if these feelings were going to lead where she thought and hoped they were, she didn't want the ever-curious Loki watching. She formed a mental picture and sent the moncat an image of him staying on the other side of the fire, facing outward.

Juelle hadn't thought it possible, but moncats could pout. Or at least Loki could. He stared at her and didn't move. Juelle sighed and sent him another picture he *could* understand—an absurd one of Juelle and Eron lying close together, their nonexistent tails wrapped around each other, and a wall of privacy around them.

Astonishment crossed Loki's face as he stared incredulously at Eron's backside, for all the world as if he expected a tail to sprout there.

For heaven's sake, didn't anyone on this planet understand metaphors? She repeated the scene, and Loki finally seemed to understand, for he scampered off into the night.

"What was that all about?" Eron asked.

Juelle snuggled closer, burrowing into his chest as his arms enveloped her. "Oh, nothing. He was picking up on my emotions and amplifying them. I asked him to stop, and he went off in a huff."

"Emotions?"

Trust the man to pick up on the one key word in that sentence. "Yes, emotions." She tugged his shirt loose and slid her hand inside, feeling the muscles under his warm skin grow taut as she stroked his back. "You remember those. We discussed them yesterday."

His arms tightened around her. "Yes, I remember."

"And, if you'll recall, we have some . . . unfinished business, too." She grew bolder, moving her hands to his front and caressing the hair on his chest, teasing his nipples.

Eron inhaled sharply and his hands tightened on her shoulders. "Yes," he hissed. "I remember that, too. But . . ."

"But what?"

"A pythia only makes love to her life-mate." His tone was regretful, as if he'd just now recalled that and wasn't at all pleased with himself for doing so.

Encouraged by the fact that he didn't move away from her caressing hands, Juelle said, "But I'm not your ordinary pythia. Besides, that's true only *after* life-mating, not before, isn't it?"

"Technically, yes. Until she's life-mated, a pythia may dally with any man. But, traditionally, it isn't done."

"You mean no pythia has ever tried out a potential life-mate ahead of time? I don't believe it. Hell, I would—especially since the life-mate ritual is irrevocable."

He glanced down at her and grinned. "Come to think of it, I don't believe it either."

He pulled her to him until she straddled his waist, smiling at how easy it had been to convince him. She pushed his shirt up so she could feel more of him, and he impatiently pulled it off. She ran her hands through the crisp hair on his chest, glorying in the feel of it, and rose to kiss a soft, vulnerable spot on his neck, right behind his ear.

As he tensed, she ran her tongue over that spot and whispered, "This time, there's no one around to interrupt us."

She leaned back, and he stared into her eyes with a darkening need as he bent to kiss her. Juelle met him halfway. She'd had enough exploratory, frustrating kisses from this man—she wanted him hard and fast and deep.

She opened her mouth under his and exulted when he thrust his tongue inside. She met him eagerly, sucking lightly on his tongue and doing her best to touch every square inch of his magnificent chest.

He pulled back, breathing hard, to gaze at her with a question in his eyes. There was no question in Juelle's mind. From the evidence rising beneath her, this man wanted her as much as she wanted him.

Keeping her gaze locked with his, she rose from his lap and slipped out of her one piece overall, now dressed only in her bra and panties.

Eron stared at her hungrily, and Juelle shivered, whether from the intensity of his gaze or the chill of the night, she wasn't sure. He didn't give her time to find out, as he swiftly shucked his own clothing, standing naked and proud before her.

Juelle couldn't help but let her gaze wander over his body. She'd seen him nude in the water before, but that didn't give her a clue as to *this*. With his long flowing hair, bulging tanned muscles, proud erection, and intense stare, Eron looked like a primal animal, ready to take his mate.

Juelle shivered once more and unhooked the clasp of her bra, letting it fall to the ground. As Eron watched in mesmerized silence, she slid her panties off and kicked them aside until she was standing as naked as he was. Warm moisture pooled between her legs and she thought if he didn't touch her soon, she'd scream.

Eron knelt and drew her to him, his mouth seeking her breast as his warm, tender hands massaged her back and her buttocks, leaving a trail of welcome heat in their wake.

Juelle sighed and leaned in to him, running her fingers through his silky hair as he fondled and sucked her breasts into aching need. When she could take no more, she pulled away and tugged him down onto the bedroll.

He rubbed at the goose bumps on her arm. "You're cold," he said in wonder.

"Very. Can we get inside the sleeping bag?"

"Of course."

They scrambled into it and snuggled together, shivering, until the heat of his body and the close confines of the bedroll warmed her. She rolled to her side and ran one hand down his chest. Eron sighed as she used her other hand to caress his velvet hardness.

Clasping him with a gentle but firm hand, she stroked until she could feel him trembling with the effort not to move, not to explode. When she thought he could take no more, she let go and moved to settle over his waist.

She eased down onto him until he filled her fully. Dear Lord, the man was big. This felt so good, so right. She started to move, but Eron stopped her with two firm hands on her waist.

"No," he said. "Wait."

As she straddled him, stretched to the limits with the strain of encompassing all of him, Eron reached between them. Juelle gasped when he touched her. The pleasure was fierce, swift, engrossing.

Eron stroked one taut nipple with his fingers as he massaged her intimately with his other hand. Juelle shut her eyes, letting the waves of pleasure wash over her.

The tension built, mounting until she was awash in a sea of pure sensation. It overwhelmed her, bringing her crashing over the precipice to shatter into a million tiny shards of ecstasy as she convulsed beneath his hand.

Swiftly, Eron shifted until she was beneath him, still joined together. Holding her securely by the waist, he gritted his teeth and stroked in and out—once, twice, three times. The pleasure was excruciating and she wrapped her legs around him.

He groaned and bent his head, then increased his tempo until Juelle could think of nothing else but the sweet friction of their joined bodies. The flaring rise of desire caught her by surprise, swamping her like an unexpected wave and dragging her under to shattering release. With a shuddering cry, Eron peaked too, and collapsed beside her.

Panting from the exertion, he still found time to hug her and mutter, "Sweet Apollo, that was magnificent."

Juelle buried her fingers in his long hair and kissed him. "Yes. Yes, it was." She grinned. "Let's do it again."

Chapter Twelve

As Shogril and Orgon watched, Nevan paced the confines of the room he had appropriated for himself, an almost exact duplicate of the councilman quarters he commanded at Dodona. And if his strategy proceeded as planned, he *would* command once again, but this time as Council Captain. He'd turn this abandoned pythian cave-city into the mightiest power Delphi had ever known.

Only one thing lay between him and achievement of his goal—Alexander Morgan and his stubbornness.

Orgon peered up at him. "What are we going to do? The Terran has become close-mouthed about the operation of the ship."

Nevan stopped pacing and frowned, his fists clenched. "If we could just get it in the air, we *know* how to fly to Dodona. But we must learn how to get it airborne for our plan to work."

Orgon shifted uncomfortably. "Uh, exactly what

is our plan? And why do we need the ship?"

Shogril scowled at him, obviously preparing to lecture him, but Nevan waved him off. It was a legitimate question from one of his key lieutenants. And now that his plans had gelled, Nevan didn't mind answering.

"We're going to fly to Dodona and give the upstart Council Captain an ultimatum: Either he clears me of all charges and gives up the Captainship, or we'll use the ship's weapons to destroy Dodona."

Orgon's eyes widened in shock. "But how will that make you Council Captain?"

Nevan waved a hand in dismissal. "Simple. All I need is a pliable pythia who is willing to become my life-mate."

"But the Golden Pythia—"

"Thena will no longer be the Golden Pythia. She will abdicate her position along with her Council Captain husband."

Comprehension dawned on Orgon's face. "I see. Then we just need to find the next highest ranking pythia and persuade her to be your life-mate."

Nevan gave him a tight smile. "You're half right. We only need to find a novice pythia who hasn't been tested, then ensure her tests reflect her high ranking."

It would be best, of course, if that pythia achieved gold or silver ranking on her own so the deception could be easily maintained—but he wouldn't be particular. The key lay in finding the right woman first.

His scouts were out now, scouring the pythia caverns for candidates. Of course, if all else failed, he could use Carina, his second cousin. Her tests would undoubtedly place her in one of the lower ranks, but she had the advantage of clan loyalty and pliability.

Nevan grimaced. He'd use her only as a last resort. He'd much prefer someone a little more mature, more . . . clever.

Orgon nodded. "I see. But how will we learn to get the ship airborne?"

"We'll just have to keep pressing the ambassador. But if his present mood is any indication, he won't part readily with the information. I'm afraid we can only stall him for another day or two before he becomes suspicious or leaves on his own—the coming storm will keep him here that long anyway."

Shogril frowned and slammed his fist on the table. "If he won't tell us, we'll *force* it out of him."

Nevan sighed. "I'd prefer not to. It would be so much easier if he cooperates. But, yes, if necessary, we will use force."

Eron woke, shifting in the bedroll. Juelle snuggled into his chest, and tenderness filled him at her unconscious gesture of trust. He hugged her, allowing himself to revisit the wonders of last night.

He'd never experienced anything like her wonderful spontaneity, her lack of inhibition, or her complete abandon in lovemaking. She'd turned a simple mating into a work of art that he would cherish forever. Eron stroked her back and held her close. He'd cherish *her* forever, too.

Ever since he'd met her, this precious woman, this quicksilver Terran, had insinuated herself into his being, gaining toeholds in the stronghold of his heart. Then, last night, she'd stormed the battlements and made him hers, just as surely as if they'd been life-mated.

His heart was hers, now and forever. His body was, too. Even now he felt himself stirring against her. He placed a kiss on her forehead and she moved restlessly, then turned her face to his.

Slowly, she opened her eyes.

Eron smiled and stared into her elfin face, waiting for her to wake fully so they could share the wonder of their new relationship.

She smiled and stroked his cheek. "Good morning."

He nuzzled her neck. "Good morning to you, too. How do you feel?"

She stretched and laid her head on his shoulder, sighing. "Wonderful. How about you?"

Words couldn't express how he felt—the tenderness, the protectiveness, the overpowering urge to keep this woman beside him forever. "I feel good," he said lamely.

She grinned, a mischievous smile that reached up to dance in her eyes. "You sure do," she said, and moved her liips against his hardening arousal.

Eron chuckled. "That's not what I meant."

"I know, but since the subject's come up . . ."

They spent another hour making slow, sensuous love before Eron's conscience got the better of him. After they were both sated, he kissed the top of her head. "We really need to get moving again."

She chuckled. "So soon? I thought you needed a little longer before you could do it again."

Eron laughed. "I meant we have to get moving toward Oasis again. Remember?"

Juelle pouted. "Do we hafta?"

"Yes, I'm afraid we have to."

Still grumbling, Juelle climbed out of the bedroll and dressed. They ate a quick meal of journeybread the village had supplied and packed up the camp to move on.

As they finished, Loki and Seri came scampering out of the trees. The harried expression on Seri's face and the exasperated one on Loki's indicated that their night hadn't been as enjoyable as Eron's and Juelle's.

To give poor Seri a break, Eron encouraged her to ride with him while Loki rode with Juelle. They all mounted and resumed their journey.

Eron took a deep breath of the morning air and grinned. He felt wonderful. Nothing could mar his mood this morning—not even the grim landscape at the edge of the desert or the threatening storm clouds on the horizon. If he'd known falling in love would have this effect on him, he would've tried it before.

His high spirits didn't even lessen when Juelle resumed her litany of the Republic's benefits. Instead, he realized he admired her for not giving up and for not letting their relationship get in the way of her principles.

But admiration and tolerance could only go so far, so long. "How long are you going to badger me on this subject?" he asked mildly.

"Until you give in," she said as if it were obvious.

"I'm *not* going to give in—and you know why."

"Because of that damned prophecy."

"That's right. The Golden Pythia's own prophecy that foretold the destruction of Delphi if we joined the Republic."

"Thena's prophecy? Are you sure?"

"Yes, I'm positive." But that was off the subject. "I thought you agreed to stop trying to convince me once the trip is over."

"Well, I did say I'd try to convince you between Dodona and Oasis, but I never said I'd stop afterward."

Eron frowned. "So you plan to continue hounding me on this subject even after we're life-mated?"

Loki and Seri came to full alert as Juelle reined

in her horse. "Whoa. Back up a moment. What do you mean, life-mated?"

He stopped to face her. "I mean you and me, bonded forever, in the Delphian life-mate ritual."

Juelle shook her head. "That's what I thought you meant. What makes you think we're going to be life-mated?"

"Last night . . ." He floundered, not understanding and not knowing what to say.

"What about last night?"

"Well, we made love . . ."

"We sure did. But where does it say that means we're tied together for the rest of our lives?"

"Nowhere, but it's customary—"

"Maybe in *your* customs, but not where I come from."

Eron frowned, trying to comprehend what she was saying. "When two people love each other . . ."

Juelle gave him a look full of compassion. "Oh, Eron," she said on a sigh.

He felt as though he'd just been knifed in the chest, but he had to know the truth, no matter how much it hurt. "You mean you don't?"

"Look, I'm sorry if I misled you, but in the society I come from, two people can make love without being in love—without committing to a lifetime together."

"So it was merely a . . . physical release for you?"

"Oh, no, Eron. It was so much more than that. I don't sleep with every man I meet, you know."

"I didn't think you did." He knew her better than that.

"Eron, I admire you greatly—I think you're a wonderful man. You're warm, considerate, compassionate . . . and incredibly sexy. I don't see how any woman could resist you."

Any woman, that is, but the one he wanted. "But

not wonderful enough to be your life-mate," he said in a flat tone.

"Right now I don't want to be mated to *anyone* for life. I don't know you that well. Certainly not well enough to make a permanent lifetime commitment. At least, not on the basis of a week's acquaintance and one night's loving."

Juelle reached down to soothe Loki's agitated fur. "Given time, I might come to love you, but—"

Eron spurred his horse into action. He'd heard enough, and didn't want to hear any more platitudes or apologies. Like a fool, he'd bared his soul to her, assuming his feelings were reciprocated.

Shame filled him. Shame . . . and anger. Talking wouldn't solve anything. The thing to do was to get as far away from her as possible. That was impossible until they reached Oasis so, for now, he had to concentrate on closing the distance between here and there as quickly as possible.

If the weather cooperated, that is. He glanced up at the windswept sky. It had darkened to a threatening gray that mirrored his mood.

Juelle watched him with a sinking feeling. *Terrific move, Shanard*. For a psychiatrist, she'd made a pretty stupid mistake. Assuming the customs and mores of this society, many light-years away from Earth, were the same as Earth's was dumb—especially since Delphi hadn't been in contact with Earth for more than two hundred years. It was a damned good thing all her patients had been Terrans, or she might have really screwed them up.

In resignation, she kicked her horse into gear and followed hard on his heels. The wind whipped black sand in off the desert, stinging her eyes and making her a little uneasy. She knew it was silly, but storms always made her nervous. The last thing she wanted was to be stranded alone out here in the middle of God-knows-where, in what promised to be a raging thunderstorm.

And alone she'd be if she didn't catch up. "Eron, wait!"

He didn't even slow down. She cursed beneath her breath and urged her horse to greater effort, afraid she'd lose the pigheaded councilman in the murky surroundings. When she was within a few lengths of him, she shouted again. "Dammit, wait for me."

Still no reaction. Stars. It was just like the man to assume action or brute force would solve all his problems. Well, she wasn't going to let him leave her—not in the middle of a storm anyway. She urged her horse to its maximum effort, knowing the oppressed steed couldn't take much more. With luck, it wouldn't have to.

She caught up to Eron, the wind whipping moisture into her face now along with the fine grit. Grabbing his reins, she yanked hard. "Stop!"

His horse slowed to a stop at Juelle's urging and Eron whipped around to face her, dark hair flying in the wind. He jerked the reins out of her hands. "*Never* do that again, woman."

Woman? That was taking denial and depersonalization just a little too far. Loki snarled, and Juelle realized the moncat was mirroring her emotions. Suppressing her own anger, she said in the most reasonable tone she could muster, "Wait. Let's talk about this."

"I've heard enough."

"Maybe you have, but I haven't."

He pinned her with a scowl. "Are you going to badger me about this, too?"

"Yes—if that's what it takes."

"Well, I don't have to listen to it."

He turned away, but Juelle grabbed his reins before he could spur his horse into motion. "What the hell do you think you're doing?" she yelled over the howling of the wind.

His deep voice boomed out, easily discerned over the elements. "Riding to Oasis."

Short and succinct, yes, but hardly accurate. "Riding away from me, you mean."

His gaze narrowed and she could tell by the tensing of his muscles that he longed to be doing something, anything, to express the feelings he wouldn't admit to. "I don't think so. I need you to cure Lera."

So that's all he'd admit, huh? "Well, if you don't slow down, you're going to lose me in this weather." She gestured down at her horse whose sides were still heaving with exertion. "My horse just can't keep up with yours."

Eron glanced around, surprise on his face as if he just now realized the weather had changed.

Thunder boomed overhead and lightning slashed across the sky, leaving burning afterimages in its wake. Juelle couldn't help but cringe. She tried to pass it off, but Loki's wide-eyed howl gave her away. The moncat's reaction was right on—it was exactly how Juelle felt.

Eron reached out to her, but Juelle scowled and he aborted the motion. She didn't need comforting like a child. She'd survive this quite well, thank you very much.

Lightning flashed again, and with the thunder came rain. Juelle cringed once more, and Loki let loose another howl that made Seri give them both concerned looks. Great. If the elements weren't her undoing, well-meaning moncats would be.

Eron frowned and moved his horse close so she could hear him above the storm. "We've got to find shelter."

No kidding. The rain was coming down hard and

fast now. "Where?" She saw nothing but rocky desert and scrub brush—not a sign of human habitation anywhere.

Eron frowned for a moment, then his face lit. "I just remembered—there are some caves nearby. We can find shelter there."

"How far?" she yelled over the howling of the wind.

"Not far—you'll see." He wheeled his horse and grabbed her reins. "This way I won't lose you. Hold on."

Juelle shivered in the cold rain and held tight to the pommel as Eron spurred their horses into movement. At least their pace was a little slower now, though the thought gave her no comfort. Without the reins, she felt lost, out of control, not knowing what her mount was going to do next and unable to see anything in front of her but Eron's broad back, bent low over his horse's neck as he strove to get them to safety.

Juelle emulated him, bending to shield Loki from the worst of the storm, stuffing him inside her shirt. The poor moncat, feeling her roiling emotions without the ability to understand and deal with them, was much worse off than she. Juelle concentrated on controlling them, more for Loki's sake than her own.

Thunder exploded overhead and reverberated through her, leaving terror in its wake. Loki's muted howl, instead of fueling the fear, served to make Juelle more conscious of her need to lock it down, suppress it, for his sake. Though she wanted to howl herself, she struggled with her emotions.

As she pounded through the rising storm, unable to see more than a few feet ahead of her, Juelle tried to reason with herself. The storm couldn't hurt her—she needn't be afraid.

Jagged lightning slashed across the sky, leaving the stink of ozone in its wake as it struck a tree a half mile away. The resulting burst of light remained imprinted on her retina as the tree exploded.

Yeah, right, the storm couldn't hurt her. Now wet clear through, she huddled even closer to the horse and tried to suppress a whimper. Poor Loki just shook within the confines of her shirt. Doggedly, Juelle gritted her teeth and got her emotions under control.

Don't think about the storm. Think about something else. Something distracting. Something like . . . Eron. Now there's a distraction if she'd ever seen one. The man was stubborn, opinionated, hopelessly mired in outdated custom, and prone to bulling his way through any obstacle as if sheer force could solve any problem. Just like he was bulling his way through this storm . . .

No, don't think about that. She turned her mind back to Eron. Okay, so those were his faults. What were his good points? Surely he had some.

Well, there was his drop-dead gorgeous looks, of course. And his smile. His sexy, intimate smile. Tenderness, too. She smiled as she thought about last night. He'd been so caring, so gentle, so responsive to her every desire. She'd never had a night like that before in her life, and doubted she ever would again.

Who would have imagined the pigheaded councilman would be such a tender, considerate lover? Certainly not Juelle.

Loki ceased trembling, and Juelle stroked the little moncat through her shirt as she gave herself permission to wallow in the heady emotions of desire and sweet arousal. Anything to keep this storm at bay.

Eron slowed their pace and yelled something over his shoulder, but she missed it.

"What did you say?"

He dropped back level with her and brought his face close to hers, the rain dripping off the tip of his nose. "See those cliffs? The caves are just ahead. Be careful and follow me."

Eron handed back her reins, motioning her to follow him. They picked their way through the rugged outcroppings while the storm slashed and beat at them. Another flash of lightning showed a black hole yawning in the cliff face beside them. "There," Eron shouted.

Juelle nodded and followed him in. Though she wasn't crazy about heading into the unknown dangers of the cave, it was far preferable to the raging storm.

They entered in pitch blackness and Juelle sagged with relief. She hadn't realized how tense she'd become. But now that her back was no longer bowed against the onslaught of rain, wind, and stinging sand, she could feel some of the tension drain away. Of course, she was still wet and miserable, but it was a definite improvement.

Now what? She couldn't see a thing.

She heard Eron fumbling in his saddlebags, then a scrape. An old-fashioned match flared to brilliance, lighting the cavern with flickering shadows. Eron's gaze darted around the cavern until the light went out. "Stay there," he said.

Before Juelle could voice a protest, he lit another one, then dismounted and found some brush, coaxing it into flame. He moved off into a dark corner. "There's some wood over here," he said. "Undoubtedly left by a previous occupant." He dragged it over to the fire.

Juelle dismounted, too, releasing Loki to go exploring on his own. Shivering, but wanting to do something to help, she took over feeding the fire while Eron took care of the horses.

Once the fire was crackling merrily, she sighed. There was something about a fire that helped keep the terrors at bay. She could almost ignore the raging weather outside as she relaxed and glanced around the cavern.

The small entrance, barely large enough for a horse and its rider, was about twenty feet long, then opened up into a large chamber about the size of a two-bedroom house on Earth.

A natural chimney drew up the smoke from the fire, and three tunnels led off in various directions from the large inner chamber, hinting at unknown dangers. Juelle's gaze slid away from them. She didn't feel even remotely tempted to explore their dark secrets. "Is it safe here?" She couldn't help the quaver in her voice, and hoped Eron hadn't noticed it.

Eron glanced up from where he rubbed down her horse. "Safer than outside."

He had a point. And now that they were here, one of her first priorities had to be to get out of these wet, clammy clothes. As Eron unpacked the horses, Juelle proceeded to strip.

Eron scowled at her. "What do you think you're doing?"

She slanted a glance at him. "Getting dry." What did he think she was doing? Trying to seduce him? Well, at any other time she might consider it, but after their earlier conversation, she doubted he was in the mood.

Eron dropped the bedrolls next to the fire and tossed her a towel. Luckily, the oilcloths protecting their belongings had kept them dry. Juelle peeled down to her skin, laid her clothing on a nearby rock to dry, and rubbed herself with the towel.

Eron ignored her as she sat next to the fire and wrapped herself in the warmth of one of the bedrolls. She began toweling off the two bedraggled moncats, who held still for the treatment—barely—then settled down next to her to groom their matted fur.

Hearing a muted splat behind her, Juelle turned to see Eron shedding his wet clothes as well. She watched unashamedly as he stripped, and admired the view. They'd been wrapped up in the bedclothes most of last night, and the one brief glimpse she'd caught of him hadn't been nearly enough. Or rather, it had been just enough to whet her appetite.

He was beautiful, even from the rear. With his broad, tanned shoulders, a muscled back tapering to a narrow waist, and firm, white buttocks supported by legs the size of tree trunks, Juelle could be forgiven for harboring a bit of lust in her heart.

But, unashamedly, she yearned to see more. *Turn around*, she begged silently.

As if he'd heard her, Eron turned toward the fire, toweling his wet hair vigorously. Juelle sucked in a breath. The front view was just as impressive as she remembered. Dark hair matted an impressively muscled chest, strong arms, and muscled thighs. Her gaze roamed inexorably to the part of him that had given her so much pleasure last night and her fingers curled with the urge to caress, to stroke him into well-remembered hardness.

Eron stilled in drying his hair, and Juelle looked up to see his gaze intently on her. He scowled, then used the towel to conceal his nudity, one giant fist clutching the cloth above his navel so as to drape the area between his thighs.

In a way, she was glad. She didn't understand why he had such an immediate effect on her libido, why the sight of his strong body should turn her knees to mush. And right now, she didn't want to think about it. Juelle smiled at him as warm moisture pooled between her legs. "Modest, now, are we?"

Though his fist tightened even more, he didn't move the cloth. "It isn't seemly to stare at me so."

Juelle almost choked. "Not seemly? After what we shared?"

"That was a momentary lapse in judgment. It won't happen again."

"Momentary? Now there's an interesting word choice. As I recall, this 'momentary' lapse occurred at least three times last night and once this morning."

"At the time, I was under the impression you shared my—" He broke off, scowling again.

"Your feelings?" she prompted.

Eron averted his gaze and strode over to drop down on the other bedroll, keeping the towel covering his lap as he held his hands out to the fire.

Irritated by his silly modesty, Juelle snapped, "For heaven's sake, you can't even say the word, can you?" When he remained silent, Juelle taunted, "I'll tell you what. I'll show you mine if you show me yours."

His swift glance of incredulous outrage was almost amusing.

"I'm talking about my *feelings*," she explained.

"That's not necessary. I can see them clearly," he said in a voice of affronted dignity.

"All right, then. Name them."

He shook his head, and Juelle pressed him further. If she could get him to name hers, to think about it instead of bulling his way through, perhaps it would be easier for him to acknowledge his own emotions. "Come on, Eron. What's the matter? Afraid you can't do it?"

"Annoyance," he snapped.

"Oh? Is that mine or yours?" When he glared at her, Juelle smiled. "Both, I think. What else?"

He studied her, then said, "Desire."

"Very good, Eron. I do feel desire. Desire for you," she added softly.

He met her gaze with an enigmatic gaze of his own. "You also feel a little superior."

Juelle acknowledged his hit with an inclination of her head.

"But that's all only to mask your fear."

She chuckled. "Fear of you? I don't think so."

"Not of me." He gestured toward the entrance. "Of the storm."

Juelle ducked her head. He was only too right. She realized she'd been taunting him to keep the storm at bay, to push it out of her awareness. But with his simple words, that all came crashing back in upon her.

Through the silence, above the crackling of the fire, she could hear the storm's fury increase, the wind howling like the legendary banshees of Earth. A sharp crack of thunder sounded close by and she jumped, shivering. "Right again," she whispered. "You're better at this than I thought."

She cast an uneasy glance at the entrance. "We're safe here," she muttered, trying to reassure herself and the jittery moncats.

"Words cannot keep you safe," Eron said.

"Maybe not, but they might be able to lessen my fear."

He cast her an annoyed glance. "Why do you always resort to words to solve your problems?"

"Why do you always resort to physical violence?" she retorted.

His eyebrows rose. "Perhaps a little of the physical is what you need right now."

Annoyed, she snapped, "I think I know what I need better than you do."

"I doubt it. You're upsetting the moncats."

Juelle grimaced. He was right. Loki and Seri were almost shaking with the intensity of her suppressed emotions. She was just lucky Loki hadn't started enhancing any of them. Then she'd really be in trouble.

It might be better all the way around if she sent him away for a while. Containing her fear as best she could, she took Loki into her lap and focused on projecting an image of him and Seri exploring the caves. Not only would it give her the freedom to let her emotions go, it would allow Loki more time to press his courtship with Seri.

The impression she received back was mixed. Loki obviously liked the idea of getting out of the range of her emotions—with Seri—but wasn't sure he should leave his pythia in this condition.

Juelle reassured him with an image of Eron consoling her, and Loki seemed to sigh in relief. He turned to confer with Seri in soft chittering sounds. Then, after one long assessing look at the two of them, Loki took off down the far right tunnel, Seri right behind him.

"You sent them off?" Eron asked.

"Yes. I figured neither one of us wanted to be around if Loki started enhancing any of my emotions."

"True. You know—"

Thunder crashed again and a brilliant flare of lightning lit the cave. Juelle crouched in her bedroll and whimpered, glancing up only when she felt Eron settle down beside her.

"Come here," he said, and offered her his open arms.

To hell with pretending she didn't want him, didn't need him. She sighed in relief and went willingly into his arms.

Chapter Thirteen

Eron would have to be made of stone to resist the vulnerability and pure need showing in Juelle's eyes. To see this quicksilver bit of a woman, strong and fearless as any man, reduced to cringing like a child pulled at him, tugging at his heartstrings.

Ignoring the harsh words they'd exchanged, he gathered her into his lap, trying to provide comfort and shelter with his large body. She shivered and he pulled her closer, rubbing her back to ward off the chill.

It worked only too well. Between the warmth of the fire and their shared body heat, he had become very warm—and very aware of Juelle's body pressed intimately against his. His towel had slipped to one side and Juelle had dropped her covering, leaving them nestled skin to skin.

Juelle wound her arms about his neck, laying her head on his shoulder as trustingly as a child. But this was no child's body he was holding. Her breasts pressed against his chest and her bare buttocks rested on his lap.

Inevitably, Eron felt himself harden and grow until he was pushing against the underside of her thigh. He groaned inwardly. Now was not the time for his body to betray him—not when Juelle was in need of nothing more than comfort. Not when he had no way of hiding his body's reaction.

Though he wanted nothing more than to bury himself inside her, he knew it was wrong. He was a councilman, an observer, with a duty to find a life-mate among the pythias of Delphi. Though he would some day lose his council position to his sister's life-mate, he had hoped that he would have a life-mate of his own by that time—a high-ranking pythia who would stand by his side and give him the ability to aspire to another Council position.

He didn't crave power; exercising it could be uncomfortable at times. But he'd seen what good he and his sister had been able to accomplish in the short time they'd presided over Oasis. He loved his world and its people, and this was the best way he knew to have a part in ensuring its future prosperity.

He glanced down at Juelle. In the past couple of days he'd come to hope this woman would be that pythia. But it was not to be. Not only was she forbidden to prophesy, she didn't even care enough to be his life-mate.

Juelle shifted within his embrace, and Eron wondered if she'd become as aware of him as he was of her. When she released her stranglehold on his neck and kissed the hollow of his throat, he no longer had any doubts.

Yearning cascaded through him, and he froze, hoping she would cease teasing him if he showed no response. But his lack of reaction didn't deter her. She seemed fascinated with the hair on his chest as she tangled her fingers in it and rubbed her breasts against him. When she scraped her fingernails against his nipples and trailed her hand even lower, Eron could endure no more.

He stood in one swift motion, dumping her from his lap. The raging storm outside echoed the roar in his blood as he took a shuddering breath and spoke. "No," was all he managed to choke out.

"No?" Juelle repeated. "Why not?"

Eron made the mistake of looking down at her. She lay sprawled where he had dumped her, on one hip. The rosy firelight played across her fair skin, making her appear flushed with desire. Her breasts were pebbled, thrusting upward in hard peaks, and he imagined that secret area between her legs grown warm and moist with desire.

He clenched his hands into fists and closed his eyes, willing the visions away. "No," he repeated. Yes, he loved her. And, even more compelling at this moment, he lusted after her, but she needed to understand his reservations. "Councilmen do not seduce pythias unless they intend to become their life-mates," he grated out.

Juelle rose to her knees and gazed up at him from perhaps a foot away. "Not even when that pythia wants to be seduced?"

"Not even then. Once a pythia becomes life-mated, she can never mate with another man without losing her moncat's rapport."

"I'm aware of that, but I'm not life-mated yet."

Eron pretended he hadn't heard her. "And it is unwise for her to dally with a man she does not intend to mate with for life, so she is not tempted later—by him or any other man."

Juelle moved toward him, still on her knees. "That's ridiculous. If I ever decide to become life-mated to a man, I will never want another."

"How can you be so sure?"

"I just am." She moved closer still, until she was only a hands-breadth away from him, and stared up into his face from the level of his hip. "Until then, I will make love to whomever I please."

So saying, she ran her hands up his legs and made sensuous circles on the inside of his thighs, eyeing the rigid evidence of his desire. "Providing he's willing, of course."

Oh, he was willing all right. Eron's breathing became labored and he suddenly realized how very stupid he'd been to initiate this conversation while both of them were still unclothed. He couldn't think straight while in this state. He had to get covered up—now.

He started to turn away, but Juelle captured his hardness in her hand and stroked. He groaned at her touch, but Apollo help him, he couldn't turn away from the need in her eyes—or the answering need within his soul.

Thunder rolled and lightning flashed, but she didn't seem to notice as she stared up at him. "Stay," she pleaded.

Eron heaved a sigh. Which would he regret more? Staying or leaving? He didn't know, but he did realize that leaving would be the hardest thing he'd ever done.

He clenched his hands into fists, knowing if he touched her now, his options would be gone, for he would be lost. Drawing a deep breath, he firmed his resolve to remove her hand so he could escape from her thrall. But she looked up into his eyes and smiled, then moved her hand to cup him and take him into her mouth.

Eron gasped with the sheer pleasure of it and all thoughts of stopping her fled. All thoughts fled, period, and his world narrowed to the sensations she was engendering with her hand, mouth, and clever tongue.

Time stood still as he remained quiescent, letting the witch work her magic. With each soft lick, each silken caress of her tongue, excitement shivered through him, bringing him to an aching pitch of awareness.

He glanced down to see her intent on giving him the ultimate pleasure, her silvery blonde hair gleaming in the firelight. Erotic thrills surged through him as he reached down to capture those silken strands in his hands.

The feel of her head in his hands as she held him captive in her mouth was too much. He moaned and found himself massaging her scalp between his fingers, holding her fast, and thrusting his hips uncontrollably. Unable to do, to think of anything else, he gasped for breath as waves of sheer elation washed over him.

Then, when he thought it couldn't get any better, overwhelming bliss carried him to a new height of sensation. He clutched the air in upraised fists and roared his ecstasy to the heavens, convulsing in blessed release, again and again.

Then, when he was spent and his sides heaved with the exertion, he glanced down to see Juelle gazing up at him, one hand still massaging him intimately as she gave him a satisfied smile.

His trembling legs could hold him no longer and he sank down upon the bedroll, lying on his back, too drained to do more than gather her against his side as he struggled to remember how to breathe.

Juelle snuggled up to him, and he rested his cheek briefly against the top of her head, then kissed her forehead. His awareness returned to the here and now and he realized the storm's frenzy had abated. So, too, had his—but Juelle had yet to be satisfied.

Experimentally, he used his free hand to stroke her exposed breast and flicked her nipple with his thumb. It peaked in his hand and he smiled at the soft sound of pleasure she made. Turning onto his side, he gently pushed Juelle onto her back and continued to toy with her breast. "Your argument was very persuasive."

She chuckled. "I thought it might be." Her lips sought his and he kissed her, a long, lingering, deep affirmation of his love that removed any need or inclination for conversation.

When he finally released her, Juelle cradled his jaw in her hand, giving him a luminous smile full of need and another emotion. If he didn't know better, he would swear it was love.

He blinked and the expression was gone, wiped away by an expression of pure sensuality. He kissed his way down her neck, then trailed his lips lower to take her breast in his mouth and suckle it. She arched against him, and Eron ran his hand down over her stomach to dip his finger in the folds of her womanhood.

She was hot and slick and incredibly wet. He moved his fingers within her and Juelle moaned, moving her hips in time with his thrusts. He found the small bud that would give her pleasure and caressed it, loving the feel of her quivering flesh beneath his hands.

He rose to get a better look and drank in the sight of her. He'd never seen anything so beautiful as Juelle lying nude beside him, the firelight playing across her white skin as she laid with her head thrown back in ecstasy, his own hand buried between her legs.

He hadn't thought it possible, but he felt himself

grow hard once more. He leaned down to suckle her breast and smiled when she moaned in pleasure. Evidently feeling his arousal against her thigh, Juelle pushed him over to lie on his back and straddled him, taking him deep inside her.

Eron sighed as she surrounded him in comforting, erotic warmth. Unable to resist, he thrust his hips toward her and she began rocking against him in an age-old rhythm.

Aware of nothing but the sweet ecstasy engendered by the joining of their bodies, he surrendered himself to the sensations spiraling through him and gripped Juelle's hips in his hands to increase the tempo of their joining.

The world expanded, then contracted and exploded in a burst of blinding light. His cries mingled with hers as they both came to a shuddering release. Panting, Juelle collapsed next to him. Then, exhausted from fighting the storms both inside and out, Eron fell asleep.

Juelle woke to find herself snuggled up to Eron's warmth. She glanced around. It was late afternoon and the storm seemed to have abated. The horses were drowsing and the moncats were nowhere in sight. They were off, presumedly exploring or maybe even indulging in some loving of their own.

Juelle frowned and glanced down at Eron who still lay sleeping, in magnificent nude splendor. Loving . . . She didn't want to connect that word with this man.

Sex. That's all it had been. Just sex. Okay, so it was great sex. The best she'd ever had, in fact, but that didn't mean she was in love with the guy, for heaven's sake.

She stood and jerked her gaze away, determined not to let the sight of his body and the remembrance of how it moved against hers sway her feelings or her judgment.

Judgment? What judgment? Her psychiatrist's mind kicked in and she automatically analyzed her own reaction. Hmm—suppressed emotions, denial, a touch of anger. If she were her own patient, she'd advise herself she was hiding from something.

Hiding from what? She sheered off from that thought and pulled some dry clothing from the saddlebags, deciding she'd think better with some clothes on.

Once she was dressed, she felt better, but it didn't stop the war going on in her mind. One side desperately tried to keep her feelings at bay while the other coldly analyzed those same emotions.

Juelle sighed. What kind of psychiatrist would she be if she allowed this to go on? She needed to resolve this now.

Grabbing a blanket, she sat down behind a rock out of sight of Eron and began to explore her own emotions. She opened her mind and relaxed, letting them come as they wanted.

Foremost was trepidation, with a touch of anger. She shunted it aside. That, she knew, was caused by her own analytical actions. Once she dissected her feelings, the fear would disappear.

With that taken care of, she waited for another emotion to show itself. The next one was easy to recognize. *Lust.* Too easy. She knew she felt lust, even if it was subdued right now. Eron had stirred *those* feelings in her from the first moment she'd seen him. What else?

The others tried to hide behind the overpowering monoliths of fear and lust, but she wouldn't allow that. Patiently, she coaxed the others into the light. What was she hiding from?

Longing.

Now there was an odd one. What was she longing *for*? The fear peaked again, and Juelle smiled. Ah, that was the question, wasn't it?

An image popped into her mind. Eron, gazing tenderly down into her face as she ran gentle fingers along the strong line of his jaw.

The longing intensified and the image focused more clearly on the love in Eron's eyes—love for her.

Juelle sighed in relief. So she longed for love, did she? Well, there was nothing wrong with that. Every human being longed to be loved, or they weren't truly human. It was perfectly normal, yet somehow . . . incomplete.

She frowned. Where had that thought come from? Incomplete? What was she missing? She ran the image through her mind several times before she finally realized what it was.

If she longed merely for love, the soul-searing love between a man and a woman, then the image should be of the most passionate, complete love she knew. She should have thought of her parents' love—or Lancer and Thena's. Instead, Eron had popped into her mind.

That meant she longed for *his* love. Juelle recoiled from the thought. She'd never thought of herself as one of those parasites who fed off others' emotions, always taking, never giving. Is that what she was hiding from?

No, that didn't feel right, either. She wasn't an emotional vulture. If she was, she never would've lasted in the psychiatric profession. Besides, she cared too much about Eron to do that to him.

She cared too much? Fear spiked again, and Juelle realized she was on the right track. That was the key—how *did* she feel about Eron? She concentrated on that and, all of a sudden, her hidden emotions burst forth and spilled into her waiting consciousness. *Longing ... tenderness ... joy ... affection ... protectiveness ... love.*

Love? That rocked her back on her heels. Dear Lord, she did. She loved Eron. She glanced around, hoping it had been Loki's emotions she'd felt, but no such luck.

They were all hers.

Her mouth twisted in bitterness. Why hadn't she left well enough alone and kept those emotions hidden? Why now? Why him?

Foolish questions, she knew, but like many of her patients, Juelle couldn't help but voice them. The timing was incredibly bad, but love had no respect for timing or circumstances—or the wishes of its hapless victims.

Instead, it attacked with no thought of the consequences, no regard for how painful it might be for a cerebral Terran to fall in love with a barbaric Delphian Councilman. Or how difficult it would be for a pythia who couldn't prophesy to mate for life to a man who had to have a powerful pythia by his side.

Juelle slumped. The fear and anger were gone. In their place, love and despair lay entwined like a lump in her stomach. Now that she'd finally found love, she had to keep it hidden, abandon it ... for Eron's sake. And Delphi's.

Oh, she suspected Eron would insist on becoming her life-mate if he knew, but she couldn't do that to him. He needed a strong pythia by his side and Delphi needed him. His idealism, vision, and yes, even his stubborness, was just what the Council needed to bring them safely into the Republic. He couldn't throw away his Council position by hooking up with her.

Of course, he did have that one blind spot about

the Republic's technology, but she planned to wear him down until he gave in.

"Juelle?"

Eron's voice startled Juelle into awareness. "Over here," she said and rose from her position behind the rock so he could see her. She'd been so intent on her thoughts that she hadn't heard him stir.

Fully dressed, Eron regarded her with a curious expression. "Is something wrong?

Juelle hesitated. How *did* you go about speaking to the person you loved? It was a new experience for her, and doubly confusing since she was not only trying to suppress those feelings, but ensure that Eron never saw them. How should she react?

"Juelle?"

She shook her head in disgust. For heaven's sake, nothing had really changed. She should just be herself—sassy, persistent, and annoying. That ought to throw him off. After all, it had worked so far—even on her. "I'm okay," she said. "Just a little distracted. Sorry."

"Are you ready to eat?"

Eat? Good grief, he'd even fixed dinner while she wallowed in her emotions? "Uh, sure."

They ate in silence. Juelle didn't know what to say, and apparently Eron didn't either. He cast her doubtful glances from time to time, obviously puzzled at her behavior. Juelle didn't know how to explain why she was so standoffish after practically attacking him earlier, so she kept her mouth shut.

He glanced around the cavern in curiosity and cleared his throat. "I believe this must be the original Oasis."

Relieved that the silence was broken, she asked, "What do you mean?"

"The first Oasis was situated elsewhere, until the desert encroached upon the caves, and the springs below the caverns began to shrink. I can still see patches of remaining lightmoss and—" He broke off and sat up straight, staring at something on the ground.

"What is it?"

"Wait." He rose and peered at the tunnel openings and the exit. "We may not be alone."

She had no problem identifying the terror now sweeping through her. Had the storm driven them in, only to be attacked by whatever cave-dwelling beast lived here? "What . . . what is it?"

He glanced up and must have seen her stricken face, for he said, "It's all right. I just found some footprints. Human footprints. Between the storm and our . . . exhaustion, I just now noticed them."

Juelle relaxed. "Are you sure they're not ours?"

"Yes, I'm sure. Most of these prints are smaller than mine, yet larger than yours."

"Maybe they're from the original inhabitants of Oasis?"

He frowned. "No—they're more recent." Appearing to come to a sudden decision, Eron hurried over to the horses and began saddling them.

"What's wrong?"

He slung a saddlebag over his horse. "It might be the bandits and, if so, they might still be here."

Oh, Lord, she'd forgotten about them. Juelle bent to gather their belongings from around the campfire, saying a small prayer of thanksgiving that the storm had kept the bandits away from the cave entrance while the two of them had been lying naked and vulnerable.

She froze in the act of picking up. Where were the moncats? They couldn't leave without them. "Eron? When do you think the bandits will return? I can't leave Loki—"

She broke off when she saw Eron crumple to the

ground, hit from behind by a man wielding a rock. Juelle emitted a stifled scream, then her protective instincts screamed to the fore. Dropping their belongings, she rushed to his defense, only to be pounced upon in turn by three men from the shadows of the left-most tunnel.

Fear beat a sharp tattoo in her chest as they captured her arms and rendered her immobile. She saw the man raise the rock again above Eron's unconscious head and screamed out, "No! Wait."

When the man hesitated for a moment, she spoke so fast the words were almost tumbling over themselves. "He's a councilman—you can hold him for ransom, but only if he's not dead."

The man grinned. "Nice try, lady, but he ain't no councilman."

He raised the rock again, and Juelle shrieked, "Don't hurt him," as she struggled for freedom from her captors, to no avail.

"Drop the rock," came a voice from the shadows.

The man dropped his weapon, and Juelle breathed a sigh of relief. She turned toward Eron's savior and inhaled sharply when the man stepped from the shadows. *Nevan.*

The tall, blond outlaw gave her a cool smile and bowed mockingly. "How very touching. We meet again, Terran." He flicked a quick glance at her attire and around at their belongings, apparently satisfied when he saw no indication of anyone else. "And this time, I'll ensure you don't escape."

He motioned to a man who had come up beside him. Orgon, if Juelle remembered correctly, the former observer who had followed Nevan into exile. Nevan motioned toward Eron and Orgon went to stand over him with a knife held at the ready. Fear spiked through her and she darted Nevan a questioning glance. Surely he wouldn't . . .

Nevan smiled again, reminding her of an oily sandsnake. "Release her."

"Sir?" questioned one of the two men holding her, but his grip didn't relax.

"Release her, I said. Orgon will slit the man's throat if she so much as makes one threatening move. But she won't." His eyes glinted in the light cast by the flickering torches of his men. "Isn't that right, my dear?"

Juelle nodded reluctantly. Even if she didn't love Eron, just the threat of having anyone's death on her hands was enough to make her do exactly as Nevan said . . . for now.

The men released her, and they stepped back as she rubbed her bruised flesh. Nevan gave her another half-bow and made a sweeping gesture to encompass the people in the room who numbered about a dozen by now. "I'd like you all to meet Juelle Shanard, Terran healer, and a good friend of our esteemed Council Captain."

All eyes riveted on her, which only made her hold her head up higher.

Nevan added, "She's also one of the traitors who assisted the upstart Council Captain in deposing me."

Uh-oh. She was in for it now. Wisely, she kept her mouth shut.

"We'll . . . suitably reward you later," he said, his silky voice at odds with his meaning. It sent shivers up and down her spine. "But for now, tell me, who is this man?"

"I told you—he's a councilman. A new one."

Nevan's eyebrows rose. "Is he Dodona's councilman . . . my replacement? They brought in an outsider?" Though his expression didn't change, his tone revealed outrage at the thought.

"No, Ketori took over as Councilman of Dodona

when Lancer became Captain."

Nevan relaxed and nodded. "That's as expected. Then who is this?"

Juelle didn't see any reason to withhold the information, since she'd already blurted out the important part. "Eron, Councilman of Oasis."

"Oasis? But Homal rules Oasis."

It was just like Nevan to think of councilmen as ruling their respective regions when, in reality, they merely held it in trust for their people.

"Not anymore. Homal retired when Lina did—Eron took his place."

"And the pythia?"

"His sister, Alyssa."

"Ah, yes, I remember Alyssa. A silver pythia. And, if her brother heads Oasis's council, that means she is not yet life-mated." He smiled and another chill ran up Juelle's spine. "She's very attractive, too."

Nevan turned to Orgon. "Don't hurt him yet—I might just find a use for him." He turned back to Juelle and granted her another chilling smile. "You, on the other hand—"

"Sir?" one of her former captors said, shifting from foot to foot.

"Yes, what is it, Ivar?" Nevan snapped. It appeared the exile didn't care to have his dramatic posturing interrupted—it disturbed the nice flow of terror he was so obviously trying to arouse in her.

The man gulped, but continued despite Nevan's glare. "When . . . when we came in, she was saying they had to wait for someone."

Nevan's gaze snapped back to her. "Is that true?" he demanded. "Are there others in your party?"

What others? "No, we're alone."

Nevan pierced Ivar with a glare. "What did she say?"

218

Ivar shrugged. "Something like they had to wait for . . . Okie."

Comprehension dawned on Juelle's face before she could mask it. Too late—Nevan saw it. "And who is Okie?"

"Not Okie. Loki. Loki is my moncat."

"*Your* moncat?" he repeated with an upraised eyebrow.

"Yes. I'm a pythia now." She showed him her wrist, waiting for the inevitable crack about her age.

It didn't come. Instead, Nevan grabbed her arm and examined it closely. "I see," he said shortly and gave her a long assessing glance from head to foot that made her feel slimed all over. "This changes things."

Chapter Fourteen

"How does this change things?" Juelle asked. Did this mean he wouldn't just kill them out of hand? Remembering the last time he'd captured her, Juelle knew he was ruthless, but wasn't sure if he was capable of murder.

Ignoring her, Nevan said, "Lock them up until I decide what to do with them."

"Where?" Ivar asked.

Juelle wondered about that herself. Most rooms in Delphian caves had only drapes covering the entrances.

Nevan thought for a moment. "The storeroom—it has a door."

Ivar glanced at Eron, obviously measuring the councilman's size. "Is it strong enough to hold him?"

"It should be. But just in case . . ." Nevan glanced around, and jerked his thumb at one of the other men. "You. Get the chains. Now."

A thrill of foreboding shivered through her. Why had Nevan found it necessary to have chains on hand? She glanced at Eron. *He's okay,* she told herself. He had to be. She couldn't lose him now.

"That ought to relieve your mind," Nevan told Ivar. "And to make doubly sure, we'll let you guard them."

Relief shimmered through her as she realized they wouldn't be so worried about confining Eron if he were dead.

"What about our visitor?" Ivar asked. "The other Ter—"

Nevan whirled on him so fast that Ivar almost seemed to swallow his tongue.

"Don't worry about *him*. Your job is to ensure these two don't escape. Understand?"

Ivar nodded, his mouth shut. Apparently, he finally realized that's what had gotten him into this situation to begin with.

Juelle frowned. What was the word Nevan had cut off? Terran? Was there another Terran here? They hadn't captured Lancer, too, had they?

"Good. Now take them away."

Two men lifted Eron and Ivar took hold of Juelle's upper arm. A hiss sounded from the right tunnel opening and she felt a surge of outrage from that direction. Her spirits lifted a fraction. Loki was back.

The men hefted their weapons and peered into the darkness of the opening while Nevan took a few steps back.

"No, wait," Juelle yelled again. "Don't hurt him—he's my moncat. Let me take care of him."

The men glanced at Nevan, who inclined his head and said, "Let her calm him. If she makes a run for it, we still have the councilman."

Juelle grimaced and approached Loki, sending

reassuring thoughts his way. He could incapacitate one man and keep another one occupied, but a dozen? No way, and that would only anger them. It was too risky while Eron was out cold. She preferred to keep her options open.

She approached the moncat, sending him soothing thoughts and crooning reassuring words more for the benefit of Nevan's twitchy men than for Loki. She moved slowly, not wanting to give them any reason to attack.

Once she got close enough, she could see a vague outline of the moncat in the darkness of the tunnel. His yellow eyes glowed and his tail twitched as he stared at the men and uttered a low, menacing growl.

Behind him, hidden in the shadows, Seri crouched. Juelle sighed in relief. She'd been afraid the Golden Pythia's moncat would come charging out after Nevan. After all, Seri had plenty of reason to dislike the deposed councilman, and Juelle was afraid she wouldn't be able to control her.

But the moncat was being cagey, very smart. Juelle could use this. Using Loki as a conduit, she broadcast a picture to Seri. Was Lancer being held here, too?

The answer was a distinct negative. Well, Seri ought to know if her pythia's life-mate was anywhere near. Perhaps Juelle had misunderstood. No matter—other things were more important now.

Poor Loki was obviously torn between his concern for Juelle and Seri and was having difficulty trying to figure out whom to protect first. Juelle made it easy for him.

So far, the men didn't know Seri was here, and Juelle wanted to keep it that way. They needed any extra edge they could get. Since the moncats could see the situation behind her, she didn't bother to explain. Instead, she sent a mental picture of Seri staying hidden, then going to Riverfork for help.

Both moncats seemed to understand. Seri scampered off the way she had come. After a single glance back, Loki seemed to lose some of his anxiety. He stopped growling, and Juelle mentally beseeched him to calm down and behave himself, for Eron's sake.

She seemed to get some sort of reluctant agreement, so she straightened and beckoned Loki to her. He took a running jump and leapt to her shoulder in one bound. The men behind her gasped and the back of her neck prickled. "It's okay," she said and turned around slowly.

Loki gave the men a disdainful hiss, and they lowered their weapons, though they kept a wary eye on the moncat. Studiously ignoring them, Loki pretended to examine Juelle's hair and face for injury. Juelle almost chuckled at Loki's antics, but this was no laughing matter. They had to get out of here.

"All right," Nevan said. "Take them to the storeroom."

Juelle moved toward the saddlebags, but Orgon blocked her path. "Take nothing with you."

She glared up at him. "I need my medical kit."

"No." His tone was uncompromising.

Juelle turned toward Nevan. "You know I'm a healer—I need that kit to determine the extent of Eron's injuries. It's no weapon."

Nevan regarded her with an assessing look. "Men have survived being hit on the head before. I'm sure he'll be fine."

With Eron's thick skull, Nevan was undoubtedly right, but she couldn't be sure until she examined him. "But—"

"If he appears to need it, I'll reconsider. Now, no more stalling."

Juelle frowned but gave in. It was obvious she wasn't going to get anywhere. Too bad. She'd lied—a medkit was rife with weapons. Well, maybe she could persuade them to let her have it later.

They dragged Eron's unconscious body down the left hand corridor and Ivar came up behind Juelle. "Please, Miss," he said in a polite tone. He didn't touch her and eyed the moncat on her shoulder, keeping a safe distance.

Juelle took her cue from Loki and held her head high, pretending a nonchalance she didn't feel as she followed Eron. In this, she would cooperate. There was no way she was letting Eron out of her sight.

They dumped him in the small storeroom and one man approached with his arms full of a heavy chain, each end terminating in a manacle. Juelle watched helplessly as they looped the twenty foot chain through two iron rings in adjacent corners, then snapped the manacles on Eron's wrists and locked them, leaving him lying on the floor. Ivar pocketed the key and they closed the wooden door and shot the bolt.

As soon as they were gone, Juelle fell to her knees beside Eron to assess his condition. The bioluminescent lightmoss was still working here at about half strength, giving her enough light to see by.

Placing him in a more comfortable position, she examined him, then breathed a sigh of relief. He was breathing fine and didn't appear to be suffering too many ill effects, but he'd have a hell of a headache when he woke.

When he did, their first order of business would be to find a way out. To that end, Juelle began to explore the storeroom, hoping to find something, anything, that would help them escape.

* * *

Eron came to and held a hand to his aching head. Sweet Apollo, what hit him?

Loki and Juelle leaned over him, matching concern in their eyes. "How do you feel?" Juelle asked.

"My head hurts. What happened?" He glanced around at the dimly lit cavern, but didn't recognize his surroundings. "Where are we?"

Juelle peered into his eyes and felt the bump on his head. "Do you feel nauseous?"

"No—just pain. What *happened?*"

"You were right about the bandits—they found us."

Fear jolted through him. "Did they hurt you?"

"No, no, I'm fine. You're the one who got hit from behind with a rock."

No wonder his head hurt.

"And it was one of my old friends—Nevan."

That got his attention. "Nevan? The councilman who was banished for trying to force the Golden Pythia to be his life-mate?"

"That's not all he was banished for—"

Eron leapt to his feet. "We've got to get out of here." He felt an unexpected weight on his arms and looked down in befuddlement. How had those chains gotten there? His gaze followed their length and he noted with a frown that he was tethered to the wall. "What the hell?"

Juelle grabbed his arms. "Shh. There's a guard just outside the door."

Eron lowered his voice. "So?"

"We might be able to distract him, catch him off guard, and get the key to your chains—but only if he thinks you're still incapacitated. He seemed a little wary of your size and wasn't too crazy about Loki either."

"Did Loki bite anyone? Or Seri?" Would their captors be out for revenge?

Pam McCutcheon

"No—and they don't know about Seri. I sent her to Riverfork for help. The villagers are smart enough to figure out that something's wrong if we send her back alone."

"An excellent idea—but that will take time, time we may not have." He glanced around. "What is this place?"

"It's a storeroom." When he got up to search through the supplies, Juelle added, "I already looked. All they have in here are bolts of cloth and food. No weapons."

The chain was long enough to allow him to roam most of the storeroom. Eron examined one large grain sack and frowned when he noticed it had Riverfork's emblem on it. He examined the others—they all bore emblems from other villages in his domain. "Well, it appears that they are also the bandits."

"Looks that way."

"Perhaps I can break down the door." Eron strode over to examine it, then shook his head. "It's the same as those on our storerooms. It's too thick—and the bolt too long. I won't be able to move it."

"What do you suggest we do?"

"I'll pretend to be unconscious, and you call the guard in on some pretext, then I'll overpower him."

She placed her hands on her hips and shook her head.

"What's wrong?"

"I should've guessed that any plan of yours would involve physical violence."

Why was she digging at him when their lives were at stake? "Do you have a better idea?"

"No, but I'm sure I could come up with one if I *thought* about it logically."

"If we take time to think, we may never get out

226

of here. You had the whole time I was unconscious to use your logic. If you don't have anything better to suggest, why don't we try my idea?"

"All right. Lie back down and I'll call Ivar."

"Ivar? You know him?

"Oh, yeah, we're great chums." She rolled her eyes. "No, of course not. I just heard Nevan mention his name."

"Maybe you'd better have Loki conceal himself, so he won't intimidate the guard either. You can call him out when we need him."

"Good idea." She communed silently with Loki, and the moncat concealed himself among the stores.

"Make sure he doesn't come out until you call," Eron said.

"I did already. Now lie down."

Eron sprawled on the floor and closed his eyes, keeping them open just a slit so he could see.

Juelle moved to the door and called, "Ivar. Ivar, I need help."

"What?" a muffled voice shouted through the door.

"Open up," Juelle yelled.

"Why?"

Damn. The man was too suspicious. Juelle looked at Eron in inquiry and he shrugged. She was on her own—he had come up with the meat of the plan. She could damned well use her logic to figure out the rest. Besides, Eron couldn't say anything for fear Ivar would hear him.

"Water," she called out. "I need water."

"Hold on," came the muffled voice.

Juelle pressed her ear to the door. For a good twenty minutes, nothing happened, then she motioned for Eron to close his eyes. "Someone's coming," she whispered.

Eron tensed when the door opened and prepared to spring to his feet, but hesitated when he saw how many men there were. Two he could handle, but didn't think he'd be able to take on four dagger-wielding men.

Instead, he clutched his head and moaned. One of the guards shoved a vessel at Juelle. She took it with a murmured word of thanks, then held it to Eron's lips.

"Here, drink," she said for their benefit. Lowering her voice so only he could hear, she said, "Okay, now what?"

He sipped and whispered back. "I suppose we use your logic. Do you have any ideas?"

"So," came a voice from the doorway. "The councilman awakes." The new arrival, a tall patrician blond man, bowed mockingly toward Juelle. "You see, my dear? I told you he'd survive."

From his arrogant bearing and his familiarity with Juelle, Eron surmised he must be Nevan.

Juelle scowled at him. "No thanks to your men. You could have killed him."

"Ah, we couldn't have that, could we?" Nevan tapped a dagger thoughtfully against his palm, then gestured two of the men out of the room. The two who remained bore a strong family resemblance to him. He glanced at Eron. "So you're the new Oasis Councilman."

Eron forbore to respond, though Juelle didn't seem to feel the same constraint. "Oh, forgive me for forgetting the courtesies," she said in a tone that was anything but repentant. "Eron, Oasis Councilman, meet Nevan, former councilman of Dodona, his father Shogril, and his cousin Orgon. You've heard of them, haven't you, Eron? The ones who were banished from Dodona—"

"Enough," Shogril said.

It seemed Juelle had found a sore point. But if Shogril thought a simple word, no matter how rude, would shut Juelle up, he was mistaken.

Eron decided to let Juelle do the talking. He continued playing dumb, hoping they'd think his wits were addled, or that he'd had none to begin with.

Juelle's eyes narrowed. "What are you going to do with us?"

"That remains to be seen. There's no doubt you're a pythia, though you're a little older—"

"Why do people keep harping on that?" Juelle demanded. "All right, so I'm not a teenager and I'm not Delphian. So what? If the moncats don't care, why should you?"

Nevan raised an eyebrow, apparently amused by her vehemence. "Frankly, I don't. As I was saying, since you're older than any pythia in history, I wonder how that will affect your ranking. Theory suggests your abilities could be much stronger than the average . . . or much weaker." He glanced at her wrist. "The bite looks fresh. Have you been tested yet?"

Juelle shook her head.

"Then we'll do that here."

Eron could keep silent no longer. "No—you can't test her."

"Oh? Why not?"

Juelle appeared puzzled, too, so Eron explained. "The testing requires you to prophesy."

"Oh," Juelle said with a downcast look. "I see." It was obvious she, too, wanted to know how strong her abilities were.

"Why is that a problem?" Nevan asked.

Eron stood to make his point. Though Nevan was tall, Eron still topped him by a full head. "There's a prophecy that says all pythias will lose their powers if Juelle ever willingly prophesies." Eron caught himself before he added the word "again." To his knowledge, Nevan didn't know about the formula, and Eron wanted to keep it that way.

Nevan cocked his head in inquiry. "Who gave you this prophecy?"

Before Juelle could answer, Eron blurted out, "My sister."

Juelle gave him an odd look, but seemed to understand why he didn't want Nevan to know the prophecy had come from the formula, so she kept her mouth shut.

"Ah, yes, the new silver pythia of Oasis," Nevan said. He tapped the dagger against his palm again and slanted them a cold smile. "The accuracy is high, then. What an . . . interesting weapon to hold over Delphi."

Eron's blood ran cold at the utter lack of concern in Nevan's voice. How could he have been a councilman yet show so little lack of concern for his own people?

"Well," Nevan said, clasping his hands behind his back. "Then we'll just have to ensure she doesn't prophesy willingly, won't we?"

Eron cursed his unruly tongue. *Why* had he revealed that? He could have kept that back and no one would have been the wiser. Juelle was right—sometimes he needed to think before he leapt into action. "I won't let you hurt her," Eron growled, meaning every word.

Nevan laughed softly. "You won't be able to stop me."

Eron's blood ran hot and he lunged for Nevan.

"Eron, no," Juelle shouted.

He glanced down to see two knives poised at his throat—the swift action of Nevan's two remaining guards. He forcibly subdued his rage. She was right—he couldn't help her or Delphi if he were dead or injured. He backed off, glaring at Nevan and his men in impotent fury.

Nevan frowned. "Immobilize him."

Orgon and Shogril each grabbed a section of the chain and pulled, yanking Eron ignominiously back against the wall. Once the chain was taut against both wrists and he was spread-eagled against the far wall, they looped the chains around the rings, anchoring him in place. Eron tugged on them to no avail, fuming helplessly.

Nevan granted him a mocking smile. "Don't worry. We won't hurt her. There are ways other than physical pain to coerce a person."

Eron scowled, but Juelle intervened once more. "*Why* do you want to test me?"

"That's none of your concern," Shogril snapped.

Nevan waved him down. "No, that's quite all right. After all, if she is to rule beside me, she'll need to understand what's going on. And if not . . ." He let his voice trail off suggestively.

Eron clenched his fists and seethed in silent frustration. Unfortunately, he couldn't do anything about it while he was staked out like an animal waiting for the stew pot. But at the first sign of weakness . . . "What do you mean, rule?" he asked.

"Oh, Nevan's up to his old tricks again, aren't you, Nevan?" Juelle said in a mocking tone.

"I wouldn't use quite that word."

Luckily, Nevan still seemed amused by them. If he weren't, Eron didn't know what might happen. Those two thugs behind him appeared as though they'd relish using their knives on human—and moncat—flesh.

Juelle placed her hands on her hips. "You don't like tricks? Then try treason. Or maybe treachery."

"Silence, woman," Shogril roared.

Juelle ignored him. "Or how about betrayal?"

231

That broke Orgon out of his imitation of a gargoyle. "Betrayal? It's the people of Delphi who were betrayed when our Golden Pythia took a Terran as life-mate."

Nevan raised his hands to placate his supporters. "It's all right, gentlemen. The lady is entitled to her opinion, though she has a somewhat . . . limited understanding of the situation."

Juelle snorted. "What's to know? You tried to wrest control of Delphi from its rightful rulers—people who trusted you and depended on you. On Earth we call that betrayal. What do you call it?"

"Delphi's political system is outdated, old-fashioned. It's based on a two-hundred-year-old policy that worked when our ancestors landed here, but which is obsolete now." Nevan was patient with her, but then he could afford to be—he had the upper hand.

"It's worked for two hundred years, hasn't it?" Juelle asked.

Eron couldn't believe his ears. She was actually defending Delphi's system.

"Yes," Nevan said, "but think about it. Delphi is governed by the relatives and life-mates of women whose only claim to fame is that they are good at prophesying."

"But Ketori's genetic studies have shown that the moncats choose only the cream of the crop to be pythias—the best."

"It's not the women I'm concerned with. It's the men. Does it make sense that a man should be Council Captain simply because he sleeps with one of these women? Regardless of the fact that she is the highest ranking pythia on Delphi?"

"At first blush, it may appear odd, but—"

"And the councilmen are chosen because they are the close relatives of other high-ranking women.

What other qualifications do they have?"

Juelle sneered. "Those same qualifications got *you* into power."

Nevan laughed. "You merely prove my point."

"No, wait. There is some basis for this, you know. These relatives are trained as observers, which includes training for holding office. And the same genes that produced the pythia also produced her relatives. If you concede that the pythias are the cream of the crop, you'll have to concede their relatives are, too."

"Not necessarily." Sweet Apollo, Nevan actually seemed to be enjoying this battle of wits. He smiled and spoke to Juelle as if her opinion mattered to him. "Even you will have to admit that intelligence and ability do not always run true in families."

"True, but the majority of the time they do."

"Your argument has some merit," Nevan conceded, "but it doesn't hold true for life-mates. Simply because a young girl craves a young man's body, that is insufficient reason for him to take power."

"But the pythia's moncat must approve her choice before the life-mating can occur."

Nevan smiled then and Eron had the feeling Juelle had just fallen into a carefully laid trap.

"So," Nevan said, "you would have Delphi ruled by the whim of the moncats—small parasites who aren't half as intelligent as the men they serve?"

He'd obviously caught Juelle off guard. She frowned, thinking. Even Eron had to admit he had a point, though there were enough safeguards in the system to ensure an incompetent man didn't take office. Juelle was probably unfamiliar with them, since they weren't common knowledge. He opened his mouth to say so, but was forestalled once more by her hasty tongue.

"So what do you propose as an alternative?"

Nevan bowed once again and gestured toward himself. "Me."

"As what?" she demanded. "Council Captain?"

"Oh, no, not Council Captain. That's an antiquated term left over from the shipboard days of our ancestors. I prefer the title of 'emperor' myself."

"Emperor Nevan?" Juelle burst out laughing.

Nevan reddened a bit, but maintained his aplomb.

"Emperor Nevan. Oh, that's rich. And I suppose your relatives and supporters will be whatever you now call the councilmen."

"Oh, they'll remain counselors—men who *counsel* the emperor, not decide. Only I will have decision-making power."

"And I suppose your successor will be one of your progeny, assuming you have any."

Nevan inclined his head, looking every bit the part he claimed for himself.

"Your system is no better than theirs," she jeered. "It's based on the same premise—a man rules by virtue of the people he's related to. How is that better?"

Nevan smiled. "Because it's *my* family who rules."

Juelle's mouth dropped open as if she didn't know how to counter such a self-serving argument.

"You see," Nevan said, "I *know* that we are superior, that we are destined to rule."

Eron decided to enter the conversation and steer it back to more immediate matters. "How does this affect Juelle—and the tests?"

"I need a pythia," Nevan explained. "If Juelle's rating is high enough, then she may have the honor of being my life-mate."

"Honor?" Juelle snorted. "Thanks, but I think I'll pass."

When Nevan merely smiled in reply, Juelle said, "If this system's so antiquated and you're going to declare yourself emperor and trash it anyway, why do you need a pythia?"

"First I have to depose the current regime. I don't think they'd just give it up without a fight, do you?"

"Hardly," Juelle concurred.

"My preferred method of taking power is to work within the current system. By life-mating myself to a high-ranking pythia, I can become Council Captain, then gradually change things to the new order."

"What about Lancer and Thena?" Juelle demanded. "And other pythias who might be higher ranking?"

"I think I can persuade them to see things my way." He flicked an assessing glance at the two of them. "After all, I have a few bargaining chips they're rather fond of. And once I get the Council on my side, the rest will follow."

"But what about the people? Don't you care about them?"

Nevan shrugged. "They'll see little difference. We've already seen they have few objections to having a Terran in power, so they shouldn't balk at having you as their Golden Pythia. And, as long as I hold your councilman, I'm sure you'll cooperate."

Eron gritted his teeth. Nevan had everything figured out, everything but—"What if she's not high-ranking enough?"

"Then I'll—" He broke off, then continued. "I guess I'll just have to find another pythia to do the job, won't I? Thena is the only gold-ranked pythia I know of, but there are a few silvers who have not life-mated as yet. If Juelle tests out as a lowly blue or green then I'll find one of them. Perhaps even . . . your sister."

Pam McCutcheon

Eron struggled against his bonds. The thought of Nevan's cold lips against Juelle's or Alyssa's was enough to make Eron fume in impotent rage. If he could only get free, he'd tear the bastard limb from limb.

Nevan chuckled. "You see the beauty of it? To keep Juelle safe, you must cooperate. To keep you safe, she must cooperate. And since joining the Republic is inevitable, having her as my life-mate will only help cement my position with them. I must thank the two of you for dropping in and settling this little problem for me."

"Joining the Republic is *not* inevitable," Eron bit out. "In fact, it will be the destruction of Delphi."

Nevan eyed him curiously. "Another prophecy?"

"Yes—the prophecy said Gaea's discoveries shall bring Apollo to certain ruin." At the doubtful expression on Nevan's face, Eron said, "I can prove it. I keep a copy of the prophecy inside my tunic."

Nevan gestured toward Orgon and the man approached Eron with caution, then reached inside his shirt to the pocket sewn there and drew out the paper.

"Yes, that's it," Eron said.

Orgon handed the paper to Nevan. Nevan took one glance at the paper, smirked, then crumpled it and tossed it aside.

Angry at seeing precious parchment—and the prophecy—tossed aside so cavalierly, Eron said, "That's the Golden Pythia's own prophecy."

"Actually, it's not. I'm assuming you don't recall the prophecy yourself, so you obtained this copy from the Dodona archives?"

Eron nodded.

"Well, I remember this prophecy. You see, I was Thena's observer at the time."

"Then you know it's true."

Nevan's expression turned odd, as if he wanted to say something but didn't quite know how to go about it.

Juelle interrupted. "Not necessarily. Didn't you hear the whole story about Nevan's banishment?"

Eron hadn't wanted to hear anything that put the Delphians in a bad light while glorifying the Terrans, so he hadn't paid much attention. "No. What don't I know?"

"Nevan falsified many of Thena's prophecies, trying to discredit her so he could install one of his own pythias in her place."

"You mean *this* is one of those prophecies?"

The man smirked again. "I'm afraid so. As I said, I remember this one. The oracle actually said Gaia's discoveries would bring Apollo to certain prosperity."

"Prosperity," Eron echoed dumbly. He didn't pay attention to the rest of the short conversation and barely noticed when Nevan departed with his cronies.

Eron hung his head in chagrin. All this time, he had based his reason for being on that prophecy, spending his entire time and energy—his very soul—on fighting Delphi's entrance into the Republic.

All this time . . . and it had been nothing but a lie.

Chapter Fifteen

Once Nevan left, Juelle tried to release Eron's bonds, but the chains were secured by a primitive padlock at both wrists. She was able to unhook the chains from the rings, though, giving him freedom of movement.

Loki came out from hiding to inspect Eron and, if his emotions were any judge, the moncat didn't seem worried about Eron's physical health. But his mental health was something else entirely.

"What's wrong?" Juelle asked. With his eyes closed and a sick look on his face, Eron appeared stunned.

He turned remorseful eyes on her. "It was a lie?"

She nodded.

"Then all this time I objected to Delphi entering the Republic, I was wrong. Totally wrong."

Juelle nodded again, glad he was finally seeing reason. But this wasn't the way she wanted to win the argument. She'd wanted the fun of convincing

238

the hard-headed councilman herself.

Instead, he closed his eyes as if in pain and laid his head back against the wall. "I just realized something," he said with a grimace. "My prophecy and the one Lancer spoke of are one and the same. Only I was too dumb to realize it."

"Don't worry about it," she said. "You had no way of knowing."

"If I'd only listened to the stories about Nevan, I would have checked on the accuracy of that prophecy. I would have known it was false and we could have avoided this whole situation." He gave her another apologetic look. "Instead, I have led us both into danger."

Juelle patted his hand. She had to concede that when he admitted he was wrong, he did it all the way. "There's no sense in worrying about might-have-beens. I'd rather you focus your energy on finding a way to get us out of here."

Eron rattled his chains. "That's going to be difficult when I'm tied up like this."

"I know. I'll just have to watch for an opportunity to see if I can get the key from Ivar."

Ivar didn't give Juelle a chance to get close. That evening, he brought armed guards with him before he dared open the door to shove food at them. After an uncomfortable night's sleep huddled up against Eron with only grain sacks for bedding, Juelle was unsurprised when Ivar did the same thing at breakfast the next day.

Late that morning, the door opened again and Nevan entered with three men. They immediately grabbed Eron's chains and slammed him against the wall, immobilizing him again.

"Is that necessary?" she asked in outrage.

"Oh, they think so," Nevan said. "My men are quite terrified of him, you see."

239

Suddenly apprehensive, she asked, "What are you going to do to him?"

"Nothing . . . if you cooperate. We're just making sure he doesn't interfere." His eyes gleamed with an emotion she couldn't define. "Are you ready for the testing?"

Despite herself, Juelle's heart leapt in anticipation. Finally, she was going to be able to put her newfound abilities to the test, if only this one time. She glanced at Eron and he nodded at her. They'd discussed this during the night and had come to the conclusion that acquiescing to Nevan's plan was the only way of keeping them both safe long enough until they found a way to escape.

She raised her chin and nodded at Nevan, refusing to let him intimidate her. Ivar grabbed hold of her arm, pulling her toward the door.

"Let go of me." When he didn't budge, she twisted to grab his elbow at a sensitive spot and pressed. If she did it right, his arm ought to go numb.

He released her. "What . . . what'd you do?" he whispered.

Juelle straightened and gave him a disdainful look, ignoring his question. When another man approached her with the obvious intention of taking up where Ivar had left off, Juelle said, "I wouldn't if I were you."

He kept coming, so she summoned Loki. The moncat leapt to her shoulder and hissed, his ears laid back with his fangs and claws poised to strike. The man backed off, keeping a wary eye on the irate moncat.

No one else seemed inclined to try it, so Juelle nodded at Nevan and said, "We can go now." If she was going to be forced to prophesy, she was damned well going to do it *her* way.

Appearing amused, he offered her his arm—on

the opposite side from where Loki sat fuming. Taking Nevan's arm with the most regal air she could summon, given her lack of appropriate attire and her need of a bath, Juelle allowed him to escort her out of the cell.

She longed to glance back at Eron, but didn't want to give Nevan the satisfaction of knowing he'd rattled her. Instead, she made polite noises as Nevan glanced down at her in appreciation and chatted inconsequentially about the weather and other harmless subjects.

As they walked, the lighting improved, and so did the condition of the caverns. Juelle looked around in interest. The lightmoss here was thriving under renewed care, and the corridors were free of debris. The farther they walked, the better it appeared.

It puzzled her for a while until she realized the bandits didn't want to advertise their presence, which they would have done had they cleaned up the entrance as well as this area. This way gave them a chance to sneak up on intruders. Her mouth twisted in a wry smile. It worked only too well.

Soon, they came to another large open cavern and her entourage halted, as did Nevan's smooth flow of patter. He released her arm and gestured toward an opening on the far wall. "Beyond lie our querent caverns. If you're ready . . . ?"

Juelle took a deep breath and nodded. She entered the antechamber, followed by Nevan and Orgon. The others remained outside. Having participated in traditional Delphian rituals, she knew only the pythia, observer, and the querent should experience what they considered sacred. At least Nevan was still following custom in that area.

She assessed her chances of escape. With her martial arts knowledge, she'd probably be able to take both of them, but what was the use? Eron was still locked up and she didn't know if she could make it to him past the others. Best not to risk it now.

Nevan, whose gesture encompassed the entire chamber, said, "I apologize for not providing you with an attendant, but we have no women in our camp."

Juelle waved dismissively and gazed around the antechamber. Like its Dodona counterpart, it was sparse, free of ornamentation save for the massive altar in the center. Juelle's eyebrows rose. She doubted Nevan had commissioned and installed the piece in the short time he'd been banished. Why hadn't the original occupants taken this when they left?

She ran her hand over its smooth surface. Carved of morlawood and polished to a high gloss that showed Nevan's surprising reverence, the altar resembled Dodona's. It, too, was dedicated to Apollo, depicting the god's slaying of the monster python on Earth at the first Delphi—the act that had given pythias their title. This altar, however, also showed the colonists' landing on Delphi and what she presumed to be the selection of the first pythia.

Why would they leave such a treasure behind? Glancing back at the entrance, she realized the altar was too heavy and too large to fit through the passageway. It must have been carved and assembled in this room.

Nevan waited until she had finished examining the altar, then gestured for her to take her place in front of it. "Shall we begin?"

She started to move to the front of the altar, then stopped.

A small frown appeared on Nevan's face. "What's the matter?"

"I-I can't." She was far too eager to perform this

ritual, far too eager to make the oracle believe she'd come to prophesy unwillingly. A feeling of decisiveness welled within her. She had to refuse, for the good of Delphi.

Orgon raised the back of his hand to her, but Nevan forestalled him. "Not here."

Taking her outside, back where the other two men waited, Nevan said in clipped tones, "Why can't you?"

"I'm far too willing," she answered with a shrug. "If I prophesy now, every last pythia on Delphi will lose her powers." And who knew what the oracle would do to her for daring to defy its decree?

Nevan scowled and her blood ran cold at the realization that the thought was no deterrent to him. Quickly, she added, "And your pythias are your only real chance of existing on an equal basis with the rest of the Republic."

That hit home, she noted in relief.

Nevan frowned. "We'll just have to force you, then."

It's what she'd expected. He motioned to one of the men, who approached her with a menacing scowl. He stopped at Loki's low growl and gave Nevan a questioning glance.

Obviously impatient, Nevan waved him away. "No, that won't work."

The man pulled his knife. "Maybe if I cut the moncat?"

Juelle rolled her eyes. If this wasn't so serious, she'd be laughing hysterically by now. "Cut the moncat. Right. Then how do you suggest I perform the ritual without him?"

The man frowned in incomprehension, but Juelle was saved from answering by Nevan who said, "Never mind. Go get a few more men and bring the Oasis Councilman here."

As they waited, Juelle tested her own resolve. If they threatened to hurt Eron, would that do it? With a sinking feeling, she realized it wouldn't. It would make her fear for his life, which would make her even more willing to go on with the testing.

Soon, she heard footsteps approaching. She looked up and couldn't suppress a grin. Eron came meekly, still chained, but was escorted by at least half a dozen men. They certainly had a healthy respect for his strength if they felt it took *that* many men to subdue him.

Eron gave her a questioning look, and she shrugged, not knowing how to convey the situation to him without words. They halted a few feet away and the knife-happy man held his blade to Eron's throat. Eron's mouth turned grim, but he kept it shut. Good—brute force would not avail him here and any attempt to speak might be met by a slashed throat.

Suddenly, the threat seemed very real. Fear rose to choke her—this was the man she loved. She forced the feelings down and her mind raced for a way to get them all out of this situation. "Eron, tell them," she urged. "Tell them about your other prophecy—the one your sister gave you."

Eron glanced at Nevan, who nodded.

Eron glared down at the man with the knife until he pulled back a fraction. In a voice deep with foreboding, Eron related the prophecy, describing the pivot point Juelle represented.

On one side lay prosperity. On the other, shattered altars, destruction of Delphi's way of life, and eventual subjugation by the Republic. He then repeated her own prophecy, describing what would happen if she ever willingly prophesied again and left the rest up to their imagination.

When he was done, the men holding him shifted,

giving Nevan uncertain glances. He inclined his head, murmuring, "A moving portrait indeed. But the threat still holds." He narrowed his gaze at Juelle. "You wouldn't like to see your friend's throat cut, would you?"

"It's no good. If you threaten Eron, you only make me *more* willing to prophesy—to save him. You'll have to come up with something else—or destroy Delphi in the process."

Scowling now, Nevan snapped, "Any ideas?"

"Maybe if we drug her," Orgon said.

"No," Nevan bit out. "It might interfere with the results of the testing and her prophecy."

"*My* prophecy?" She'd forgotten about that. With mounting apprehension, she asked, "What question do you plan to ask?"

With a tight smile, Nevan said, "Why, how to ensure my plan succeeds, of course."

Rage boiled through her, seeking expression in the hissing of her loyal moncat. Nevan planned to use *her* prophecy in his nefarious plan to take over Delphi?

She shuddered at the thought of contributing, however unwillingly, to Nevan's success. "Like hell I will."

His smile widened. "That's all I needed to hear. Would you say you're not quite so willing to endure the testing now?"

"You got that right, buster. Helping you would be far worse for Delphi than anything Eron described."

He gestured toward the antechamber. "In that case, shall we proceed with the testing?"

"Didn't you hear me? There's no way I'll help you take over this planet."

Nevan's smile turned cold and nasty as he turned back to stare at Eron—and the man who still held a knife to his throat. The man moved, and a trickle of blood ran down into Eron's shirt.

Furious now, Juelle turned on Nevan. "Don't you dare hurt him."

Obviously realizing he had the upper hand now, Nevan merely raised an eyebrow. "I won't, if you cooperate."

Fuming, Juelle glared at Nevan, then turned to look at the man she loved. He stared at her unafraid, prepared to back whatever decision she made.

Damn her overconfidence. She'd been so sure there was nothing Nevan could do to force her to this, and she'd been wrong. So very wrong.

Loki jittered on her shoulder, obviously wanting to *do* something about Juelle's emotions, but still constrained by her firm resolve that he not attack any of the men present. She soothed him and made her decision.

She couldn't sacrifice Eron—Nevan would just keep on trying until he found a way to convince her, and Eron's death would be for naught. She glared at Nevan and snapped, "All right, let's get on with it."

Smirking, Nevan followed her into the antechamber, as did Orgon. She stood in front of the altar, angry and feeling empty inside. It seemed she was destined to be the doom of Delphi no matter *what* she did. Blinking back sudden tears, she barely registered Nevan's voice. "What?"

"You must calm yourself," he explained. "Before we can proceed into the preparation chamber and beyond to the querent chambers, you must clear your mind of all emotion."

"That's difficult to do when you're coercing me into this," she snapped. "You can't have it both ways."

"Nevertheless, you must do so . . . for Eron's sake."

He was right. If she didn't, Eron would suffer, and perhaps die. Loki shifted on her shoulder, and Juelle glanced at the moncat. Perhaps he could help.

She sighed and sent Loki a message, this one in feelings instead of pictures, asking him to help block her negative emotions and enter the necessary trance state.

Loki blinked at the request, but complied. She could feel him working to damp down her anger and wondered if the Delphians knew moncats could be used to subdue emotion as well as enhance it.

It took a few minutes, but soon the anger was nothing but a memory, as were most of her other emotions. Instead, she felt a bit numb.

Well, this was as good as it was going to get—might as well get this show on the road. She nodded at Nevan, and he and Orgon took their places beside her at the altar.

Assuming a prayerful expression, Nevan began the ritual. "Juelle Shanard, are you prepared to devote yourself to Apollo?"

"I am." Surprised by the depth and intensity of her response, Juelle realized she'd come to respect the Delphians' beliefs in the short time she'd spent with them. And, regardless of what she may or may not think of religion, there was something to these Delphian rituals. Something . . . magic.

Nevan continued in a melodic and measured voice. "It is necessary to be in a state of grace, for only then will He hear your plea and grant your petition to become a pythia. Clear your mind of mundane concerns and repeat after me. Gracious

Apollo, Guardian of Delphi and Patron God of Pythias, hear our plea. . . ."

A sharp thrill of excitement stabbed through her, but it felt more as if it came from Loki instead of her. Of course, this was his first participation in a ritual. Juelle couldn't blame him for being excited.

Dutifully, she repeated the words. Her mind cleared of all mundane concerns as she barely registered the droning words of the ritual.

Loki enhanced the feelings of serenity and peace that enveloped her, surrounding her as if she were being comforted by unseen arms. She relaxed and let herself go. The outcome of the ritual was unimportant. What mattered was the ritual itself, coming closer to her own state of grace.

Eventually, the words ceased, and Nevan touched her arm, gesturing her toward one of the doorways. "Do you know what to do?"

She nodded—she'd been through this before as a querent. Nevan and Orgon went through the doorway on the left, and she took the one on the right, the one reserved for pythias.

Inside the preparation room, the familiar fragrance of caroline flowers greeted her. No lightmoss was needed here, for the white and purple flowers provided their own illumination, a soft, violet light that mesmerized her while the drugging scent of the flowers captured her in its thrall.

She inhaled, letting the flowers do their work as she disrobed and slipped into the small stream running through the chamber. As in Dodona, the water must have emanated from nearby hot springs, for it was warm and silky soft against her skin. The water was much more shallow than Dodona's, and she sank deep into it to immerse her body up to her neck, letting the clear waters wash away her accumulated filth—and the last of her reservations.

She bathed and soaked, her senses captured by a multitude of sensations, until a soft chittering sound caught her attention. She opened her eyes to see Loki standing next to a pile of white cloth, urging her out of the water.

Reluctantly, she emerged and dried off with the towel provided, then donned the white chiton, somehow unsurprised to see it was the same one the villagers had given her. Once clothed, she picked Loki up and exited through the other side to find Orgon and Nevan waiting for her there.

When he saw her, Nevan exhaled a relieved sigh and escorted her into the nearest querent chamber. There, amidst a profusion of carolines, three traditional cushions rested. Nevan chose the one in the center while Orgon sat on the smaller one beside the door. Juelle settled on the remaining cushion across from Nevan, with Loki in her lap.

"Remain calm," Nevan murmured. "Clear your mind of everything but the ritual and let the oracle in."

Juelle didn't need to do as he asked, for she was already deep in a trancelike state induced by the carolines and enhanced by Loki's empathic abilities.

She drifted there for a short period of time, then became aware of another presence—an awe-inspiring immensity that made her feel humbled before it. A flash of fear surged through her, and she wondered at her own audacity in appearing before this presence once again.

The oracle, for that's who it was, reassured her wordlessly and Juelle's panic subsided. This time, at least, she was not to blame and the oracle would suffer her to prophesy.

When she was calm once more, the oracle seized control of her and intoned the familiar words of the ritual, "State your question."

She hovered expectantly, waiting for Nevan's question so she could dive into action. Instead, he said, "Before you sits a new supplicant to the rank of pythia, one of your high priestesses. Will you test her and determine her worthiness?"

"I will," the oracle responded through her. "Proceed."

"In what manner of vehicle did our ancestors come to Delphi?"

As Nevan asked the question, Juelle felt the oracle stir within her, opening her mind like the petals of a flower, then encompassing it whole in one swift move. It held her mind lightly within its grasp and probed as if testing *her* worthiness as a vehicle. When it was satisfied, it gave her the answer and Juelle duly repeated it. "They arrived from the stars in a space-borne craft."

"Their original destination was far from here. What change caused them to settle on Delphi?"

Again, the oracle probed through Juelle's psyche, searching for the roots of her own change. This time she re-experienced the moncats' inquisition in full, rapid-fire detail. After what seemed like an eon, yet was only an instant, the oracle responded. "They were captured by a hole in space and redirected to Delphi."

Again, Nevan posed a question. "And their rebirth? How did that occur?"

Once more, the oracle probed her, seeking the seeds of her rebirth. It found them snuggled safe in her memory—the remembrance of waking to find herself a pythia and, later, realizing the extent of her love for Eron.

The oracle flared brightly with its answer. "When the people of Earth accepted their fate and Apollo, they were reborn in glory."

With exultation in his voice, Nevan said, "Then I name you, Juelle Shanard, silver pythia to Apollo."

Joy rose within her. She had never expected, nor hoped for, such a high rank.

The oracle flared a bright silver in her mind, agreeing with Nevan's assessment, but gave her no time to bask in her newfound rank as it intoned, "The silver pythia has been tested and found worthy. State your question."

Nevan took a deep breath. "What must I do to assure my plan to rule the world?" he asked in a voice of surprising intensity.

Juelle almost gasped aloud at Nevan's effrontery in stating his question so baldly. Inside, she could feel the oracle's anger, held in check.

Though angry, the oracle did its duty and Juelle felt the presence shift. One moment she was in her mind, and the next she dove into another's. Down she raced, the path clear before her. Besieged and buffeted on all sides by the intense emotions in Nevan's mind, she raced for the center.

But not fast enough. The emotions became more active, whirling and striking at her. She fought back and her passage began to feel like an aerial dogfight—with her the underdog.

Juelle chastised herself. This was no way for a psychiatrist to react. She paused and tried to analyze the emotions besieging her, sensing a deep-seated need for healing. Nevan, too, was human, with human foibles and fears. Perhaps if she treated him as a patient, she could cure the monomania that held him in its grip.

More confident now, she counterattacked with understanding. The emotions backed off and regrouped, as if unwilling to let themselves be understood. Reaching out in fascination, Juelle followed them, hoping to learn more about them, to heal them.

Instead, the oracle yanked her from her detour and sent her speeding down the main path again. The feeling she received was that it didn't disapprove of her actions, it just didn't think this was the proper time to apply her newfound knowledge.

Accepting its verdict, Juelle gave up the fight. This time, the emotions left her alone and she came to the path's end in an instant, and was ejected into the void. She floated there in the center and tried to catch her breath, wondering what would happen next. Soon, many paths appeared, leading into Nevan's past and all his probable futures.

Though she longed to explore his past to learn what had shaped the man he had become, Juelle waited for a sign, something to tell her which path to choose. As if it had only awaited her wish, a bright silver light appeared and illuminated one of the paths. In jubilance, Juelle sped down it to the end and found the answer for the question Nevan asked.

The oracle intoned the answer, and she gasped in horror before she lost consciousness.

Juelle came slowly to her senses and placed a hand against her throbbing head. She'd forgotten what these caroline hangovers were like. Easing open her eyelids, she found herself staring nose to nose with an anxious Loki. She smiled and reassured him that she was going to live, then looked around and sighed. She was back in the storeroom.

As she stirred, a man huddled by the doorway rose and left, presumably to inform the others of her awakening. She glanced over at the far wall and saw Eron had been spread-eagled again, his chains looped over the ring so he couldn't move. He raised his head at her movement and her heart lurched in her chest—he looked bruised and beaten. Juelle forgot her own pain as she leapt to her feet to release him.

She unhooked the chains, and Eron fell to his knees with a moan. She knelt next to him as he flexed strained muscles. "What did they do to you?"

Nevan answered from the doorway. "He brought it upon himself, trying to get to you when they brought you out of the querent cavern unconscious."

"Is that true?"

Eron nodded.

"Why? Surely you know all pythias pass out after their prophecy."

Eron shrugged, so Nevan answered for him. "It appears he forgot that for a few moments, and he was quite the animal until he could be reassured that you were still alive." He eyed them speculatively. "He must care about you a great deal to be so concerned."

"Did you have to beat him?"

Eron laughed hoarsely. "This is nothing. You should see the other guys."

Juelle glanced up and noticed that the men accompanying Nevan did appear to be sporting a few bruises and black eyes that hadn't been there before. Good for Eron. "I see." She was surprised they hadn't imprisoned him against the wall again, but noticed they all stayed as far out of his reach as possible.

"So," Nevan continued, "if your concern has been satisfied, would you like to know the results of your tests?"

Juelle wanted to say no, but couldn't. In all but a few cases—cases she'd been trained to cure—pythias couldn't remember their own prophecies. She had to know what had happened. "Yes," she answered shortly.

"Your rank is silver," he said with great satisfaction, "and a strong one at that."

Juelle exchanged a glance with Eron. Elation warred with dread within her—elation that she possessed such a high accuracy rate, yet dread of the use to which Nevan would put it. The same war seemed to be occupying Eron's battle-scarred face. Curious now, Juelle asked, "How is that determined?"

"By a series of questions," Nevan answered, appearing pleased she was asking questions. He handed her a piece of paper. "Here are the questions and your answers."

She perused it, then said, "I don't get it. Why don't you just ask what rank I am and leave it at that?"

"Because a low-ranking pythia has been known to get her answers mixed up and sometimes unintentionally claim for herself a higher ranking than she really has—or a nonexistent one. The first three questions are to test the veracity of the last answer."

"How?"

"It's not so much the answers themselves, but the way you answer them that's important."

He gave her an expectant look, and she gestured for him to continue.

"The lower the rank, the more vague the answer. For example, instead of saying our ancestors came in a space-borne ship, a blue pythia might say they arrived in a chariot of fire. Or instead of describing the hole in space, she might call it the maw of a monster."

"I see." She turned the paper over, but something was missing. "What about my prophecy?"

Nevan smiled then and her blood ran cold. If he

was pleased, what did that portend for Delphi—and for them?

"It was very clear. You said, 'If the querent continues as he has begun, he will be sole ruler of his own world.'"

As Juelle and Eron gaped in horror, Nevan's smile widened: "I will be emperor," he said softly.

Chapter Sixteen

A cold elation seized Nevan as he strode toward the Terran ship the following morning. Finally, all his plans were coming together. And now that Delphi was finally within his grasp, he would wait no longer to bring his plans to fruition.

The first step was to perform the life-mate ritual with the fiery Terran, Juelle. An unexpected thrill ran through him at the thought. Her belligerent attitude was oddly stimulating. He looked forward to the prospect of matching wits with her, of taming her into submission. And if he wasn't equal to the task, no problem. He'd just keep her drugged and compliant until he no longer needed her.

He reached the ship and found Alexander overseeing the cleaning of the filters. "Ambassador Morgan."

Alexander walked over to him. "Good morning, Apollo. I see your men are hard at work on the filters again."

"Yes, the storm yesterday made it worse."

"Now, look, it shouldn't take them more than a day to fix them. They should be done tomorrow at the latest."

"That's absolutely correct."

"That's . . . correct?"

"Yes, they should be done tomorrow. Then you can take us to Dodona." If he couldn't get the man to teach him how to take off and land, then Alexander would just have to do it for them.

Alexander's eyes narrowed. "I don't think—"

"As ambassador to Delphi, I would think it would behoove you to accommodate the new ruler of Delphi."

"And who is that?"

Nevan granted him a cool smile. "Me. I've discovered a new pythia, one powerful enough to win the title of Golden Pythia away from Thena." That wasn't true, but since when had the truth stopped Nevan from getting what he wanted? "We life-mate today, and then I shall be Council Captain."

When Alexander hesitated, Nevan added, "I can see you might be concerned that I am usurping your brother's position, but it's the way our society works. The life-mate of the most powerful pythia is the Council Captain—not even your brother can change that. As ambassador, don't you want to deal with the leading authorities?"

Alexander nodded warily, so Nevan continued. "And I'm sure I'll be just as accommodating as he when it comes to working with the Republic."

That part wasn't a lie. Joining the Republic was inevitable, so Nevan wanted to ensure he negotiated the most advantageous position for himself.

Alexander regarded him thoughtfully. "I suppose you can prove this claim."

"Yes, of course—to the Council. I'm afraid you

wouldn't understand our proof." As an added inducement, Nevan added, "The Council will be able to validate my claim immediately."

"All right," the Terran said. "If your men get those filters cleaned by tomorrow, I'll take you to Dodona."

Nevan smiled politely, but inside, he exulted. The Council *would* validate his claim. With the Terran ambassador, the Terran healer, and the Oasis Councilman as hostages, and the weapons of the ship at his disposal, they would have no choice. Then, once the Council capitulated, the common people would accept him as well and follow him.

He smiled in satisfaction. At long last, he'd redeem his family's honor and resume their rightful place as rulers of Delphi.

Juelle lay curled in Eron's arms, shivering in the thin material of the white chiton. She snuggled into his warmth and he stroked her back, his clinking chains providing an appropriate counterpoint to her misery. "You were right," she said. "I never should have prophesied."

He raised her chin with one finger to look her in the eyes. "It's all right. You haven't destroyed Delphi. Your prophecy was unwilling."

"I know that, but that prophecy confirmed Nevan's rise to power. If that doesn't doom Delphi, I don't know what will."

"Even a silver pythia's prophecies aren't infallible. There's a chance the prophecy is wrong."

She slanted him a dubious glance. "How big a chance?"

"Very small," he admitted.

Juelle was afraid of that. Even Eron thought the prophecy was true. "But Nevan has falsified prophecies before. Do you think . . . ?"

Quicksilver

"I'm afraid not. He and his minions were far too pleased, far too sure of themselves. It wouldn't do him any good to falsify that prophecy—he'd only be hurting himself."

Just as she'd feared. Juelle snuggled even deeper into Eron's arms. "So we just give up? Let him have Delphi?"

Eron snorted. "Of course not. We continue to fight. Perhaps we can change his mind, or mitigate some of the effects of his wrongdoing. We never give up until we are triumphant . . . or dead."

Juelle smiled into his shoulder. Now this was the Eron she'd grown to know and love. "What about this life-mate business? Nevan expects me to go along with it."

The thought made her cringe. She knew now that the only man she could ever contemplate spending the rest of her life with was Eron. But that was impossible. He needed a real pythia as life-mate, one who could rule beside him for the good of Delphi.

"Just pretend to agree. He must have forgotten that both the pythia *and* the moncat must acquiesce to the life-mating. If Loki searches your heart and mind, he will find no love there for Nevan."

"You got that right." A surge of agreement came from Loki in the corner.

Eron jerked as if he were startled.

"What's wrong?"

"Nothing—I just thought I felt . . . Never mind." Eron kissed her on the forehead. "So if the moncat refuses, you are not to blame."

Juelle nodded. "Then it won't do any harm to agree—"

She stopped when she heard a noise at the door and scrambled out of Eron's arms, not wanting to give their captors additional ammunition to use against her. They already knew she cared about

259

Eron, but if they suspected she loved him, it would be even worse for him.

When the door opened, they were both sitting on the floor, arms around their knees. Their jailers decided to take no chances yet again, and they shortened Eron's chains until he was once more pinned to the wall.

Nevan entered and smiled down at her. "Your waiting is finally over, my dear. It is time for the life-mate ritual."

Two goons held knives to Eron's neck. Fear combined with a slow rage within her. "There's no need for that," she said. "I'll perform the ritual willingly."

Nevan seemed taken aback and more than a little suspicious. "That's quite a change in attitude. Might I inquire what prompted it?"

She shrugged, letting her shoulders droop. "There's no point in fighting you anymore. The prophecy said so. You win."

She gazed at him out of dejected eyes, projecting despair and resigned compliance with every ounce of her being.

Nevan approached and put his arm around her. She forced herself not to stiffen, to remain passive within his embrace.

"Juelle, my dear," he said.

She gazed up at him, rigidly maintaining that compliant attitude.

"I appreciate your sentiments," he said softly, "but I can't count on them."

His grip tightened so that her arms were pinned against her sides. Panic surged through her. She'd left herself vulnerable and Nevan was too strong to resist. Before she could protest, he whisked her out the door and slammed it, leaving Eron and Loki alone inside.

Confused, and beginning to feel more than a little

frightened, she gasped out, "What—"

"Ivar," Nevan said, "bring the chela."

Wasn't that a drug? Dear Lord, what was he going to do? In a real panic now, Juelle twisted and turned, managing to escape from Nevan's hold. In a flash, she was off, running down the corridor. Too late.

She stumbled over the long hem of the chiton and two of Nevan's men overtook her. Each grabbed one arm and hauled her back to Nevan.

Her chest heaving with exertion, Juelle glanced in apprehension at Ivar, who bore a flask toward her.

"No," she cried and struggled even harder to win freedom. But the guards held fast.

"Ah, so you aren't so willing after all."

"Not to be drugged," she snapped. "Is this necessary?"

"I'm afraid so, my dear. It's the only way I can assure you will be fully compliant."

"What . . . what does it do?"

"Don't worry," he said smoothly. "The effects aren't permanent. But while it's in your body, it will leave you eager to comply with anything I wish."

In horror, Juelle watch Ivar approach even closer. He put the flask to her lips and said, "Drink."

Juelle clamped her lips shut and glared at him. Ivar cast a doubtful look at Nevan, who gestured toward her as if to tell him to get on with it.

Ivar clamped hard fingers on her face, trying to force her jaws painfully open. Enraged at the indignities they were putting her through, Juelle abandoned reason and decided to try Eron's way— brute force. With great relish, she kneed Ivar in the groin.

He went down like a sack of grain, moaning and clutching at his crotch. Unfortunately, he didn't spill any of the drug, damn the luck. She pulled her foot back to kick it out of his hand, but her captors pulled her back and away.

"Subdue her," Nevan snapped.

Knowing she had no choice, Juelle fought them like a wildcat, using her feet, her head, her teeth, any part of her body that wasn't constrained. It still did no good. She got in a couple of kicks and one or two bites, then they all piled on top of her until she was lying ignominiously on the ground, with her limbs held fast by Nevan's brutes.

"Damn you, let me go," she shouted, trying desperately to get just one hand free.

It was no use. Nevan approached, flask in hand. "Open her mouth," he ordered.

The man holding her head protested. "She bites."

Nevan's gaze narrowed. "You'll get worse than a bite if you don't do as I say."

The man yanked open her mouth. Juelle tried to close it, to bite him, to turn her head, anything. Again, to no avail.

Nevan knelt next to her with the flask. "You could have made this much easier, my dear, but this way will do just fine."

He poured the foul-tasting liquid into her mouth and Juelle gagged, but refused to swallow. She tried to spit it out, but they clamped her jaws shut so she couldn't.

Still, she refused to swallow. Nevan smiled and held her nose so she couldn't breathe. She stood it as long as she could, then had to swallow to get some air. Three more times they poured the drug into her mouth and forced her to drink, until the flask was empty.

She could hear Eron bellowing in the room beyond, and felt Loki's frantic worrying. She held onto those as if to a lifeline, but the drug took effect, making her woozy and light-headed.

She strove to free herself, but her struggles weakened as a drug-induced lassitude stole over her body, leeching away her resistance, her will to fight. Soon, she lay exhausted on the ground, her muscles relaxed.

Sluggishly, she tried to force herself to do something. She knew it was vital, but couldn't remember what it was. Remembering was too much effort, so she gave up. It would come back to her when she needed it. Instead, she closed her eyes and let the numbing lethargy take her away from all her cares, all her worries. . . .

Eron held his fear and worry in check until Nevan hurried Juelle out the door. Concern overtook him then, confirmed when he heard Nevan tell the guard to bring the chela.

Eron struggled even harder against his bonds. Chela, used by the healers to calm frenzied patients, could also be a dangerous tool in the hands of an unscrupulous person. It left its victims pliant and suggestible, willing to do anything proposed to them.

And they planned to give it to Juelle. Through the closed door, he heard a scuffle, and Loki ran to the door, trying frantically to scratch a way through to his pythia.

Dear Apollo, what were they doing to her? From the moncat's distress, she had to be putting up a fight.

Rage consumed Eron as he sought vainly to go to her aid. Damn Nevan to the netherhells—he'd chained him up like an animal and left him there to wallow in his own pain and rage. The only outlet they'd left him was his voice, and he used it fully, roaring out his rage and frustration, pulling against his bonds until he wore his wrists raw trying to get loose.

He kept it up, screaming out invectives and promises of what he would do to Nevan when he finally got his hands on him, hoping Juelle would hear him and that it would help her in her fight.

Loki never ceased his desperate measures, either, scratching at the door until his claws and paws were bloody, and howling almost as loud as Eron. With their shared fear for Juelle, Eron could feel the moncat's emotions as if they were his own, bloody raw things with a desperate edge to them. They fed off each other, making the situation more bleak until finally, Loki's desperation eased.

Eron ceased yelling, and stared at the moncat. What had caused him to change so abruptly? The moncat's brow creased into a puzzled frown as he pawed at the door and whimpered.

Realization struck Eron and he sagged against his bonds. They'd succeeded in drugging Juelle. Dear Apollo, it was the one thing that might work. If Nevan could convince Juelle in her drugged state that she was in love with him—and convince her deeply enough so she believed it—then that's what Loki would find when he searched for her willingness.

And, despite her true feelings, the moncat would undoubtedly go along with what he found in her mind—and complete the life-mate ritual.

Despair filled Eron and he tugged at his chains once more, knowing it was hopeless. The physical strength he prided himself on was of no use in this situation. His captors had assessed his strengths and weaknesses and taken advantage of both, effectively neutralizing him.

Juelle was right—brute strength wasn't always the answer. Certainly not in this situation. But what could he do? She touted the virtues of using intelligence and logic, but Eron had little practice in using them as weapons. How could you use something so . . . intangible?

He hung his head in despair. It seemed hopeless, but he had to try . . . for her sake.

Think—he had to think. He glared at his chains. If he could only pick the locks, he could get free and cut a swath through Nevan's men to get to Juelle.

No—that wouldn't work. He couldn't even get to his wrists. If only Juelle were here, to unloose them from the rings. But that was absurd—if she were here, he wouldn't be in this fix.

He thought hard. How could he get free without anyone present to release him? Loki whimpered again and Eron realized he wasn't quite alone—the moncat was still locked in with him.

Excitement surged through him. Maybe he could get Loki to unloose his chains. But how?

That tenuous connection pulled at him, tantalizing him with small snippets of the moncat's emotions. Twice, earlier, Eron had felt a surge of feeling from what had to be the moncat. Perhaps, since he and Juelle had grown close, Loki had also started to pick up on Eron's emotions.

Elation surged within him. Yes, that was possible. It was common for moncats to become sensitive to a pythia's family members, and with all they'd gone through together, Eron certainly felt like family.

Could it be? There was only one way to find out. With all his formidable will and concentration, Eron formed a thought and fired it at the moncat. Loki jumped and whirled around to stare at him.

Eron almost chuckled. The moncat's expression was comprised of equal parts of indignation and outrage. He muted the next message, sending Loki a soothing confirmation that it was indeed him.

Loki's outrage faded, and he approached Eron with curiosity and interest. Eron sent him encouraging thoughts, and tried to tell him mentally what he wanted the moncat to do.

The moncat merely blinked at him.

Eron tried again, still with no success. Then he remembered some pythias communicated with their moncats in pictures. Slowly, he constructed a picture of Loki loosening the chains from the rings, and sent that to the moncat along with an impassioned plea.

The moncat blinked again, then stared at the ring. *Yes, do it,* Eron urged. When the moncat hesitated, Eron sent him another picture, this one of Eron bashing the guards' heads together when they opened the door, then using the key to unlock the chains and rescue Juelle.

That decided him. Loki took a running leap high up the wall, but missed the ring on his first pass. Elated that the moncat had understood him and was following his instructions, Eron encouraged him to try again.

The game little animal backed up even farther, and stared at the ring with determination in his eyes. He gathered himself to run, but the door opened just then, destroying his and Eron's concentration.

Six men filed into the room and Loki retreated to the relative comfort of Eron's bulk. There were too many men for the moncat to handle so Loki played it smart. Eron confirmed that mentally, advising him to wait. Though the feisty moncat didn't make any overt moves, he stood between Eron's widespread legs, hissing at the men.

Orgon gestured at one of the men. "You, take the moncat."

"Uh-uh," the man objected. "I already got bit by the pythia. I ain't gonna be bit by no moncat, too."

Eron suppressed a satisfied smile. So Juelle had gotten some licks in herself, huh? Good for her.

Orgon glanced at the other men. They all backed away, shaking their heads and refusing to make eye contact. Orgon frowned. "One of you—pick him up."

"I told ya," the other man said. "No one's gonna risk being bitten by that moncat."

Eron just watched, enjoying the byplay.

"But Nevan needs him for the life-mate ritual."

"Then let *him* come and get him."

Orgon's expression turned cold, crafty. "I'll tell him you said that."

The man pursed his lips as if in thought, then glanced at the hissing moncat, and back at Orgon again. "Go right ahead. I figger the moncat's bite is worse'n his."

The other men chuckled, putting Orgon in a livid rage. While he yelled at them, Loki obviously saw his chance to escape and darted out the open door.

Orgon snatched at the moncat as he streaked by, but Loki dodged him and was gone.

"After him!"

"Wait," Eron yelled.

The men, all too eager to avoid chasing after a poison-fanged moncat, turned to him. "Why?" Orgon snapped.

"You don't need to chase him."

"Why not?"

"He's going right where you want him—straight to his pythia." Eron hoped he was wrong, but knowing the strength of the bond between a pythia and her moncat, he knew he was right. And, just in case

Loki was going for help, he wanted to give the mon-cat every opportunity to do so.

Orgon regarded him for a moment, then nodded. "You're probably right." He whirled back around to face his men. "But if he isn't, you're all going to pay."

The men must have cringed enough to satisfy him, for Orgon nodded, then said, "Unchain him. Nevan wants him present at the ceremony."

Eron's lip curled. So Nevan wanted an audience, did he? Well, good. That's where Eron wanted to be, instead of waiting here impotently, wondering what was going on. And, with any luck, he'd find a way to stop the ceremony before it ever began.

The men eyed him almost as warily as they had Loki. Ivar, his jailer, approached him carefully with the key. After Ivar unlocked the manacle on his left wrist, Eron let his arm fall to his side. He stretched it, trying to ease the ache.

While two men hung onto the chain on his right arm, keeping it taut against the iron ring, they pulled the chain back through the other loops. When they were done, Eron held out his left arm again, offering it for the manacle.

Orgon appeared startled, and Eron shrugged. He knew it was inevitable, and besides . . . "You're tak-ing me where *I* want to go, too."

Orgon nodded in understanding, then gestured for Ivar to continue. Eron continued to stand doc-ilely as Ivar relocked the manacle on him. Ivar kept casting him nervous glances, and Eron toyed with the idea of jerking his hand loose, just to see the shaky man's reaction, but discarded it. He didn't want anything to interfere with being allowed to attend this farce of a life-mate ceremony.

Orgon glared at him. "Kneel."

"Why?"

He held up a strip of cloth. "You can't attend the ceremony unless you're gagged."

Every nerve ending screamed a protest, but Eron bent his head for the gag. What did it matter if he couldn't speak? That was a small price to pay to be allowed to attend the ceremony.

They gagged him, then walked him down the corridor, two men on either side with one in front and one in back. Soon, they came to the antechamber to the querent chambers. By tradition, this was where the life-mating ceremony would take place, amidst the happy couple's family and friends.

Eron glanced around. What a farce. The audience consisted solely of Nevan's band of cutthroats and thieves—not a suitable audience for such a solemn, sacred occasion. Vague murmurings wafted through the chamber, though most took care to stay well away from the prisoner.

As Eron listened to their mutterings, he realized the odds were weighted heavily against him. Dread rose within him and the situation hit him with a vengeance.

This was real. In a few minutes, Nevan and Juelle would walk through that doorway and be life-mated forever in the eyes of Apollo—unless Eron did something. But what?

Once again, brute force would not avail him—not in this crowd. He had to use his mind. He weighed several plans, but soon discarded them. They all required him to be free to use his strength, his muscle. Forget that—it wasn't possible. What was?

A hush came over the gathering, and Eron looked up to see Juelle enter on Nevan's arm, her expression serene and flat as she smiled up at him and took her place by the altar. Eron's heart sank. Unfortunately, Loki rode in his proper place on her shoulder; the ceremony could proceed.

Eron thought fast. He could do nothing to stop it, so someone else had to. Loki. The moncat could still refuse to perform the ceremony. Hope rose within Eron. Maybe he could make Loki understand.

Nevan turned around and spotted Eron, then motioned him forward. Eron's guards dragged him to the altar and his lip curled. If Nevan thought the presence of a real councilman would give this ceremony credence, he was mistaken.

Nevan granted him a cool smile, though real amusement burned in his eyes. Rage rose within Eron as realization struck. The man knew how he felt, knew he loved Juelle, and was torturing him. Well, Eron would be damned if he'd let Nevan get away with it.

Carefully, he concentrated, and sent a questioning bolt at Loki. He had to get the moncat's attention, make him understand. Loki glanced sidelong at him with a confused expression on his face. Eron couldn't blame him—his pythia was agreeing to mate for life to a man she detested. No wonder he was confused.

As quickly and concisely as he could, Eron formed a picture of the true situation—a drugged Juelle being forced into the ritual. Loki cast Eron a puzzled glance, and Eron cursed under his breath. This was a difficult concept to put into a picture, but he had to do it, he had to make Loki understand.

He tried again, sending the moncat another picture. Loki's brow creased with the effort to understand, and Juelle reached up to stroke him. Loki turned away then, and Eron tensed in frustration. Had he gotten through?

Shogril took his place on the other side of the

altar and held up his arms. The chamber quieted, and Eron's dread increased.

He still didn't know if Loki had understood his message . . . and the ceremony was about to begin.

Chapter Seventeen

As the life-mate ceremony started, Eron's captors seized him in an even tighter grip, realizing, no doubt, that he may still try one last-ditch effort to save Juelle. He relaxed under their scrutiny, hoping to catch them off guard so they might relax their vigilance. If Loki hadn't understood his message, Eron would need to wrest his way free to stop the ceremony—if it were possible.

In anguish, he watched the ritual begin. When Shogril lowered his arms, Loki leapt down from his pythia's shoulder to sit on the altar, halfway between Nevan and Juelle on one side with Shogril on the other. This was a new attitude for the feisty moncat—dignified silence. It was appropriate for the occasion, but very unlike Loki.

"Gracious Apollo," Shogril said, "we are gathered together to witness the joining of . . ."

Eron tuned out the familiar words as he scrutinized the moncat, hoping for some sign that Loki had seen and understood Eron's plea, that he knew Juelle was high on chela and not in her right mind. Loki merely stared in puzzled silence at Nevan and Juelle as they placed their left hands on the altar before him, palm up in the traditional manner.

Then Shogril came to the part of the ceremony Eron had been dreading. "Do you, Juelle Shanard, take Nevan as your life-mate, to cleave only unto him until you should both be in Apollo's arms?"

Juelle hesitated, and Nevan murmured something to her.

Haltingly, she said, "By Apollo's . . . grace, I . . . do."

Eron couldn't help himself—he tensed, and the men restraining him reactivated their vigilance, grabbing his chains to hold him fast. Eron watched helplessly as Loki stared into Juelle's face, then leaned down to bite her left wrist, thereby irrevocably beginning the ritual.

No! It's not supposed to happen this way!

Eron strained against his bonds but his captors were too strong. They held him fast, and he ceased struggling only when he heard the last part of Nevan's affirmation. ". . . I do."

His heart in his throat, Eron watched as Loki gazed first at Juelle, then at Nevan, then back again. The moncat wavered, then seemed to come to a sudden decision. He leaned down toward Nevan's hand and Eron screamed in silent frustration.

Then, without warning, Loki leapt for Nevan's face. Grabbing Nevan's ears for support, the moncat chomped him viciously on the nose.

The room erupted in a frenzy of howling and surprised cries. Exulting inside, Eron almost laughed aloud as Loki dodged the men who charged toward the moncat with murderous intent. Instead, Loki leapt for the one man left holding Eron's left arm, fangs bared.

The man jerked backward, dropping Eron's arm, and Eron caught the moncat in midair. Loki grabbed for a secure hold on Eron's left arm with all four paws and his tail. Casting Eron what could only be described as a moncat grin, Loki bit him on the wrist. Mission completed, he scrambled for the safety of Eron's shoulder, far above the crowd.

Eron froze momentarily in surprise. The moncat had just initiated the life-mate ritual . . . with him. Elation sang through him as he fought to get to Juelle. Loki wouldn't have chosen him if he didn't know, somehow, that they were destined for each other.

Juelle stood, unaware, her hand still poised on the altar, waiting for the completion of the ceremony as chaos reigned around her. Joyously, Eron took the few steps necessary to reach her and pressed their wrists together to complete the ceremonial part of the ritual and seal them together for all time.

He clasped her hand in his and their blood began to mingle. As it did, he felt an odd tingling sensation where their wrists were joined together, then hot needles speared through his blood.

So intent was he on their joining that he blocked out all extraneous activity. That was a mistake. As Nevan convulsed on the ground next to him in the throes of Loki's poison, Shogril glanced up from where he was bending over his son and gave them a murderous look.

Yelling at the nearest men to grab them, he spat out, "Get them out of this sacred place before I forget where I am and slay them where they stand."

Though Eron was still conscious of voices, he couldn't react or even acknowledge anything beyond the roaring in his blood, urging him to complete the ritual. Instead, Nevan's minions thrust them back into their cell, but not before looping Eron's chains through the rings once more, and slamming him against the wall.

He remained there, helpless. He was still gagged, so he couldn't even call out to Juelle. His blood burned, singing with the need for release, for completion. It occupied his thoughts to the exclusion of all else save Juelle and his need. But she lay drugged, sprawling on her back where they had shoved her across the grain sacks, her moncat bent over her in solicitous concern.

With every fiber of his being, Eron yearned toward Juelle, his entire attention focused on her. He could only hope the power of the moncat's bite and the fierce need to complete the ritual would wake her before his senses were overwhelmed by the crying need.

After what seemed like an eternity but, in reality, was only a few minutes, Juelle blinked and her face lost some of the placid expression he associated with chela. She sat up and held her head groggily then peered up at him. "What . . ."

"Mrphm umph," he muttered around his gag.

Juelle's expression was uncomprehending as she stared at him with a crease between her brows. Loki chittered anxiously, then ran up Eron's body to land on his shoulder, and plucked at the gag.

Juelle blinked again, then levered herself to her feet and stood swaying for a moment before she headed for Eron.

Reaching up, she untied the gag and pulled it from his mouth. Eron ran his tongue around his dry mouth and lips and despite the imperative in his blood, croaked in a voice suddenly gone hoarse, "Are you all right?"

275

"I-I think so. I feel light-headed . . . and there's a burning sensation inside me that seems to *want* something."

He forced the need back, trying to speak rationally. "It's perfectly natural. You were drugged—that's why you feel woozy."

"And the burning?"

"That's natural, too—it's part of the life-mate ritual." He held himself rigidly in abeyance, knowing she needed answers.

Her eyes grew round in horror. "You mean Nevan and I . . . ?"

"No—Loki bit him on the nose instead of the wrist."

Loki appeared smug and Juelle chuckled, then stopped abruptly. Her eyes widened and she leaned against Eron for support. "What's happening to me?" She glanced up at him as if in sudden realization. "And who am I life-mated to?"

"To me," Eron said, dreading her reaction.

As her eyes turned cloudy and she sought to take it all in, her hands slid under Eron's shirt and roamed his chest, as if she were unaware what they were doing.

Her hands felt like soft fire blazing across his skin. Eron almost moaned aloud. The ritual. They had to complete the ritual.

"Why to you?" she asked.

Surprised by the mildness of her question, Eron said, "That was Loki's decision." He left the rest unsaid. Surely she knew enough to know that moncats would only choose those worthy of their pythias—or those whom they truly loved. Usually both. In this case, he understood that the moncat found him worthy, but whether Juelle loved him was another matter.

She peered at Loki who appeared to be pleased

with himself. Some sort of communication seemed to pass between them, then she nodded. "And we have to complete it?"

"*Yes.* You feel that burning, that yearning inside you?"

She nodded again, and her hands continued their caressing journey of his body.

"The chela is dampening the effects, but soon your blood will be raging with the need."

She glanced up at him with a questioning look. "Is yours?"

He declined to answer the obvious, since her fingers were now curled around the evidence of that need. He thought he would almost explode with the force of holding back.

"As yours will be soon," he gasped out. "Even now your hands roam my body."

She glanced down at her hands, seeming shocked they had caressed him so intimately without her knowledge. It didn't stop her, though. She continued fondling him, as if she couldn't help herself. "What do we have to do?"

"The moncat bites have been administered, and our blood has flowed together. Now there is nothing left but the consummation of our union."

Juelle thought about it for a minute and Eron held his breath, afraid she would refuse. If she did, he would surely die.

Giving him a mischievous glance, she said, "I think I can manage that."

Eron released the breath he had been holding. Now. He needed to consummate their union now. "Then release me from this wall."

He could feel her emotions now, through the tenuous bond of their life-mating. Though excitement thrummed through her, the chela still numbed her responses and she was nowhere near as aroused as he—yet.

She gave him another mischievous glance as she loosened the bonds of his clothing until he was bare from his chest to his knees. "I'm not sure . . . I think it might be more fun this way," she said in a teasing manner as she trailed a blazing path down his body with her mouth and hands.

Any other time, he would be willing to play this game with her, but not now—not when the need raged within him, demanding release. He begged her to free him, but she just laughed and continued teasing him, slowly removing her clothing until she stood nude before him.

Frustrated beyond anything he had ever experienced, Eron called upon Loki. Desperate now, he begged the moncat to release his chains from the rings. The moncat complied, and Eron almost gasped with the relief when one arm fell free. Moments later, the other did as well.

Simultaneously, the clever moncat began enhancing Juelle's emotions, damping down the chela, and making Juelle's need as fierce as Eron's.

He exulted when she gasped and he could feel her desire surge to match his. Without finesse, he bore her down to the floor, then entered her in one swift movement.

She cried out and, bonded as they were, Eron knew it was a cry of ecstasy as fierce as his own. He crushed her lips beneath his and held on, wanting her close, surrounding him, deeply entrenched in each other's hearts and minds.

The need drove him to a savage coupling, far more violent than any he had ever experienced. Juelle met him with a frenzy that matched his own, demanding he move harder, faster. He complied, and soon felt the world spinning out of control as his world . . . her world . . . their world . . . burst into light, refracting their joy in an endless series of reflections.

It stayed that way for one timeless instant, then coalesced and reformed into a single unit—something new . . . something better . . . something wonderful.

Sated, Juelle stroked Eron's cheek. He was so large, so primitive, so . . . everything she thought she'd never want in a man. But she'd come to know and love him during this trip. His world had crumbled around him, yet he hadn't crumbled with it. He'd stood steady as a rock—and she knew he'd weather all of life's disappointments and disasters the same way.

His physical strength masked a sensitivity he tried hard to hide, but was evident every time he spoke to his people, dealt kindly with his young cousin, and made love to her. The pigheaded barbarian was nothing but a big softie, and she loved him for it.

She glanced down at his half-naked body. He wasn't bad to look at, either—with or without his clothes.

Eron stirred and gazed down at her with concern in his eyes. "I-I . . . Did I hurt you?"

She chuckled and squeezed as much of his chest as she could reach. "No, not really."

"I'm sorry."

"Don't be. I don't think you—or either of us— were in control there."

Eron nodded, then stroked her cheek with a tender motion. "How do you feel about us?"

She smiled up at him, saying, "I feel just fine."

He hesitated, then said, "You do realize we're mated now . . . for life?"

279

"Yes."

"And that doesn't bother you?"

"Nope."

Eron frowned and Juelle smiled to herself. She didn't think he was getting quite the answers he expected. That's all right—give him long enough, and he'd figure it out. But there was no time to play games.

She chuckled then said, "Yes, Eron, I'm aware I can no longer mate with any man but you or risk losing Loki. I know that, and accept it. It's not a problem."

When he still appeared blank, she gave it to him straight. "That's because I love you, dummy."

The slow smile that spread across his face was a work of art, expressing delight, wonder, and sheer joy. Juelle's heart flipped over at the sight, and she blessed her lucky stars that she'd found such a special man—one who shared the fierce love she felt for him.

He was hers—her life-mate. If anyone could capture and hold her heart forever, this man could.

He grabbed her in a bone-crushing hug and rained tiny kisses all over her face. Laughing, Juelle endured it until he finally captured her lips with his in a kiss of exquisite gentleness and sweetness. She sighed, knowing that if she hadn't been in love with him before, she would be now. But, unfortunately, now was not the time to plan the future. *If we have a future.*

"We may not," Eron said.

Startled, Juelle glanced at him, not realizing she'd spoken that last thought aloud. "True." Reluctantly, she disengaged herself from his arms and began to dress. "They won't be happy with Loki for biting Nevan, and once they remember us, they'll be back." She gave him a wry look. "What do you think are our chances of surviving this?"

He regarded her gravely as he fastened his clothing. "Not good. Even if they were inclined to be lenient with us since Loki actually did the biting, your life-mating to me changes Nevan's plans. *That* is likely to cause the most problems."

Once they were both dressed, Juelle put her arms around him as far as they would go and leaned her head against his chest. "I wish . . ."

Eron stroked her hair. "I know. I wish it, too. I wish we could be far away from here, together."

Juelle nodded, though she knew that wouldn't solve their problems. There was still the small matter of her being the doom of Delphi if she ever prophesied again. How would they be able to reconcile that with Eron's desire to be a leader of his people? She didn't want to take that away from him . . . or them.

Suddenly, the door slammed open and Shogril entered, followed closely by Ivar. Grabbing Eron's chains, they jerked him back against the wall. Eron hit it with a thud and a muffled groan.

Juelle whirled on Shogril. "Good Lord, haven't you done enough?"

"Not nearly enough," Shogril sneered with a wild-eyed look, and pulled a sword from a scabbard that hadn't been there before. "But I'm going to rectify that now."

Fear stabbed through her at the sight of the weapon. Even Ivar took a cautious step back. "Now, wait," she said in as reasonable a tone as she could muster. "There's no need for violence."

"Where's the beast?" Shogril asked.

"What?"

"The moncat. Where is it?"

Juelle felt for Loki. He'd been sleeping between a couple of grain sacks and was just now waking. She sent him a sharp mental command to stay still. Obediently, Loki froze.

"I don't know," Juelle lied, playing for time. "He didn't come back here with us."

Shogril's gaze scanned the room with an intent, focused stare. "He's in here somewhere. I know it." He gestured back at Ivar. "Close the door and help me catch him."

"M-Me?"

Shogril paused in scanning the room to give Ivar a contemptuous glare. "The moncat's venom needs another hour to regenerate. You're safe. Now *find* it."

Ivar began a cautious search of the stores at the far end of the room while Shogril stabbed his sword randomly through various sacks, uncaring that the grain spilled onto the dirt floor.

Think, Juelle advised herself. What could she do to get Loki—and them—out of this in one piece? "You don't really want to kill the moncat," she said in a reasonable tone. "He's sacred to Apollo, your god."

"The moncat has blasphemed against Apollo, wounding him grievously."

Uh-oh. It sounded like Shogril wasn't grounded in reality anymore. Not if he thought his son was Apollo. Even Ivar eyed him doubtfully.

"But Apollo is a fair and forgiving god," Juelle ventured.

Shogril took aim at another grain sack, coming closer to Loki's hiding place. "I am the instrument of his revenge. Through me, he shall be avenged upon all those who have wronged him. Starting with the beast."

Damn. This wasn't working. They didn't even seem to be participating in the same conversation. She glanced at Eron, wondering why he was so quiet. He stood motionless, watching Shogril with an intense, predatory gaze.

Juelle realized that he hoped Shogril would forget about him and come a little too close. She knew Eron well enough to realize he must figure the odds were better now. Two men, one armed, against Eron, who had only the minor inconvenience of being chained to the wall.

Great odds. Yeah, right. And, just as obviously, they all discounted her presence as being help *or* hindrance.

Well, she wouldn't jeopardize Eron's shot at it, but she didn't hold forth any hope that it would work. She glanced at Shogril again, wondering what she could say that would penetrate his fixated mind, and suddenly realized his arm was raised to stab in the spot where Loki was hiding.

Terrified, Juelle screamed out mental and verbal warnings. "Run, Loki." The moncat leapt up, evaded the blade, and scurried out of his hiding place, running straight for the door.

"Grab him," yelled Shogril.

The closed door balked the moncat, and he whirled around to confront Ivar and Shogril, hissing. Ivar shuffled toward the door, his arms stretched wide to catch the moncat if he shot by.

Juelle looked at Shogril and was dismayed to see an expression of glee and utter madness in his eyes. He raised the sword to chop down at Loki. Now, Juelle had finally had enough of this creep.

With every ounce of her strength, she hurled herself at him. She deflected the sword, then knocked it out of his hand and chopped at the side of his neck to render him unconscious.

Swiftly, she turned to Ivar, who had his hands full with a spitting, hissing, clawing Loki. Encouraging Loki to keep him distracted, she darted behind Ivar and administered the same blow to him. He fell at her feet, and she searched his pockets.

"Where did you learn to do that?" Eron asked in an awe-filled voice.

She found the key and moved toward him. "My father taught me. He thought it might come in handy sometime to discourage unwanted . . . attentions."

She unfastened the chains from the rings to lower Eron's wrists to where she could reach them, and unlocked his manacles.

He rubbed his wrists, saying, "Thank you. Why didn't you do that before?"

She gave him an exasperated look. "Because violence is not a solution."

Eron glanced at the two unconscious men on the floor and raised his eyebrow. Loki, too, appeared confused. She could tell he was wondering why she was making such a big deal out of something that was so necessary.

Juelle felt her face warm. "Okay, *sometimes* it's a solution."

"If you say so," he murmured.

Juelle ignored him. She wasn't going to rise to *that* bait. "We'd better get out of here while we still can."

"Right." Eron headed for the door, and opened it a crack, listening.

He opened the door farther. "There's no one out there," he whispered. "Let's go."

Juelle nodded and scooped Loki up off the floor, giving the moncat a few well-deserved caresses.

They headed back up the corridor, toward the entrance. Though Juelle wished they could take the time to find their horses and packs—including her medkit—she knew it wasn't feasible.

Halfway there, they heard voices coming toward

them down the corridor. A strangely familiar voice said, ". . . filters *now*."

As another voice responded in tones too low to understand, Eron and Juelle glanced around for an avenue of escape. There was none. The nearest branching corridor was a hundred feet behind them. There was no way they could make it there before the party approaching them rounded the bend.

From the expression on Eron's face, it appeared he'd come to the same conclusion. "We're going to have to stand our ground," he whispered. "Do you think you might be able to produce a little more violence for a good cause?"

She threw him an exasperated glance. She might as well finish what she'd started. She nodded, just in time to see the party round the corner.

The man in the lead said, "That is *not*—"

He broke off when he saw Eron charging at them. He sidestepped the big Delphian neatly, and Juelle gaped in astonishment. "Alexander! What are you doing here?"

Alexander's eyes grew round with surprise, but whatever he had planned to say was lost in the melee behind him as Eron waded in with his big fists, aided by Loki with his sharp claws and teeth. Unfortunately, they were outnumbered ten to two and needed help.

"Never mind," Juelle snapped. "No time for that now."

With that, she joined in the fray, jabbing one man in the kidneys and taking another one out with a blow to the neck. She was just reaching for another when a brute grabbed her from behind and held her in an unbreakable arm and headlock.

She stopped struggling in order to breathe and saw Eron on the floor, pinned by six men, but still struggling. Loki had somehow been captured in a sack and was even now writhing to get out. Even Alexander, sporting a black eye, was being held by two men.

As she watched in horror, one of the men grabbed a nearby rock and brought it down hard on Eron's head. Eron's body went limp, and a small stream of blood trickled down his face.

Stars above, had they killed him? Juelle struggled once more to be free, to run to her life-mate, but her captor was too strong.

To top it all off, Shogril came staggering down the corridor just then, holding his head. He pointed his sword at the group and shouted, "Hold them. They *will* meet Apollo's justice."

Juelle redoubled her efforts to escape, but the man had a good headlock on her and she couldn't get free.

Shogril slowed as he neared, an avid expression on his face and fire in his eyes. His eyes narrowed when he spotted Juelle and the tip of the sword wavered in her direction. "You," he said. "You brought my son to this."

The frenzy in his eyes made Juelle realize that seeing his son felled by the moncat bite must have sent the man over the edge. He was no longer sane.

"He brought it upon himself," Juelle snapped, "when he attempted to take what was not his."

"Apollo has judged you and found you all wanting," Shogril intoned, his sword now leveled at Eron's throat. "And I shall execute his will."

"Damn you," she shouted. "You would kill an unconscious man? Where's your pride, your honor?"

Shogril's eyes narrowed. "The two of you have taken it from me. I have no more honor until my son is avenged."

Desperately, she sought to delay him. "Wait. Remember the prophecy?"

"What prophecy?"

"My prophecy—the one that predicted your son's ruling the world."

Out of the corner of her eye, she saw Alexander dart her a startled glance. She didn't have time to explain now—she had to find a way to save Eron's life . . . and her own.

"What about it?" Shogril growled, though the tip of his sword wavered. "With you life-mated to him," he nodded at Eron, "my son's plans lay in ruins."

"My, my," Alexander murmured, his eyebrow raised. "You have been busy, haven't you, Ju?"

Juelle shot him an exasperated glance, then ignored him. "But he told us the prophecy said he need only proceed as planned, and he would win control of the world. Think about it," she said. "His plans never included our death. If you change his plans, you change the outcome of the prophecy. And how can you expect to win the people's support if you kill a councilman . . . and a pythia?"

"Not to mention the Terran Ambassador," Alexander added.

Juelle flashed a look of surprise at him. "Looks like you've been busy, too," she murmured.

Alexander merely shrugged as Shogril frowned in thought. "Perhaps. Perhaps not." His eyes turned cunning and an evil smile graced his mouth. "I have a better idea. Take them to the ship."

"Now wait a minute," Alexander protested. "That's my ship."

"And I am commandeering it in the name of Apollo."

"In the name of your son?"

Juelle flashed Alexander a puzzled look. "Apollo is their god. Nevan is his son."

"The same Nevan who falsified Thena's prophecies and tried to steal her from Lancer?"

Juelle nodded.

Alexander shook his head in resignation. "I thought it was odd that he was named after their god. I should've known. And all this time I've been helping—"

"Silence," thundered Shogril. "Take them to the ship. Now. You three,"—he gestured with the sword to three of the men who had been sitting on Eron—"get some rope."

The men did as he ordered, and the others picked up the unconscious Eron and a strangely subdued moncat. Juelle was concerned for a moment, then realized Loki was biding his time, waiting for a moment to spring loose from the sack.

Shogril's men manhandled Juelle and Alexander out of the caves and across the rough terrain, then down into a gully where Alexander's ship waited. Some men were working on it, and looked up at their approach.

"I trust the filters are complete now," Shogril said, his tone daring them to say otherwise.

"Yes, sir," one of the men replied, darting a guilty glance at Alexander.

Shogril glared at Alexander. "Open the ship."

"Why?"

"Do as I say."

"No," Alexander said. "First tell me why."

The tip of the sword swung to Alexander's throat. "Open it," Shogril repeated.

Alexander was equally stubborn. "Killing me won't do you any good. You can't open it without my voice command."

Shogril's mouth firmed into a straight line and he glared at Alexander. All of a sudden, he flew into a rage, chopping at a desert plant with a sword and hacking it to pieces. When he was done, he picked up a handful of black sand and flung it full into Alexander's face.

Alexander yelped in pain and shook his head, trying to reach his eyes, but his captors restrained him. "I can't see."

"I am the eyes of Apollo," Shogril said. "You have no need to see. Open the ship or the woman will die."

Alexander froze. "But you wouldn't—"

"We are all going to die soon. Whether she dies now or later is up to you."

The men around them cast Shogril doubtful glances, and a cold chill crept up Juelle's spine as she wondered what he meant by that. If it were up to her, she'd just as soon take her chances on later.

Alexander visibly wavered, then pitched his voice louder and said, "Ship, open."

The side of the ship opened and a ramp slid out.

"Get them inside," Shogril ordered. They did so, and he snapped, "Now, tie them up."

The men went to work on them, using the rope to tie their feet and fasten their hands behind them. The man holding Loki's sack dropped him in a corner, apparently thinking the moncat was no threat. As Juelle and Alexander sat on the floor against the bulkhead, she silently urged the impatient moncat to remain still.

Loki was their ace in the hole, and Juelle didn't want to play that card prematurely. She told him to remain patient, and passed the time by keeping him informed via mental pictures of what was going on in the cabin of the ship.

Once they were all tied up, with the exception of the moncat, Shogril motioned the rest of the men outside. "Go now."

Orgon hesitated. "But won't you need me?"

Pam McCutcheon

"No, they're harmless now. Nothing will be served by your death. You must stay here to aid my son when he recovers from his illness."

Death? What did he mean by that?

Orgon must have wondered the same thing, for his eyes grew round, but he gulped and nodded, then exited the ship, followed by everyone but Shogril and his captives.

Once they were all off, Shogril pulled the lever to pull up the ramp and close the door. Juelle's eyes widened. How had he learned to do that? Suddenly, fear filled her. This might be more serious than she thought.

"Now, you," Shogril said and manhandled Alexander over to the console. "Show me how to take it up."

"How can I? You've blinded me."

"It's only temporary. I will be your eyes. Just tell me what to do."

When Alexander hesitated, Shogril added, "Tell me . . . or the woman dies."

Slowly, Alexander began detailing what Shogril had to do. Since the terms were unfamiliar to the Delphian, Juelle had a feeling it would take a while before they achieved liftoff. And while Shogril was distracted . . .

She called Loki silently and explained what he had to do. The moncat's emotions surged with elation at finally having something to do. She urged caution, and he heeded her, worrying open the neck of the loosely tied sack to creep out of it.

Juelle kept her attention on Shogril and Alexander, not wanting to draw attention to Loki's activities should Shogril glance back at them. Instead, she followed Loki's progress mentally.

Keeping a wary eye on Shogril, Loki made a scurrying dash across the room, then darted into the small space between Juelle's back and the wall. She glanced at Shogril. Good. He hadn't seen him. Surreptitiously, she inched away from the wall to give Loki more room, then urged him to use his sharp teeth on the ropes binding her hands.

Loki went to it with a will as Juelle continued to watch the other two. Eron was still out cold, and she worried about him, though Loki assured her he was unconscious and not dead. But head injuries were always iffy—and he'd been hit twice in the span of a couple days.

Soon, she felt the engines vibrate and sensed the high-pitched whine that indicated an imminent liftoff. No—it was too soon. She wasn't free yet. She braced herself and told Loki to do the same as Shogril and Alexander took their seats in the pilot chairs. She urged Loki to further exertions. He chewed as fast as he could, but the rope was thick and the moncat was trying hard not to bite his pythia.

The ship took off, and the force of it sent Juelle sliding across the floor to sprawl in the opposite corner. Loki followed her, sliding ignominiously on his back the whole way. Despite himself, he squealed in protest.

The ship stabilized, and Juelle righted herself as Loki hid behind her in the corner. Shogril turned toward her. "What was that?"

"Nothing," she answered, "I-I was just surprised when the ship took off."

Shogril's eyes narrowed. To head him off, she asked, "Where are we going?"

"Dodona."

"I, uh, don't remember those coordinates," Alexander protested, obviously stalling for time.

"You don't need to," Shogril said. "When you showed us earlier how to set the . . . autopilot," he

291

stumbled over the unfamiliar word, "you set up a code for Dodona."

Alexander's jaw slackened in dismay. Shogril turned toward the autopilot and keyed in a command with great concentration. Loki finished chewing through her bonds, and Juelle shook her hands until the ropes fell to the floor behind her. Now the only thing left were the ropes binding her ankles.

Rubbing her wrists and giving Loki mental strokes, Juelle asked, "And what's going to happen once we get there?"

Shogril's mad eyes turned cunning. "If my son can't win his way into the Council Captainship by life-mating to a pythia, we'll just have to find another way to create a vacancy in the position."

She didn't like the sound of that. "Like what?"

"According to him," Shogril nodded at Alexander, "if I take no action to disable the autopilot and land the ship, it will crash into Dodona."

"But . . . that will kill everyone there," she protested.

He smiled in satisfaction. "Exactly. It will create a power vacuum my son will be able to fill so he can rebuild the power and glory of our family."

"It'll kill all of us on board the ship, too," she reminded him.

"That's a price I'm willing to pay to see our family's honor restored."

Well, I'm not, Juelle thought, but decided it probably wasn't wise to say that aloud. Now her need to win freedom from her bonds had become even more urgent. She fell silent, hoping Shogril would turn away and ignore her.

Alexander took up where she left off, urging Shogril to change his mind, painting a lurid picture of the Republic's ability when it came to investigating the deaths of its subjects, especially its ambassadors, and promising Shogril would never get away with it.

While they argued, Juelle loosened the bonds on her feet and massaged her ankles, planning her strategy. Obviously, logic wouldn't work on this madman. She sighed. It appeared physical violence was going to be the only solution once again.

Shogril stopped responding to Alexander's arguments. Instead, he picked up his sword and whipped Alexander across the head with the hilt. "I don't need you anymore," he muttered as Alexander fell to the floor, unconscious.

Stars! Was she next? It was now or never. For the third time that day, Juelle readied herself for action and, taking a deep breath, launched herself at Shogril, Loki right behind her. Some sound must have alerted him, for Shogril turned and saw her coming. He tried to bring the sword around, but the unwieldy length caught on the console.

Juelle hit him square in the chest, knocking him down. The sword fell loose, clattering to the floor. He scrabbled for it, but Juelle caught him with a glancing blow on the shoulder that should have made his arm go numb.

Loki screeched as Shogril twisted, tossing Juelle off him. She tried to hit his other shoulder in the same manner, but couldn't get a hold on the writhing man.

Instead, he used his other meaty fist to grab the sword and brought it toward her neck. She grabbed his wrist in both hands, trying to push the sword away, but it lowered inch by inch toward her throat.

Loki flashed by, and sunk his fangs—the poison now regenerated—into Shogril's thumb. Shogril howled in outrage and slackened his grip. Juelle rolled away, too late. He delivered a glancing blow to the back of her head with the sword hilt.

She fell into darkness, realizing in despair that the ship was now hurtling on a death flight toward Dodona, crewed only by four unconscious bodies . . . and one terrified moncat.

Chapter Eighteen

Eron woke, and tried to raise a hand to his throbbing head, but his hands wouldn't move. Neither would his feet. He groaned and opened his eyes, pleased to find that some part of his body was still functioning. The light was bright, painfully so, and he squinted, trying to remember where he was and how he'd gotten there.

As his eyes adjusted to the dazzling light, he glanced around at his surroundings. Nothing was familiar, and he blinked again, trying to make sense of the shining metal walls, the blinking red lights, and the images flashing by above a pair of odd-looking chairs.

Realization dawned on him. Somehow, he'd gotten aboard one of the Terran vehicles. How had that happened . . . and why? The last thing he remembered was being attacked by a dozen men as Shogril bore down on them with a sword.

Well, it seemed he had survived that. His eyes

flew open. But what about Juelle?

He scanned the room again, and saw three bodies sprawled in various postures. A stranger lay slumped next to one of the chairs, Shogril convulsed on the floor by the far wall, and Juelle lay beyond him, unmoving as Loki bent over her.

Juelle! Was she hurt?

He tried to get to her, but couldn't move fast enough, bound as he was. Loki looked up with an anxious expression and chittered urgently. Eron wiggled his way toward her. When he finally reached his destination, he could see she was still breathing. His shoulders slumped in relief. Good. She wasn't dead.

Loki scooted around toward his back, and Eron jumped when he felt the creature's soft fur against his arm. What was he doing? Soon, he realized Loki was chewing through his bonds. Eron stilled and let the moncat do his work. He couldn't help Juelle until he was free.

A few strands parted, and Eron forced the rest of them open. Swiftly, he untied the ropes around his ankles and knelt to assess Juelle's condition. From the lump forming on the back of her head, it appeared Shogril had hit her.

Eron scowled. There was nothing he could do except make her comfortable and hope she woke up soon so they could get out of this metal box.

WHOOOOP. WHOOOOP. WHOOOOP. A loud clanging noise echoed through the vehicle, startling him and making the moncat jump. A disembodied genderless voice boomed, "FIFTEEN MINUTES TO IMPACT. DISENGAGE AUTOPILOT NOW."

Impact? That didn't sound good. Eron rose and stumbled on unsteady feet to where the voice had originated—by the wall with the moving pictures.

The surface there had a hodgepodge of buttons,

dials, and levers, with flashing lights and fast-moving numbers. On the left side, a wheel-like contraption rose from the panel on a long pole, but Eron couldn't figure out the purpose of any of it.

None of it made sense, so he glanced at the wall above him. The pictures puzzled him for a moment, until he realized it was a window and he was looking down at Delphi.

Down? That must mean they were up in the air, above his world. Then this must be Juelle's scoutship. But how in Apollo's name had they gotten inside it? And where were they going?

He glanced around for a clue, and found the word, "Dodona" spelled out on a lighted panel. Well, that answered one question. They must be headed for the capital.

WHOOOOP. WHOOOOP. WHOOOOP. "TEN MINUTES TO IMPACT. DISENGAGE AUTOPILOT NOW."

Damn. He had a sinking feeling he knew exactly what they were going to "impact." "Tell me how," Eron shouted at the voice.

It didn't answer, and Eron glanced around in desperation. What the hell was he supposed to do? The only one conscious, besides himself, was the moncat, and he was no help. Loki stood pressed against the window, peering out, looking as puzzled as Eron.

Eron scanned the panel again, trying to make sense of it. Damn. If it were a runaway horse, he might be able to stop it, but how did you stop a runaway ship? Suddenly, he wished he'd paid more attention to Juelle's lectures on the benefits and usage of technology—especially the usage part.

Well, there was no use wishing for what he couldn't have. Instead, he concentrated on making sense of what was in front of him. Words. There were words—written in his own language. He peered at them, trying to understand the strange terms, then spotted the word "autopilot".

"NINE MINUTES TO IMPACT. DISENGAGE AUTOPILOT NOW."

Frantically, he stared at the red square below the autopilot. Two letters flashed mockingly at him. "ON," they declared. Damn it, he knew that. But if there was an ON, there should be an OFF. Where was it?

"EIGHT MINUTES TO IMPACT."

Great Sandsnakes, they were all going to die if he didn't figure this out soon. *Think, man, think!*

"SEVEN MINUTES TO IMPACT."

Eron's gaze darted over the rest of the panel, but he couldn't find another autopilot, or an off switch. In frustration, he pounded the red square, hating its mocking flashing light.

"SIX MINUTES . . ." The voice paused. "AUTO-PILOT DISENGAGED. PREPARE FOR LAND-ING."

In elation, Eron glanced back at the red square. It had been recessed into the panel before, but now it was raised a half inch above the panel and clearly announced OFF. He sighed in relief . . . too soon.

He felt a sinking sensation in his stomach and glanced up at the window. They were approaching the ground fast. Too fast. If he didn't do something soon, they'd hit it even though the autopilot was disengaged.

"WARNING. REDUCE AIRSPEED."

Loki chittered anxiously, and Eron shared his concern. What should he do? How could he control this thing?

Suddenly, he saw the wheel move, sliding in toward the panel as they headed inexorably down toward Delphi. Suspecting a connection, he grabbed it and pulled. They leveled off. He pulled back more, and the ship rose.

Elated, he realized maybe it *was* like a horse, and this wheel its reins. Unfortunately, this beast had the bit in its teeth and was hellbent on going somewhere—fast. Irreverently, he wondered if he would find the word "whoa" somewhere on the panel.

Eron spared a glance for the other passengers. They were still unconscious. Maybe he could keep this thing in the air until Juelle woke and—

"WARNING. FUEL LOW. INITIATE LANDING SEQUENCE."

Eron swore beneath his breath. That must be why that FUEL light was flashing. He glanced quickly over the panel to see if there were any other lights he had to worry about and was glad to see there weren't.

But this one was bad enough. He didn't have anything to feed this metal horse, so he was going to have to land it. But how? And how the hell was he going to reduce the airspeed?

He pulled back on the wheel to give himself more height. As the ship tilted, Loki lost his precarious perch by the window and slid backward, scrabbling all the way for a grip. He caught himself on the lip of the console with his forepaws and braced one foot on the lever above him.

All of a sudden, they shot forward with a jolt.

"Let go," Eron shouted. The hapless moncat yowled, then released his hold and slid off onto the floor. Eron glanced at the lever. Just as he suspected, it was the airspeed. "Thanks, Loki," he said, and pulled the lever in the other direction.

Numbers flashed by almost too fast for him to read, until he felt they'd passed the speed at which they'd been traveling before. But not too far past.

If this thing was like a horse, then bringing it to

a dead stop while it was moving so fast wouldn't be smart. It would be tantamount to getting tossed over the horse's head . . . only this toss would be fatal.

Loki's head popped up again, this time in the other chair. Eron let him be. The moncat had been useful before. He might be again. He shot a glance at his other passengers. They had rolled around a bit, but didn't seem to need immediate attention.

"WARNING. FUEL REACHING CRITICAL LEVEL. INITIATE LANDING SEQUENCE."

Eron grimaced. He'd stalled long enough. Now it was time to try landing. He gulped and spared a moment or two to think about it. Where should he land? He glanced down at the countryside. Somewhere near Dodona, so they could get help if they needed it. Yes, that's it.

But they'd passed over Dodona several minutes ago. How did you turn this thing around? If it were a horse, he'd wheel it in a circle. Wheel . . . Eron glanced down at the wheel and inched it to the right. The ship turned in the same direction.

That was it. He turned the ship in a wide circle until it was facing back toward Dodona. Good. Now he just needed to land the ship in the clearing where the Council Captain had parked his scoutship.

Eron eased the wheel forward until the ship was pointing down, and reduced the airspeed. If they were moving too fast when they landed, they'd surely crash.

"WARNING. AIRSPEED DROPPING," the voice said.

Well, of course—that's what he *wanted*. Didn't he?

"WARNING. LANDING ANGLE TOO STEEP."

Frantically, he pulled the wheel backward and leveled off, realizing that if he were leaning too far over a horse's neck and it stopped abruptly, he'd catapult over its head. The same principle must apply here.

Yes, that made sense. With more confidence now, he decreased the airspeed gradually and, just as carefully, reduced his altitude and angle of descent until he spotted the small clearing.

As he neared it, he could see two ships sitting side by side. Lancer's . . . and Juelle's? Then whom did this one belong to? He shook his head. The question was irrelevant. More to the point, how was he going to land this speeding craft in that small space?

In rising horror, he realized he couldn't. The ship would take too far to land and, at this angle, he'd take out a hundred trees before he crashed into the side of the mountain . . . exactly where the stables were. And at this time of day, the stables would be full of horses and riders.

"WARNING. FUEL LEVEL DANGEROUSLY LOW. LAND NOW."

He couldn't land—not and kill Apollo knew how many people. He'd just have to take his chances somewhere else—on the plains beneath Dodona.

Suddenly, the trees were immediately below him. He pulled up, too late. The ship clipped the treetops, and he heard something rip free on the side of the ship.

"WARNING. STARBOARD ENGINE FAILURE."

The ship wobbled and Eron cursed. He'd lost some control. He fought the wheel, and struggled to bring the ship around again. He'd just have to land on the plains.

"WARNING. FUEL LEVEL APPROACHING ZERO."

Terrific. Well, there was nothing he could do about it now. Besides, he didn't need that damned voice telling him what was wrong every few seconds. He'd already figured out he had some serious problems here.

With shaking hands, he clutched the wheel. He only had one more chance, and he had to make it good. They were fast approaching the ground and he needed all his wits about him so he could land. Keep the ship level, bring it down slowly, and he should be all right.

He repeated those words as a litany and lowered the ship toward the fast-approaching ground. As it rushed toward him, the vibration ceased. He hadn't really noticed it until it stopped. What did that signi—

"WARNING. FUEL TANKS EMPTY."

They hit the ground with a thump. The ship bounced twice, throwing objects and bodies around the room, then slid roaring on its belly across the tall grass like butter on a hot griddle.

Eron spared one thought for his poor passengers, but could do nothing for them now.

He held on tight and fought for control, but the ship resisted, bucking and swerving like a crazed beast. In dismay, Eron watched as it slid inexorably toward the base of the mountain, where the trees were more plentiful. He yanked back on the wheel, but it no longer responded.

"WARNING. IMPACT IMMINENT."

As if it had a mind of its own, the ship raced full tilt toward a small stand of trees. It clipped them, and something else ripped off as the force of the blow spun them in a new direction.

"WARN—" the voice started, then cut off.

Eron gave thanks for small blessings as the distraction ceased, but watched helplessly as the ship slid screeching through a storage shed, demolishing it to splinters. It didn't even slow the ship down as it raced directly toward the side of the mountain.

Sparks flew from the console. Seeing they were about to crash, Eron grabbed Loki from where he was cowering wide-eyed in the chair, and dove between the seats, holding his arms over his head in preparation for the collision.

They hit the trees and slid through them. The groan and shriek of rending metal assaulted his ears, and the stench of burning technology seared his nostrils as the ship tilted and spun, throwing them about the cabin.

The cacophony reached a fever pitch. Then, abruptly, they came to a crashing halt and Eron was thrown against the wall with a thud.

Juelle woke and glanced around her surroundings. For a change, she knew exactly where she was—she lay in the Healing House at Dodona, where she'd spent many hours learning the Delphian ways. But how had she gotten here?

She glanced down, glad to see that someone had dressed her in comfortable overalls. She checked her wrists, relieved to see that the healing bites on both confirmed that the events of the recent past had been real. And her medkit—someone had found her medkit and left it thoughtfully beside her bed.

A soft chittering sound caught her attention and she turned to see Loki sitting on the pillow next to her, staring at her with concern in his eyes. Stroking his soft fur, she said, "It's okay. I'm fine."

He purred in satisfaction, then leapt off the bed and scurried out of the room.

"I'm happy to see, you, too," Juelle called after the retreating moncat, then laid back down. Later, she'd get up and find some people. Answers could wait. For now, she needed to sort through her scattered wits.

Pam McCutcheon

A head ducked inside the room, and Thena smiled at her. "How do you feel?"

"Not too bad, but I'm *really* glad to see a friendly face for a change."

Thena chuckled. I'm glad to see you, too," she said, her expression half exasperated, half amused. "But I have a bone to pick with you."

"What's wrong?"

"It's that moncat of yours."

"Loki? What's he done?"

"Nothing, really, but he's been chasing Seri ever since he got her, waving that bold little tail of his all over the cavern."

Juelle laughed. "What do you expect me to do about it?"

"Nothing, but I thought you ought to know he finally caught her."

"Good for him."

"For him, maybe, but not for her. Now we're probably both going to be pregnant at the same time," Thena wailed.

Juelle laughed and Thena darted a glance down the hallway. "Well, it looks like you have another visitor. I'll talk to you later."

A moment later, a large hand swept aside the drapes covering the doorway. Eron stood there, Loki by his side. Her life-mate took one glance at her and froze, his expression a mixture of relief, anxiety, and something else she couldn't define. "How do you feel?" he whispered.

"Not too bad. I have a little headache, and I feel bruised and battered all over but, other than that, I'm fine. How about you?"

"Not bad—I've got a hard head that not even your technology can crack."

Juelle grinned, but wondered why Eron was acting so stilted. She reached a tentative hand toward

304

him. As if that were a signal, Eron's expression relaxed and he came fully into the room. Despite her dizziness, Juelle met him halfway and sighed in happiness when Eron took her into his strong arms.

He gave her an exquisitely gentle hug, then led her over to the bed. It creaked under his weight, but he held her as if she were made of fragile crystal and kissed her tenderly.

Juelle snuggled into his strong chest. This is where she belonged . . . if only it wouldn't totally ruin his life. Reluctantly, she pulled back and asked, "How did we get here?"

"In Alexander's scoutship—the new ambassador to Delphi."

"I know that, but the last I saw, there was no one conscious to land it. Did Alex wake up?"

"No, I did."

"You did? You mean to tell me *you* landed the scoutship? How?"

He grinned at her. "I don't know—I just pretended it was a horse and brought it in. Eventually, it stopped."

She chuckled at the image that conjured up. "What'd you do, say, 'Whoa, horsie'?"

"Something like that," he muttered.

"Well, I sure wish I'd been awake to see that."

"So do I—then *you* could've landed the bedamned thing. Besides, it was not a perfect landing. Ambassador Morgan said it was totaled, whatever that means."

"You mean you actually used your brain . . . and logic?"

He nodded ruefully.

"Did it hurt?" she asked in solicitous tones.

He gave her a mock frown. "No more than your using physical force did."

She winced. "Ouch. Direct hit. Well, at least you

got us down alive. See, technology isn't all that bad, is it? It's just a more advanced version of what you're already used to."

His sidelong glance was full of skepticism. "*If* you know how it works. I wouldn't care to repeat the experience."

She shuddered. "Neither would I. I assume Alex is okay, but what about Shogril?"

Eron frowned. "The Council Captain has him locked up, pending the Council's decision what to do with him. Nevan, too. Of course, neither are going anywhere until they recover from the bites Loki gave them."

The little moncat preened himself and Juelle chuckled, then rubbed his head. He had a right to be proud of himself. "But how did Nevan get here?"

"Well, when Seri made it back to Riverfork, Hermes was bright enough to figure out what had happened, and he and Ferrin led a raid on the bandits' hideout. But with Nevan out of commission and Shogril gone, they didn't put up much of a fight."

"Good for Hermes."

"After we crashed here, the ambassador was the first to recover and he explained everything to the Council Captain. Lancer flew there and took the bandits prisoner, then flew out to get all the councilmen and bring them here for an emergency session."

"Good grief . . . How long have I been unconscious?"

"A few days. We were beginning to worry."

Juelle nodded slowly. "No wonder I feel so weak."

"Do you feel up to talking to the Council?"

"Now?"

"Yes—we're in session, but we took a break when Loki arrived with the news that you were finally awake. Do you feel like joining us? They'd like to hear your side of things, to fill in some of the blank spots."

Juelle nodded. "Might as well get it over with while it's still fresh in my memory." She stood, but wavered by the bed. Eron picked her up as if she weighed nothing. When she tried to protest, he frowned her down.

Lacking the strength to complain, Juelle suffered herself to be carried as Loki scurried on behind them. They garnered quite a few curious glances and more than a few grins, but Juelle just smiled and nodded, as if being carried about by this hulking brute were an everyday thing.

Well, who knew? She might institute it as a new tradition—she rather liked being pampered and cosseted for a change.

Eron ducked through the opening of the Council Chamber, and set her gently down on a chair against the wall next to Hermes. Juelle glanced around. Not only were Ketori and the other two councilmen there, but so was Alexander, and even Ferrin.

Lancer glanced at her. "Are you okay, Ju?"

"Sure. I'm fine. It's just that my life-mate here thinks I'm made of glass."

Sharply indrawn breaths reverberated throughout the room, but Juelle only had eyes for Eron. This is the first time they'd appeared in public together, and she wanted to make it clear that she honored the Delphian way. Eron gazed back at her with love and pride in his eyes.

"So it's true?" one councilman asked. "You're really a pythia . . . and life-mated?"

"Yes, it's true," Eron said, and stood by her with one large hand on her shoulder, as if daring anyone to contradict him.

"Gentlemen," Lancer said, "since everyone is

present, perhaps we could start again?"

Hermes leaned over to whisper in her ear. "I have something important to tell you."

"Shh. Not now. Later."

"But—"

She hushed him with an upraised hand and Lancer spoke. "We're meeting here to determine the fate of Nevan and his followers. To do that, we need you to tell us exactly what happened from the time you encountered him until now. Eron, why don't you begin?"

The tale, as told by Eron, Juelle, Alexander, Ferrin, and Hermes, took several hours. They left out nothing but the formula-induced prophecy. At the end of it, Lancer called for discussion from the Council members.

One elderly gentleman said, "This calls for banishment!"

Ferrin snorted, and Eron reminded the councilman, "They're already banished. It didn't work."

The councilman frowned but fell silent.

"That's true," Ketori said, "but we don't have the facilities to hold them captive. The only other alternative is death . . . and we haven't administered that punishment for anything less than murder in two hundred years."

"If the Council pleases," Alexander interjected.

Lancer nodded at him, and Alexander said, "There's another solution. Since they kidnapped and held hostage two of the Republic's citizens, the Republic can bring them to trial under Delphi's current treaty—if you're willing."

Eron gave him a considering look. "What would that entail?"

"If found guilty, they could be sentenced to prison for up to fifteen years."

"And then what?" Eron probed.

"Then they'd be returned to their planet of origin," he admitted.

Eron frowned. "Then we merely postpone this for another fifteen years, to give them a chance to build their plans and try again."

"Yes, but in the interim—"

"Wait," Juelle interrupted Alexander. "There's another alternative." She cast Eron an apologetic glance. She had a feeling he wasn't going to like this. "If Delphi joins the Republic, then Nevan becomes a citizen and his crimes are much more serious. He can be tried under our laws for treason, kidnapping, and attempted murder."

When everyone remained silent, she added, "And if he's found guilty, the penalty is banishment for life to a prison planet, with no chance of parole."

Eron nodded in decision and stood. "All right, then I call for a vote."

Juelle felt a strange sense of déjà vu as Eron cast a sweeping glance around the room. This is where all this had begun.

"The last time we met," Eron said, "I spoke against the Republic and their technology. Not only was I reacting to an invalid prophecy—one falsified by the same man we have condemned—but I was wrong."

As Juelle listened in open-mouthed astonishment, Eron went on to offer arguments in favor of technology, much of them gleaned from conversations with her. He was very persuasive, and Juelle felt a great deal of pride. He had put aside his personal prejudices and, despite his one devastating brush with the worst part of technology, he recognized it was best for Delphi.

When Eron finished, Lancer called for further discussion. When there was none, he called for the vote to join the United Planets Republic. The councilmen filed by, each choosing a black or white ball, then dropped it in a box before Lancer.

When they were done, Lancer inspected the contents of the box and looked up, smiling. He tilted the box forward to show them its contents—five yes votes. "The motion passed."

Smiles beamed all around, and Alexander rose. "Then, if it pleases the Council, I will arrange for the transport of the prisoners to the trial." He paused, then added, "And in view of the secrecy with which we are still keeping the abilities of your pythias, I will recommend the prisoners be remanded to our newest prison planet, to be incarcerated there alone."

Juelle couldn't help but laugh.

Giving her a raised eyebrow, Lancer said, "What's so funny, Ju?"

"I just realized that Nevan's prophecy will come true. He *will* be ruler of his own world . . . just not the world he expected."

With a chuckle, Lancer called the meeting back to order. "That reminds me of another item of business. Ferrin, Alexander, would you mind leaving us?"

Ferrin and Alexander left, then Lancer turned to Juelle and Eron. "Because Juelle has tested out as a powerful silver pythia"—his quirked eyebrow showed he still wanted to know how that had happened—"normally we would test her against the other silver pythias. If she is stronger, then she would assume the ranking position in the cavern, and her life-mate would assume the councilman position."

He paused, and the other councilmen shared uneasy glances. He was talking about deposing *them*.

"However," Lancer continued, "her life-mate already has a Council position by virtue of his relationship to Alyssa—if he chooses to have two silver pythias in the Oasis caverns."

Eron stood once more. "I waive my right as Oasis Councilman, in favor of my uncle, Hermes' father."

"No," Juelle said, and all eyes turned to her. "I can't let you do that. You embody the best qualities of this planet—you're strong and brave and true. Stubborn as hell, too."

That garnered a few chuckles, but Juelle continued. "This Council is going to need that stubbornness in dealing with the Republic. You need someone who isn't afraid to stand up for what's right, who knows this planet inside and out, who knows the arguments for and against technology first hand. That man is Eron. You can't let him leave the Council."

Lancer nodded. "But if you're stronger than the other pythias, Eron will become councilman of another cavern."

"No, he won't, for I'm a pythia who can never prophesy."

A few gasps were heard around the room, and Hermes pulled on her sleeve, saying, "But—"

"Not now, Hermes, let me finish. I couldn't mention this while the others were here, but I can never be a true pythia because I—" She took a deep breath and glanced at Eron.

He stared at her with compassion in his eyes, but made no move to stop her from saying what she knew had to be said. "Because I used the formula to prophesy first."

The astonished expression on Lancer's face was almost comical. "You did *what?*"

"I used the formula to prophesy . . . and the oracle told me I could never prophesy again."

In the resulting silence, Hermes voice sounded loud and strong. "No, it didn't."

She turned to him. "What?"

"I wrote the prophecy down," Hermes explained, "and that's not what it said."

"What *did* it say?"

Hermes pulled a creased piece of paper out of his shirt. "Let me read it so I get it right. It says, 'If the Terran uses the *false elixir* to willingly prophesy again, Delphi's gift will be lost forever.'"

Juelle's hopes rose. "You mean . . ."

Hermes grinned at her. "Yes. You can prophesy as a pythia, you just can't use the formula to do so."

She whooped, and Eron laughed and swung her into his arms. "I'll never use the formula again," she swore. "And I'll destroy all my notes on it. How did the prophecy get so confused?"

Hermes shrugged. "You weren't a pythia then, so the only way you could prophesy was the formula. At the time, I assumed that meant you never could. I didn't remember the exact words, so it just slipped my mind until I read my notes."

She hugged him, too. "That's wonderful—"

"Yes," Lancer interrupted, "but that means the question still stands. What do we do with our newest silver pythia?"

Juelle glanced at Eron. "I don't want to usurp your sister's position—or anyone else's. I just want to be a healer."

The other men nodded in approval, and she added, "But you should be on the Council. They need you."

The men frowned, and Lancer grinned. "I think I might have a solution. Hoping we would agree to join the Republic, Ambassador Morgan has requested we appoint a spokesman for Delphi that he can deal with to determine trade terms, et cetera."

He paused, then added, "And Juelle has very persuasively shown why Eron should be that person.

Any objections? No? Then I suggest we appoint Eron as spokesman for Delphi, based here in Dodona, and award him a seat on the Council."

The discussion raged about him as the councilmen protested that a new Council seat had not been added in more than two hundred years. Lancer explained that progress demanded they change. Eron stayed silent through it all.

When Lancer finally pointed out the fact that having Eron on the Council in this position would ensure he didn't usurp their positions, the other councilmen turned quiet, and the vote passed.

Lancer adjourned the meeting, and the others filed out. Eron captured Juelle in his arms, love shining in his eyes. "I didn't believe it possible," he whispered.

"Neither did I," she whispered back. "But it's true. We're both getting what we want, including each other."

"Yes, but now that you've talked them into making me spokesman for Delphi, I need to learn more about technology. And the first thing I want to start with is—"

"Let me guess." She grinned. "You want to learn how to fly a scoutship."

He chuckled and shook his head. "No, I want to learn how to *land* one."

Dear Reader,

I hope you have enjoyed Juelle and Eron's story. When I wrote my first book, *Golden Prophecies,* I never intended to write a sequel, but the petite Terran psychiatrist who befriended the Golden Pythia wouldn't stay out of my mind. She kept demanding her own story, so finally, I gave it to her, and *Quicksilver* was born.

While I was at it, I realized I had to find a mate for Seri as well. What could be more fun than moncat love—especially with a feisty moncat like Loki? The moncats even inspired my brother, Geoff Luzier, to try his hand at sketching one. The result was exactly how I had pictured them, and we were both thrilled when the art department agreed to translate that vision to the cover so you, too, could see exactly what a moncat looks like.

I love writing romances and hearing from my readers. You may reach me at P.O. Box 25417, Colorado Springs, CO 80936-5417. If you wish a reply, a self-addressed stamped envelope would be appreciated.

Sincerely,

Pam McCutcheon

Futuristic Romance

Golden Prophecies

Pam McCutcheon

She is the Golden Pythia, the most accomplished oracle on her planet. Yet Thena doesn't foretell the danger one Terran man will bring to her world—or the storm of desire he will arouse in her heart.

Sent to Delphi to prevent an interstellar war, Lancer refuses to credit Thena's power of prophecy, but he can't deny the strength of his growing attraction for the silken beauty.

Enchanting believer and charming skeptic, Thena and Lancer soon learn that the wandering stars aren't the only heavenly bodies that cross in the night. But unexpected perils and deadly enemies stand between them and the sweet, sensual delight of golden prophecies.

_52005-2 $4.99 US/$5.99 CAN

Futuristic Romance

CRYSTAL FIRE

KATHLEEN MORGAN

"A unique and magical tale!"
—Janelle Taylor

The message is explicit—no other man will do but the virile warrior. Determined that Brace must join her quest, Marissa rescues him from unjust imprisonment, then nurses him back to strength. She never tells the arrogant male that he is just a pawn to exchange for her sister's freedom. But during the long, cold nights Marissa finds herself irresistibly drawn to the hard warrior's body, and as the danger-filled days fly by, she knows her desperate mission is doomed to failure. For how can she save her sister by betraying the only man she can ever love?

_52065-6 $5.50 US/$7.50 CAN